ALL TOGETHER NOW

ALSO BY HOPE LARSON

Madeleine L'Engle's
A Wrinkle in Time: The Graphic Novel

Compass South (Four Points Book 1)
Illustrations by Rebecca Mock

Knife's Edge (Four Points Book 2)
Illustrations by Rebecca Mock

All Summer Long

ALL
TOGETHER
NOW

HOPE LARSON

Farrar Straus Giroux
New York

Farrar Straus Giroux Books for Young Readers
An imprint of Macmillan Publishing Group, LLC
120 Broadway, New York, NY 10271

Copyright © 2020 by Hope Larson
All rights reserved
Printed in China by Toppan Leefung Printing Ltd.,
Dongguan City, Guangdong Province
Cover design by Molly Johanson
Series design by Andrew Arnold
Interior book design by Rob Steen
First edition, 2020
Colored by Hilary Sycamore and Karina Edwards

Paperback: 10 9 8 7 6 5 4 3 2 1
Hardcover: 10 9 8 7 6 5 4 3 2 1

mackids.com

Library of Congress Cataloging-in-Publication Data is available.
Paperback ISBN: 978-0-374-31365-4
Hardcover ISBN: 978-0-374-31162-9

Our books may be purchased in bulk for promotional, educational,
or business use. Please contact your local bookseller or the Macmillan
Corporate and Premium Sales Department at (800) 221-7945 ext. 5442
or by email at MacmillanSpecialMarkets@macmillan.com.

September

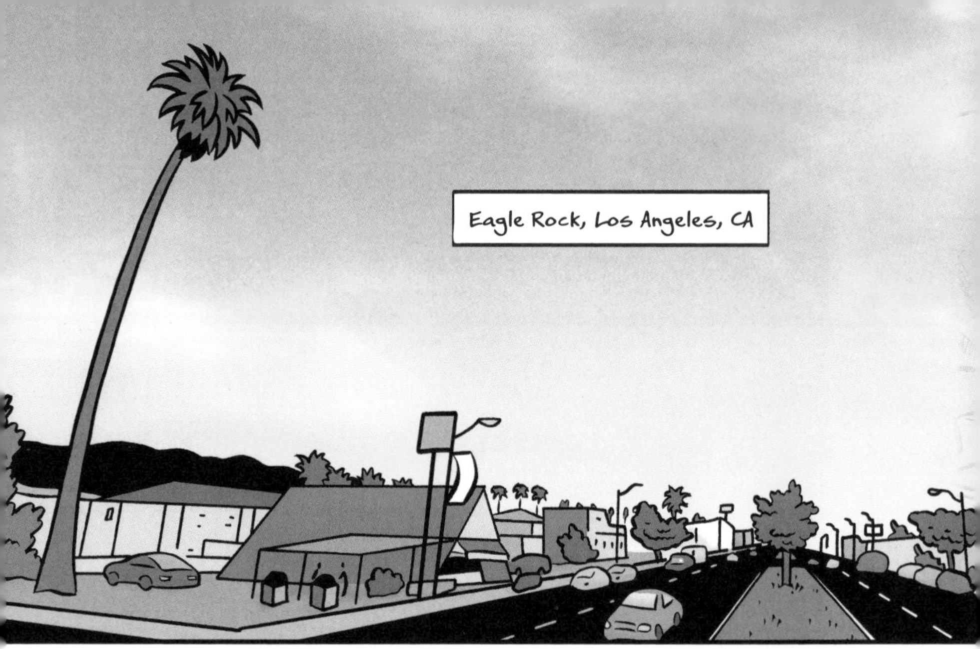
Eagle Rock, Los Angeles, CA

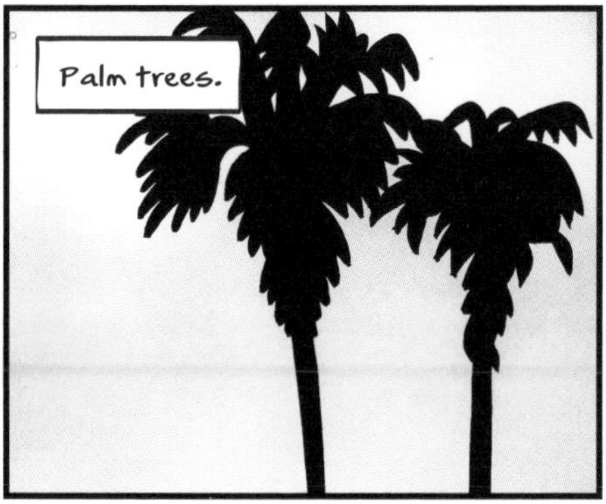
Palm trees.

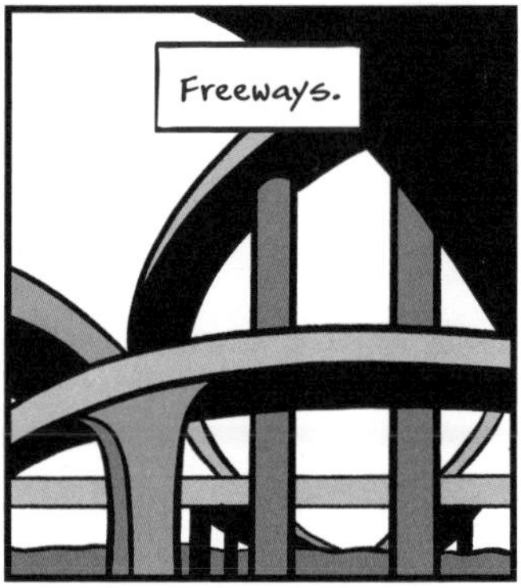
Freeways.

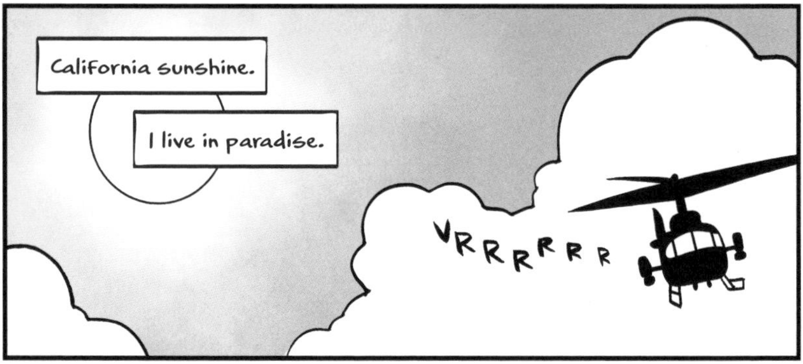
California sunshine.
I live in paradise.
VRRRRRR

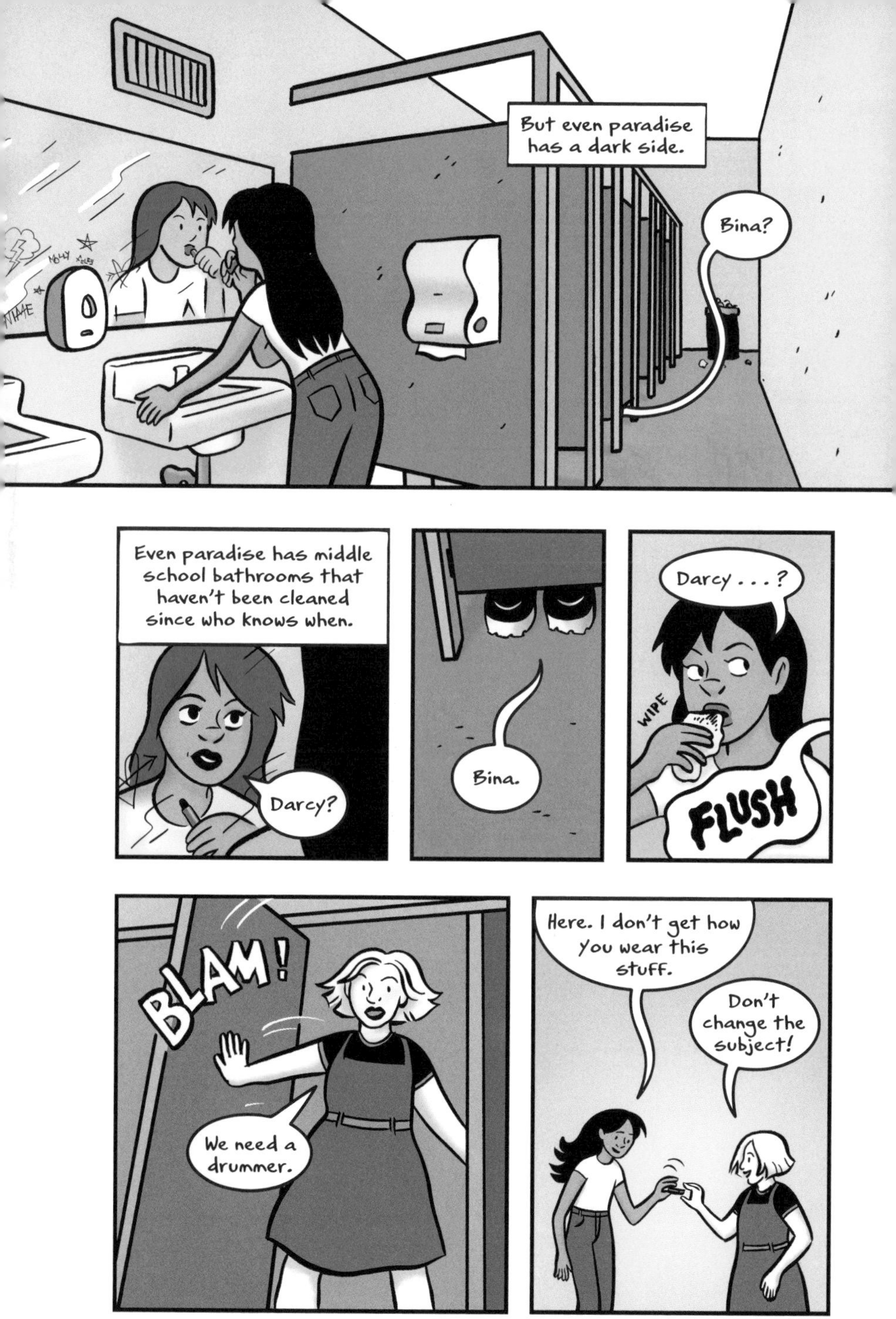
But even paradise has a dark side.
Bina?
Even paradise has middle school bathrooms that haven't been cleaned since who knows when.
Darcy?
Bina.
Darcy . . . ?
WIPE
FLUSH
BLAM!
We need a drummer.
Here. I don't get how you wear this stuff.
Don't change the subject!

Panel 1:
I just don't know that I'd File "drummer" under "need."

More like, "nice to have." We already have a drum machine.

Panel 2:
Mt. Royal Middle School

Come on. Those are the kiss of death at a live show.

When the band has to stop and fiddle with a bunch of knobs between songs?

MT. ROYA

Panel 3:
Total mood-killer.

I guess you'd know. You've seen more shows than I have.

Panel 4:
When I lived in Brooklyn, there was a great live scene.

That's what you keep saying.

Panel 5:
Sorry. I'm not trying to be cool New York girl.

But if you wanna start playing out, we need a drummer.

4

Fine, Darcy. You win. But if we get a drummer, where do we practice?
My house is out. The neighbors complain to my parents when I have my amp set too loud.
The drummer's house, obviously.
This hypothetical drummer is very committed to the band.
Well, they should be. They get to hang with us all the blah.
Blah blah blah blah? Blah blah.
Blah blah blah.
BOOMP
YEAH! Go Austin!
Jeez, girl!

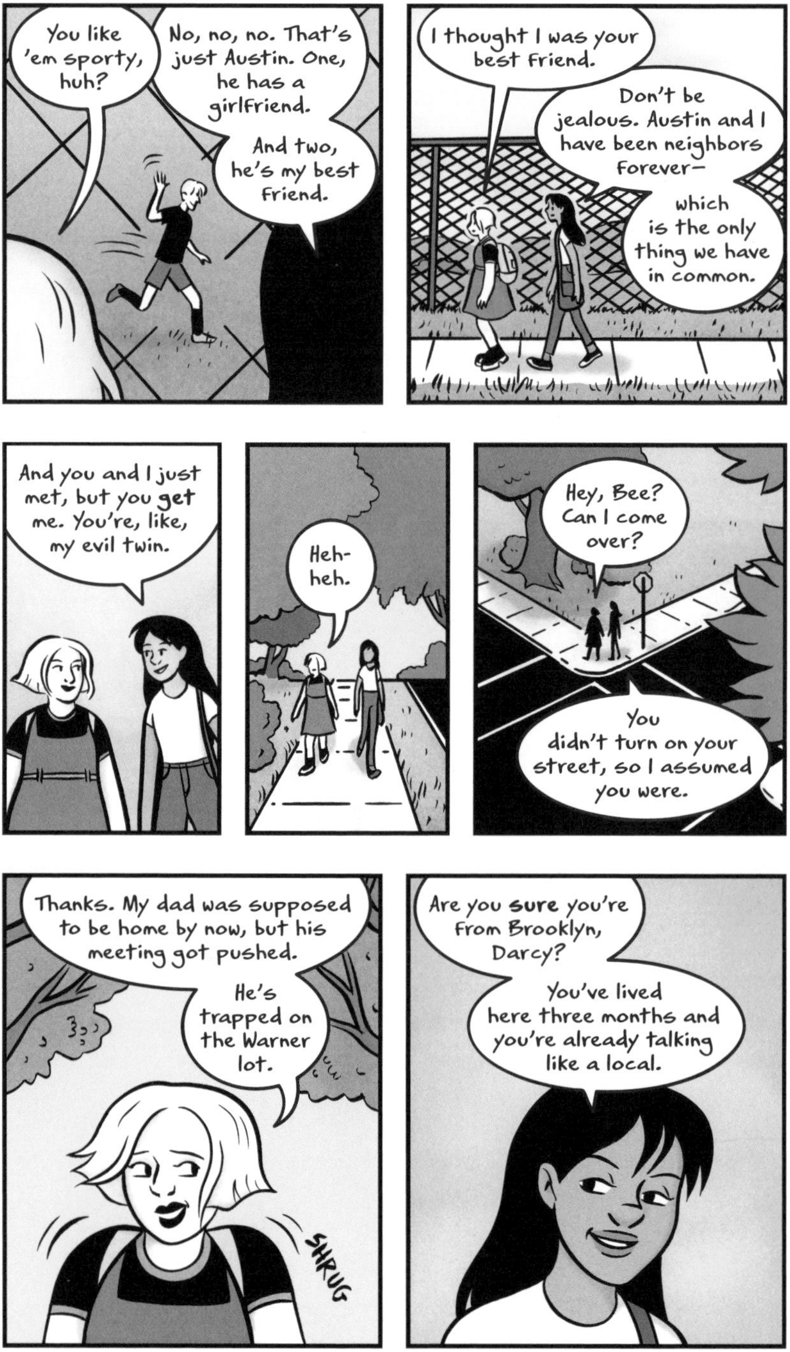
You like 'em sporty, huh?
No, no, no. That's just Austin. One, he has a girlfriend.
And two, he's my best friend.
I thought I was your best friend.
Don't be jealous. Austin and I have been neighbors forever—
which is the only thing we have in common.
And you and I just met, but you **get** me. You're, like, my evil twin.
Heh-heh.
Hey, Bee? Can I come over?
You didn't turn on your street, so I assumed you were.
Thanks. My dad was supposed to be home by now, but his meeting got pushed.
He's trapped on the Warner lot.
SHRUG
Are you **sure** you're from Brooklyn, Darcy?
You've lived here three months and you're already talking like a local.

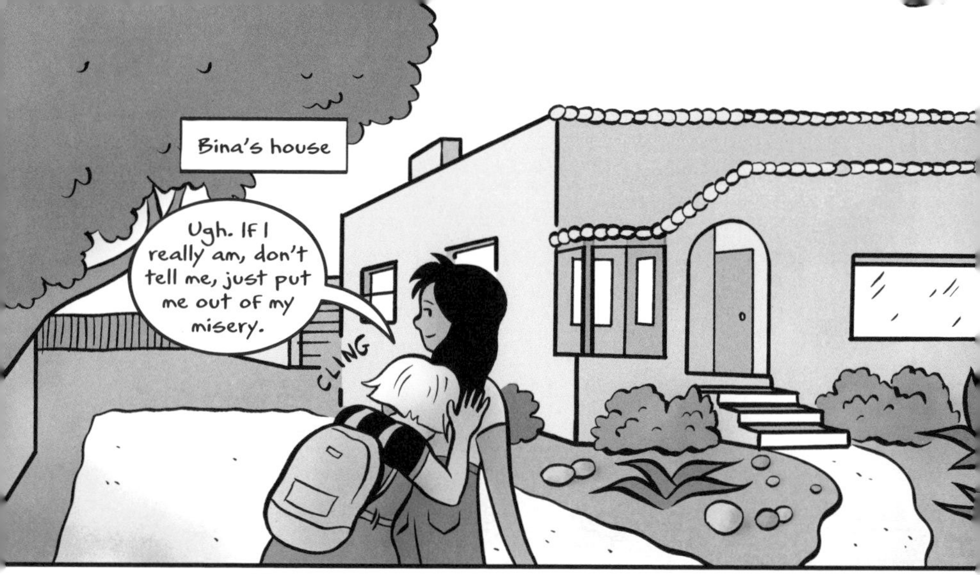
Bina's house
Ugh. If I really am, don't tell me, just put me out of my misery.
CLING

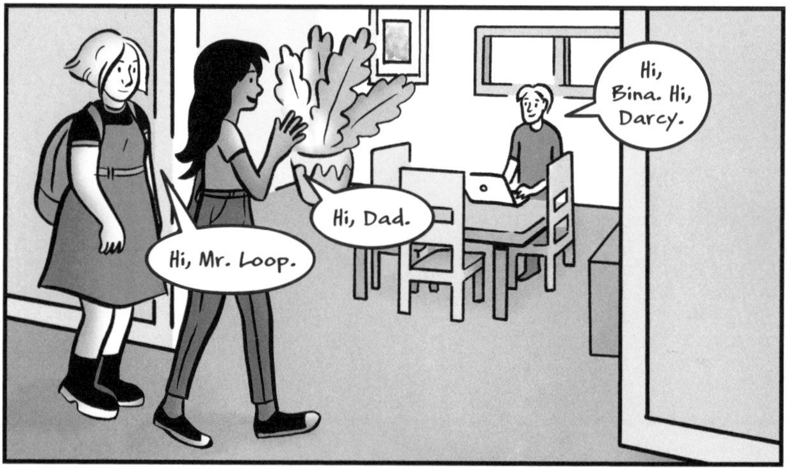
Hi, Mr. Loop.
Hi, Dad.
Hi, Bina. Hi, Darcy.

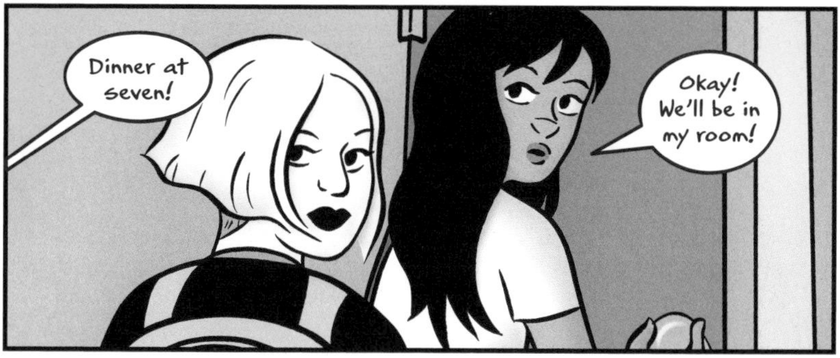
Dinner at seven!
Okay! We'll be in my room!

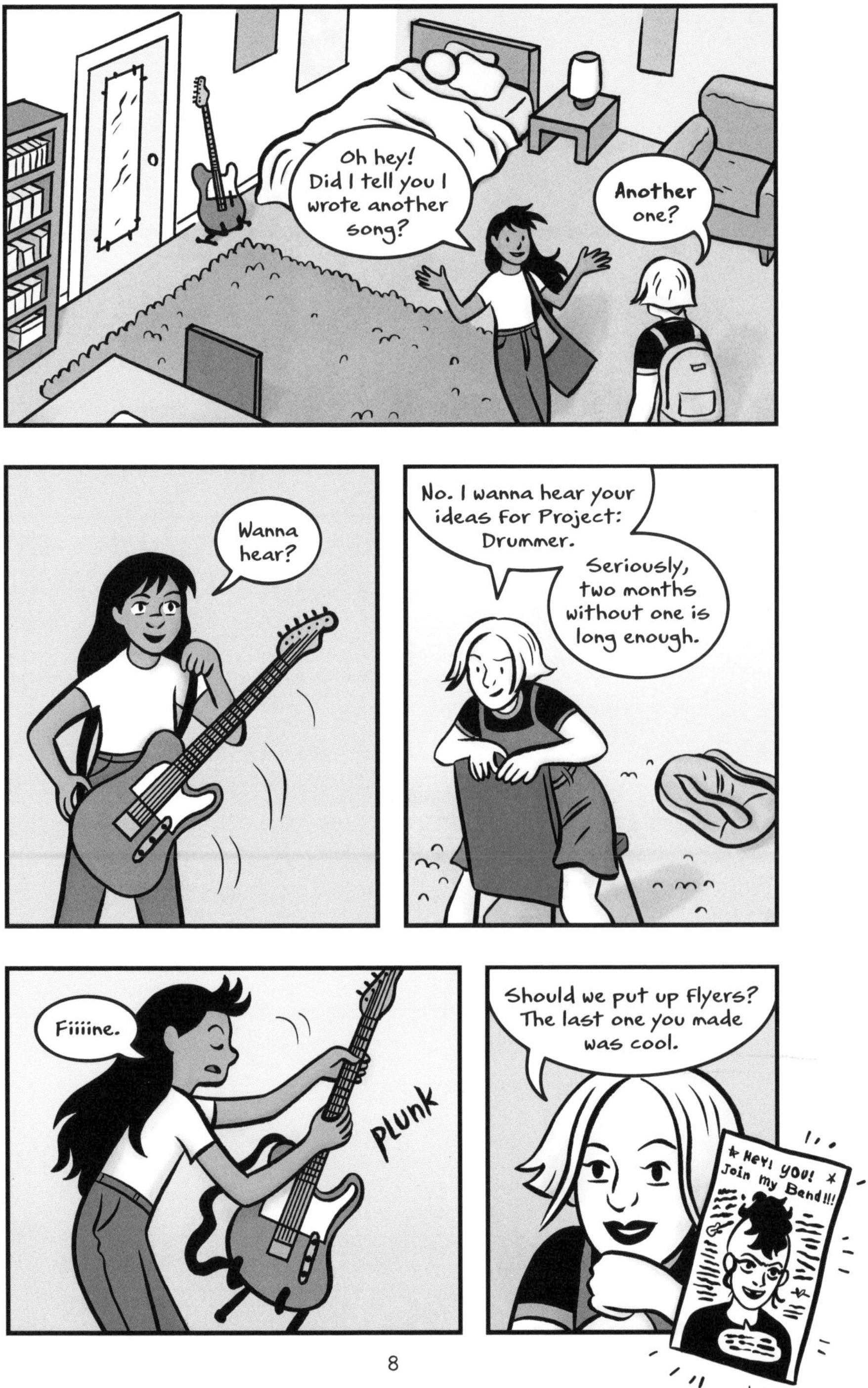
Oh hey! Did I tell you I wrote another song?
Another one?
Wanna hear?
No. I wanna hear your ideas for Project: Drummer.
Seriously, two months without one is long enough.
Fiiiine.
PLUNK
Should we put up flyers? The last one you made was cool.
★ HEY! YOU! ★ Join my Band!!!

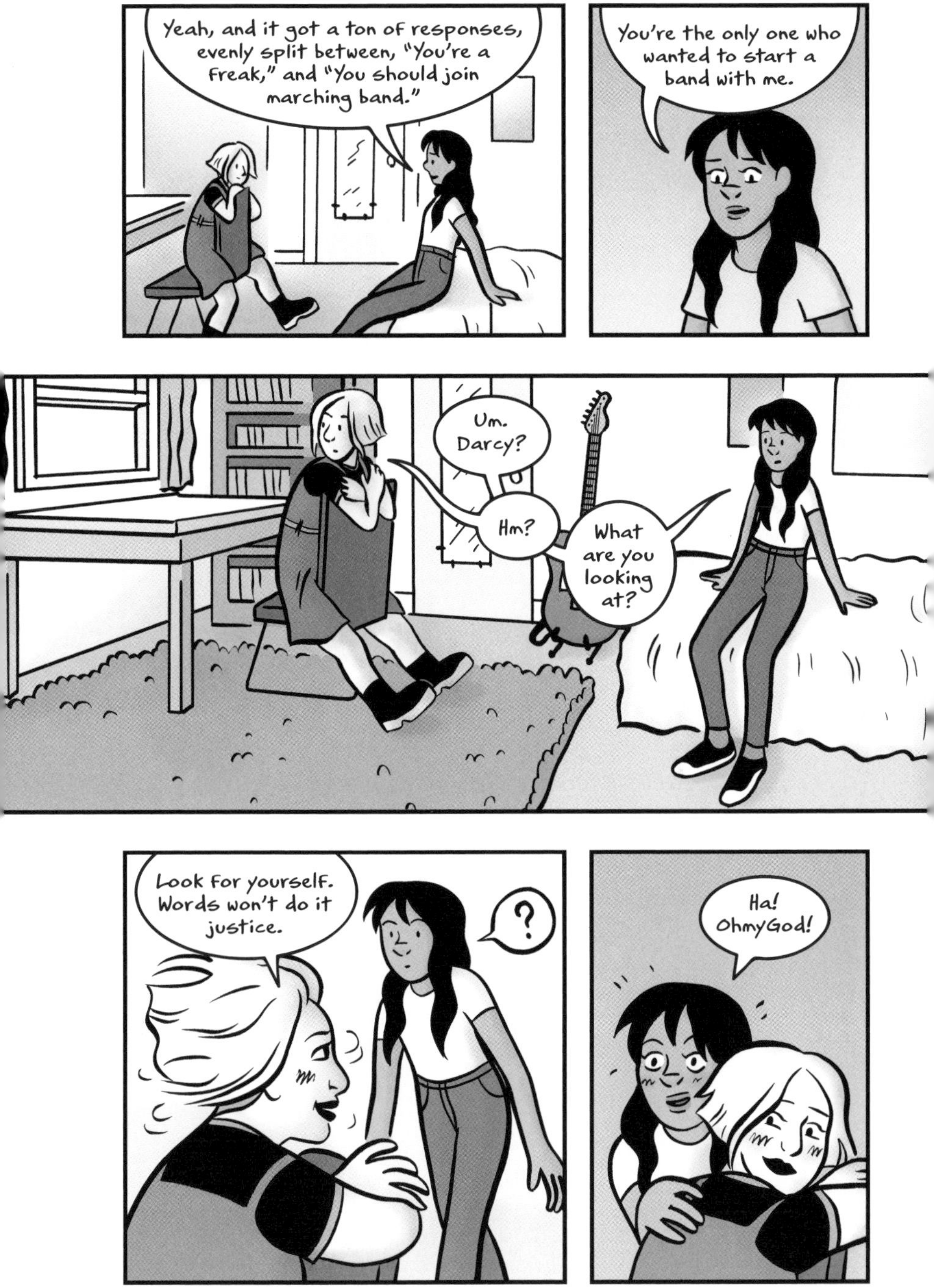
Yeah, and it got a ton of responses, evenly split between, "You're a Freak," and "You should join marching band."
You're the only one who wanted to start a band with me.
Um. Darcy?
Hm?
What are you looking at?
Look for yourself. Words won't do it justice.
?
Ha! OhmyGod!

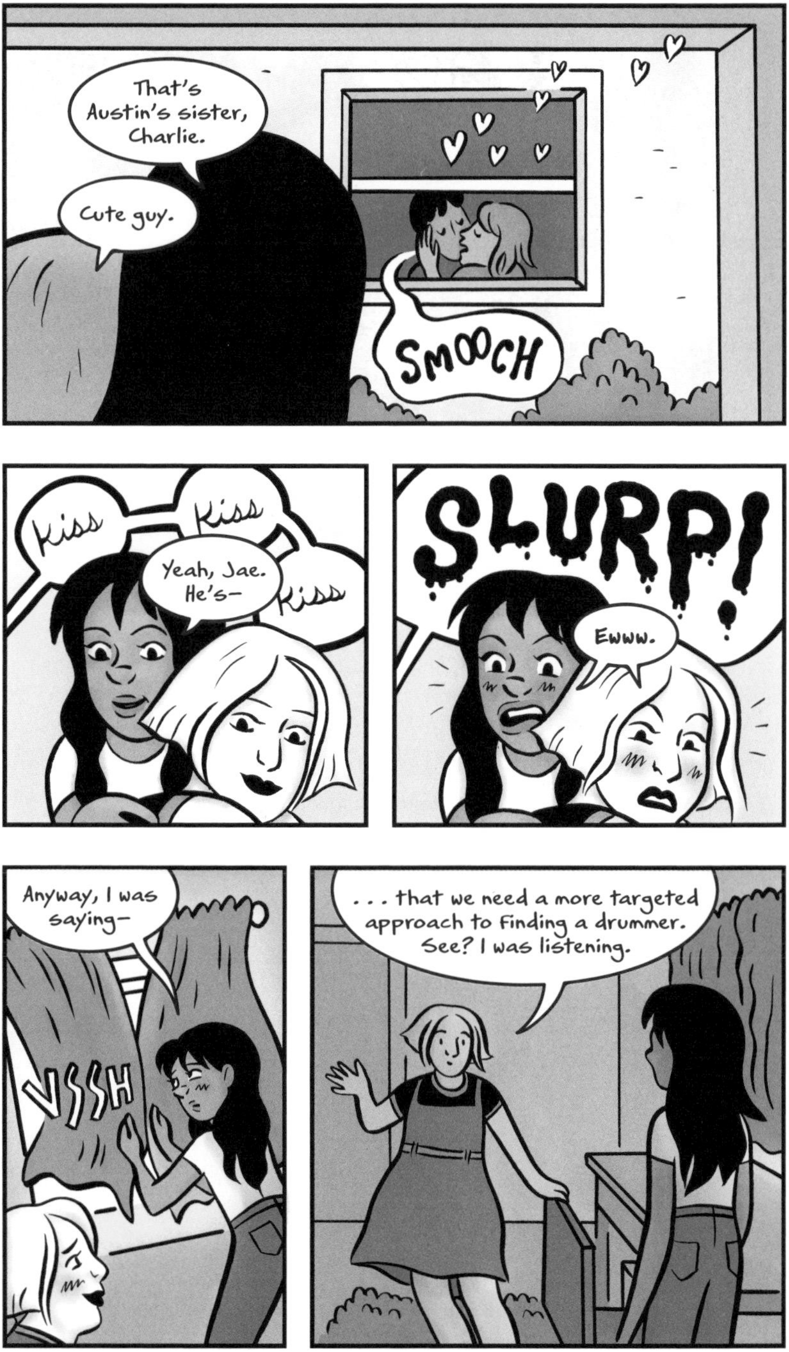
That's Austin's sister, Charlie.
Cute guy.
SMOOCH
kiss
kiss
Yeah, Jae. He's—
kiss
SLURP!
Ewww.
Anyway, I was saying—
VSSH
. . . that we need a more targeted approach to finding a drummer. See? I was listening.

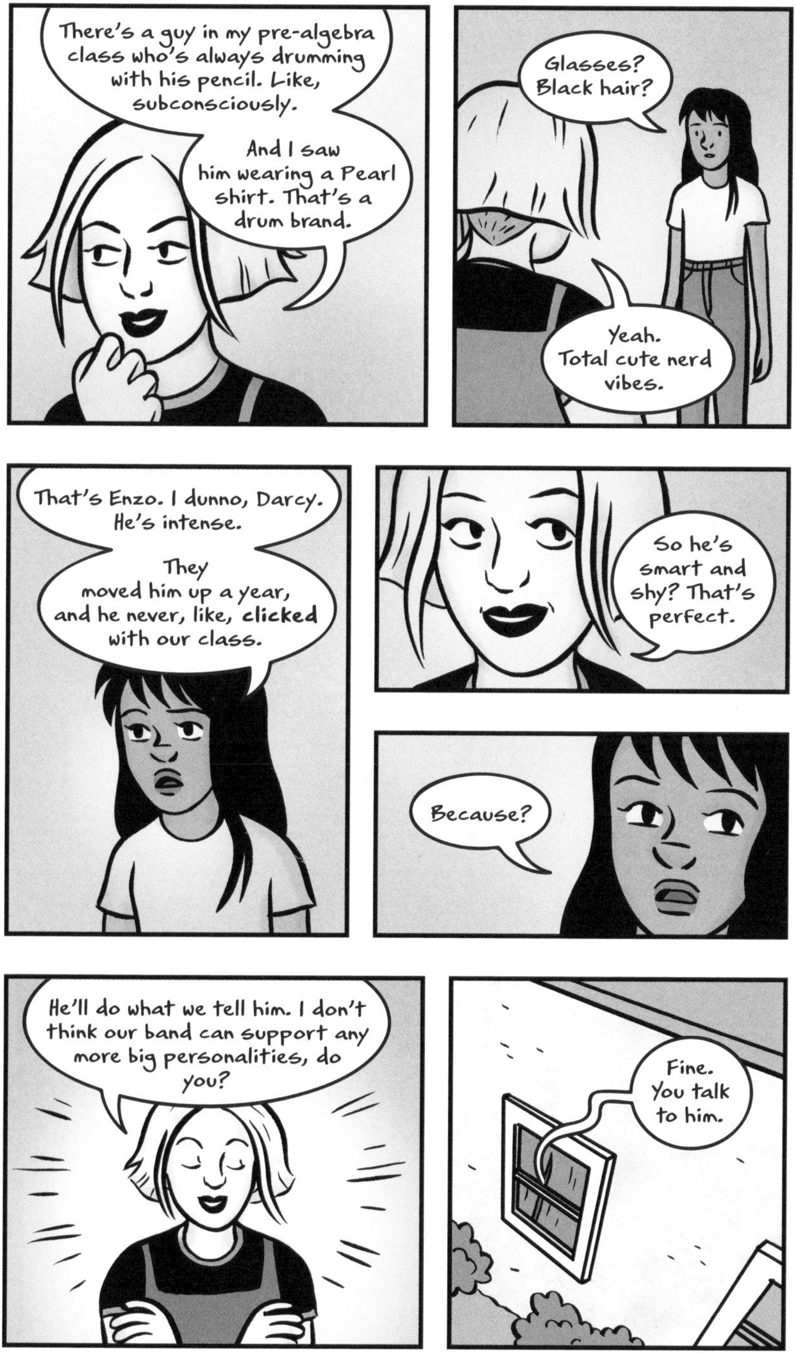
There's a guy in my pre-algebra class who's always drumming with his pencil. Like, subconsciously.
And I saw him wearing a Pearl shirt. That's a drum brand.
Glasses? Black hair?
Yeah. Total cute nerd vibes.
That's Enzo. I dunno, Darcy. He's intense.
They moved him up a year, and he never, like, **clicked** with our class.
So he's smart and shy? That's perfect.
Because?
He'll do what we tell him. I don't think our band can support any more big personalities, do you?
Fine. You talk to him.

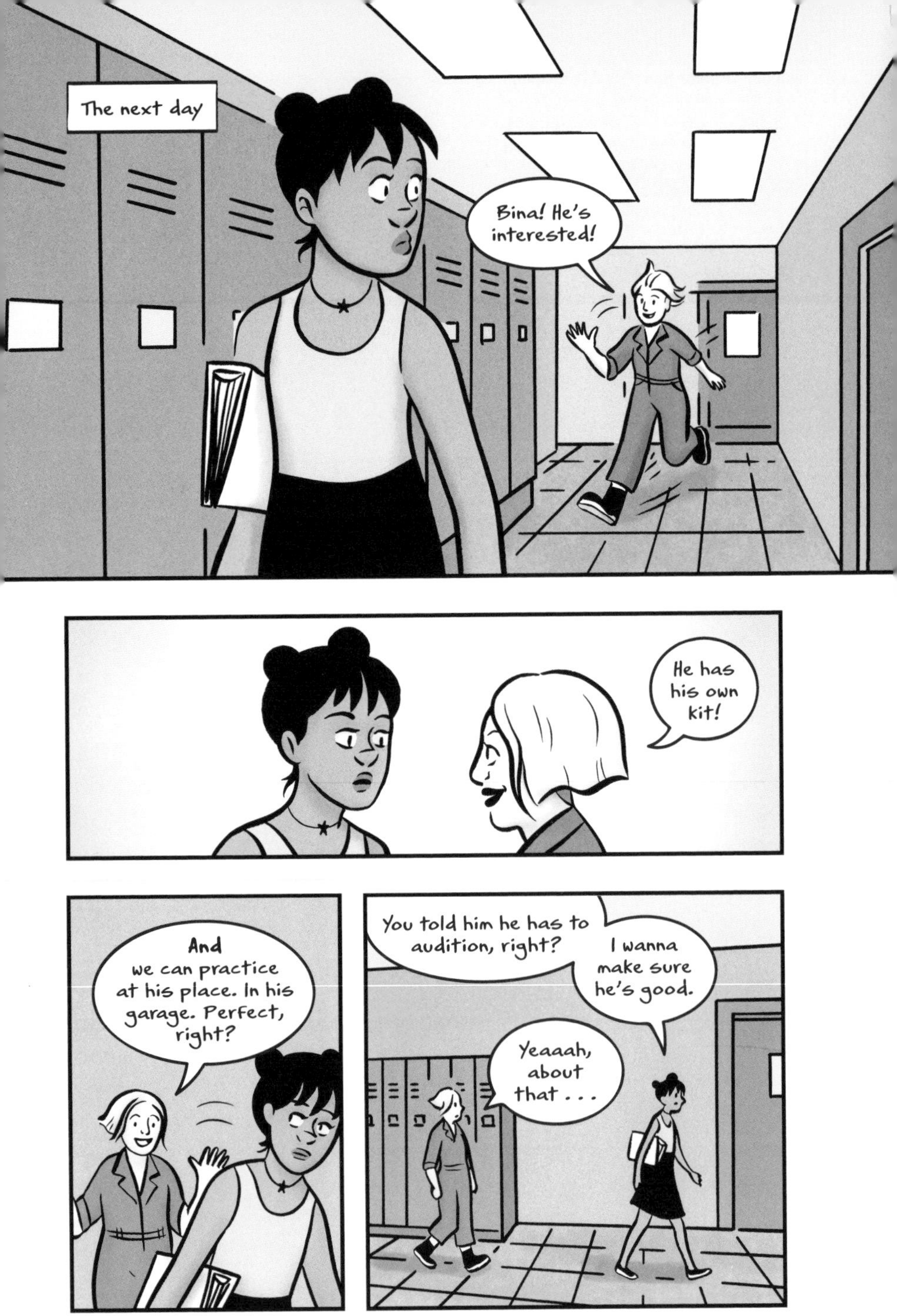
The next day
Bina! He's interested!
He has his own kit!
And we can practice at his place. In his garage. Perfect, right?
You told him he has to audition, right?
I wanna make sure he's good.
Yeaaah, about that . . .

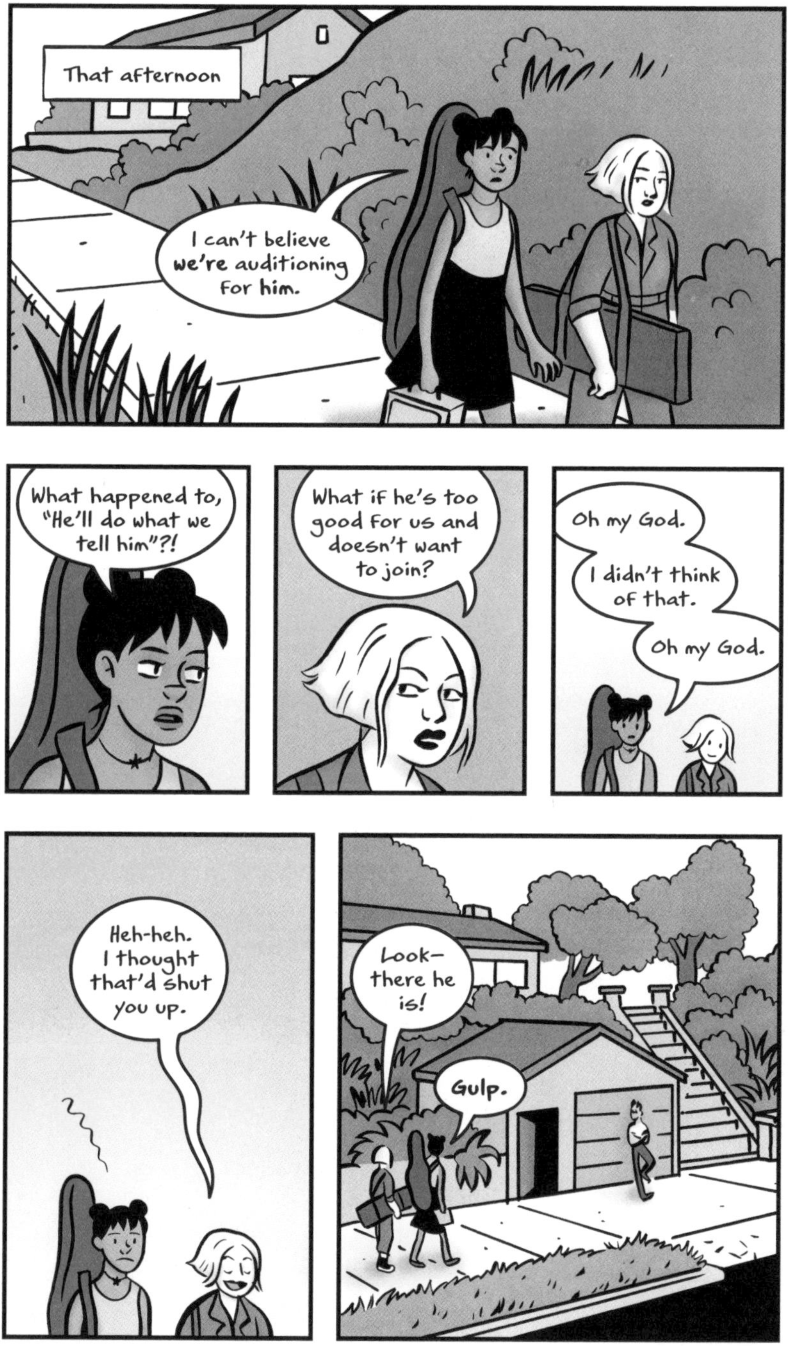
That afternoon
I can't believe we're auditioning for him.
What happened to, "He'll do what we tell him"?!
What if he's too good for us and doesn't want to join?
Oh my God.
I didn't think of that.
Oh my God.
Heh-heh. I thought that'd shut you up.
Look— there he is!
Gulp.

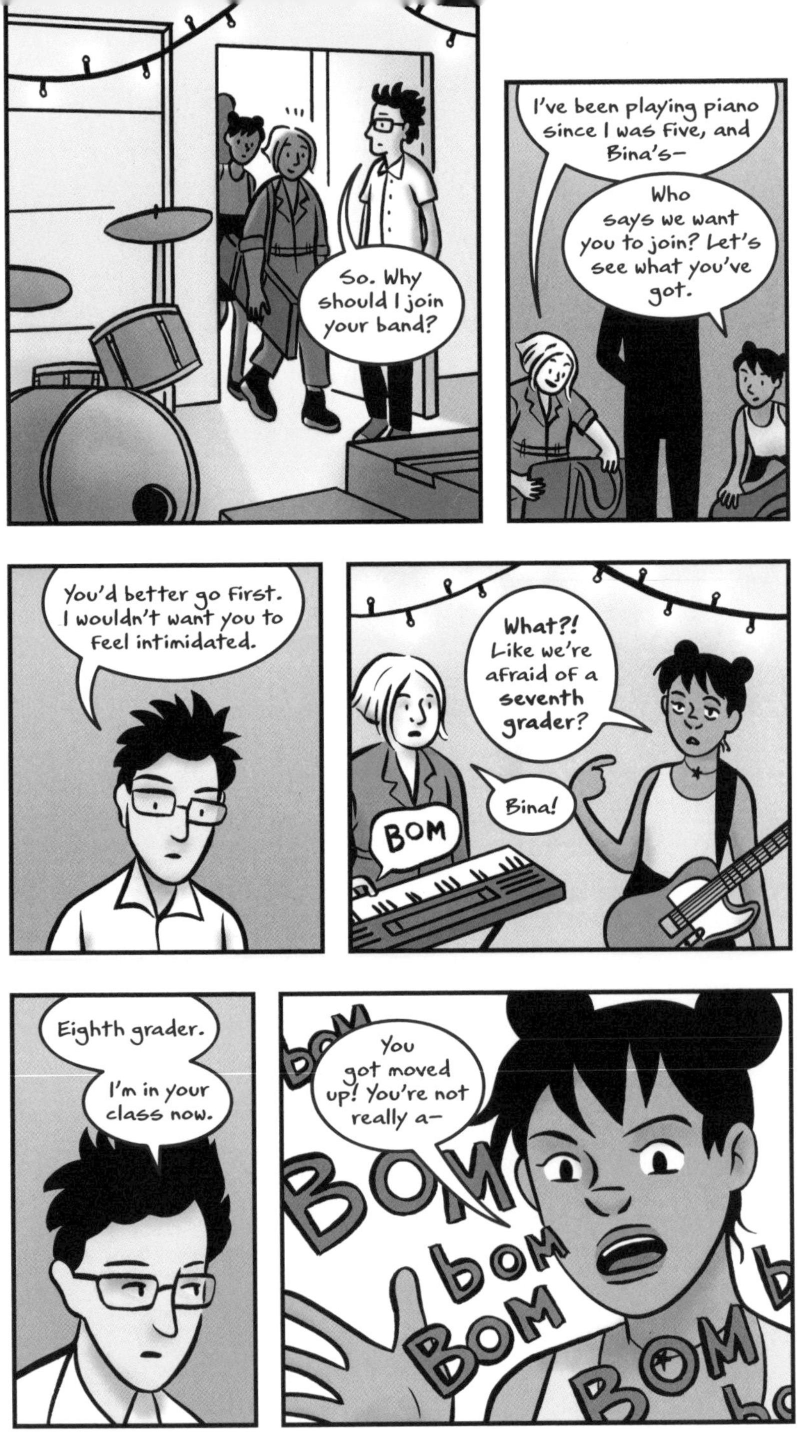
So. Why should I join your band?
I've been playing piano since I was five, and Bina's—
Who says we want you to join? Let's see what you've got.
You'd better go first. I wouldn't want you to feel intimidated.
What?! Like we're afraid of a seventh grader?
Bina!
BOM
Eighth grader.
I'm in your class now.
You got moved up! You're not really a—
BOM
bom
BOM
BOM

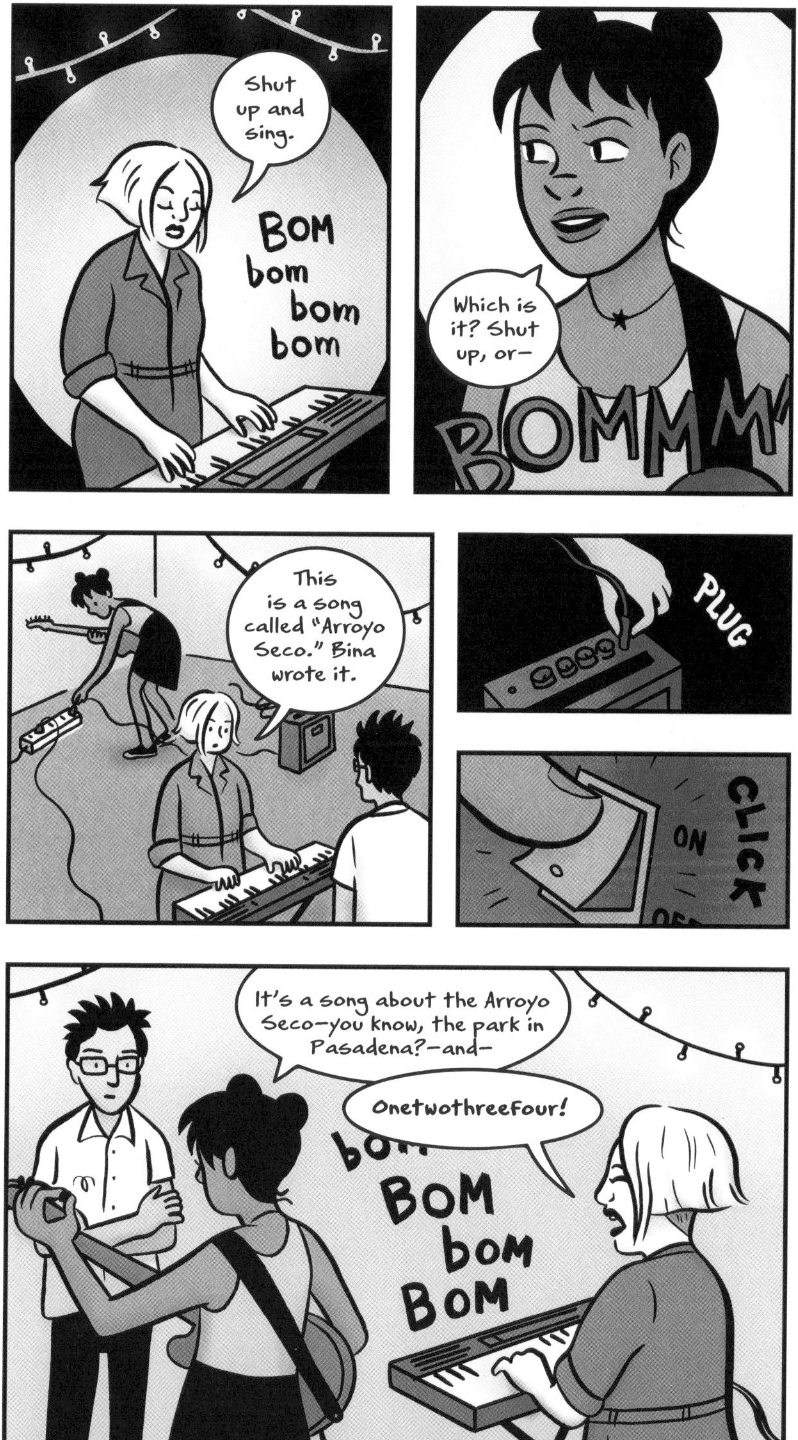

Shut up and sing.
BOM bom bom bom
Which is it? Shut up, or—
BOMMM
This is a song called "Arroyo Seco." Bina wrote it.
PLUG
CLICK
ON
It's a song about the Arroyo Seco—you know, the park in Pasadena?—and—
Onetwothreefour!
BOM bom BOM

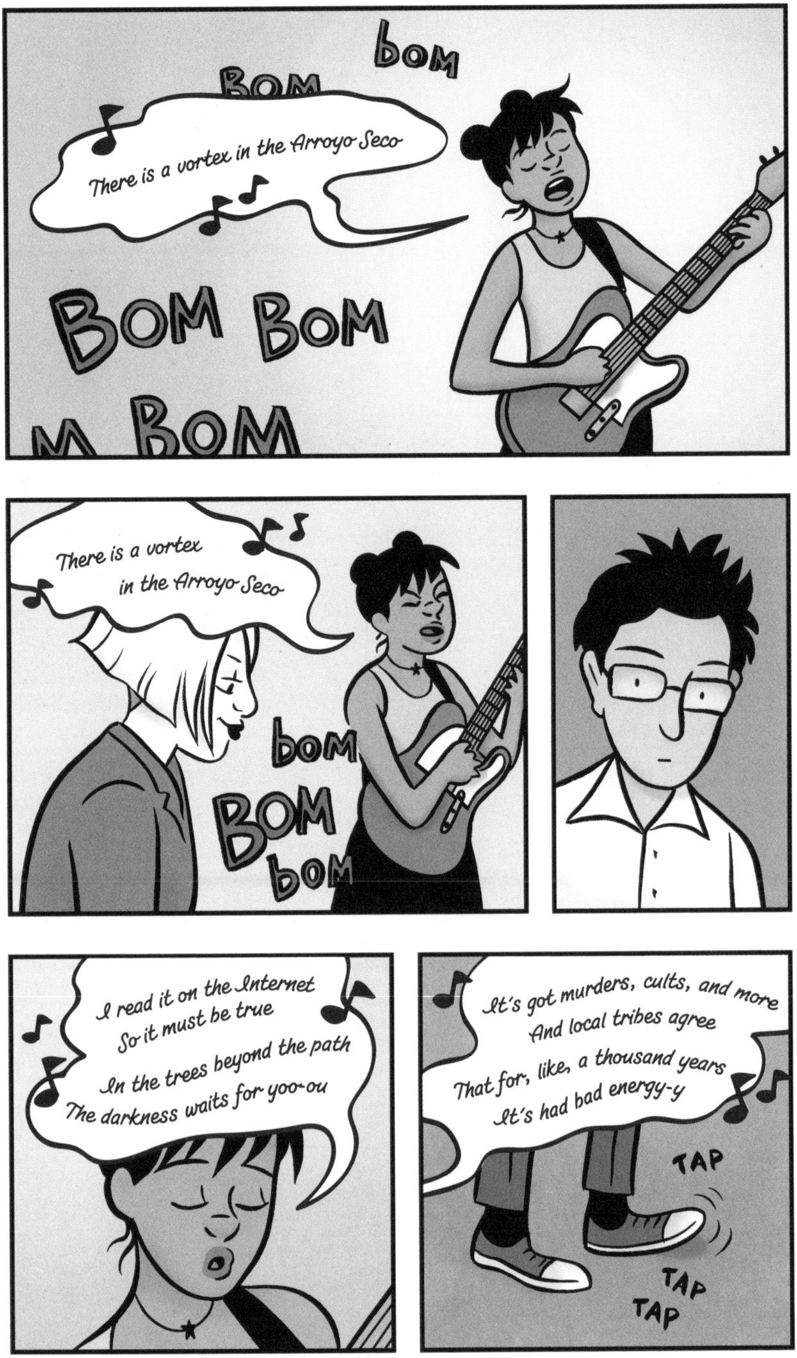
bom
BOM
There is a vortex in the Arroyo Seco
BOM BOM
m BOM
There is a vortex in the Arroyo Seco
bom
BOM
bom
I read it on the Internet So it must be true
In the trees beyond the path The darkness waits for yoo-ou
It's got murders, cults, and more And local tribes agree
That for, like, a thousand years It's had bad energy-y
TAP
TAP
TAP

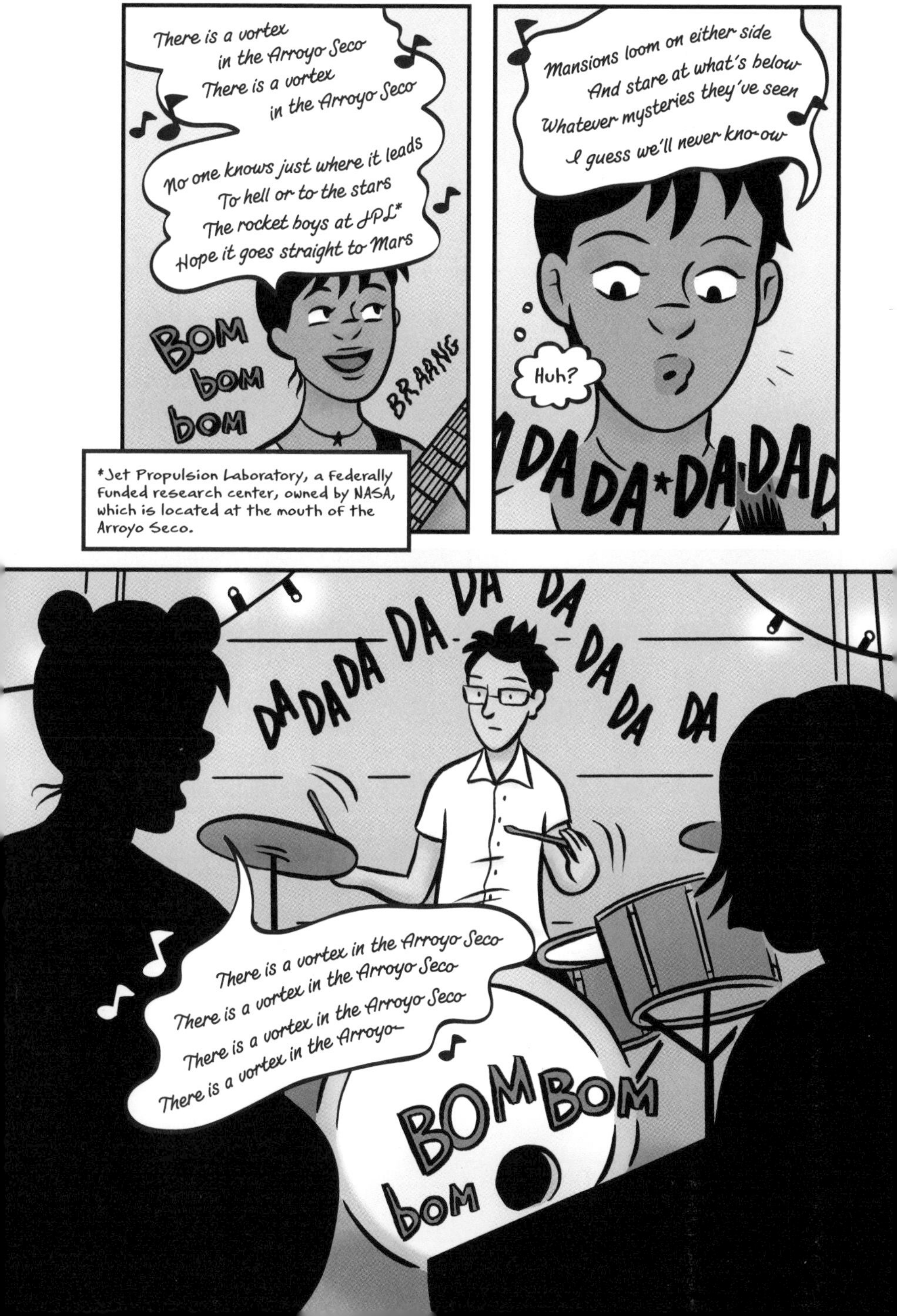

There is a vortex in the Arroyo Seco There is a vortex in the Arroyo Seco
No one knows just where it leads To hell or to the stars The rocket boys at JPL* Hope it goes straight to Mars
BOM bom bom
BRAANG
*Jet Propulsion Laboratory, a federally funded research center, owned by NASA, which is located at the mouth of the Arroyo Seco.
Mansions loom on either side And stare at what's below Whatever mysteries they've seen I guess we'll never kno-ow
Huh?
DA DA DA DA DA
DA DA DA DA DA DA DA DA DA
There is a vortex in the Arroyo Seco There is a vortex in the Arroyo Seco There is a vortex in the Arroyo Seco There is a vortex in the Arroyo—
BOM BOM bom

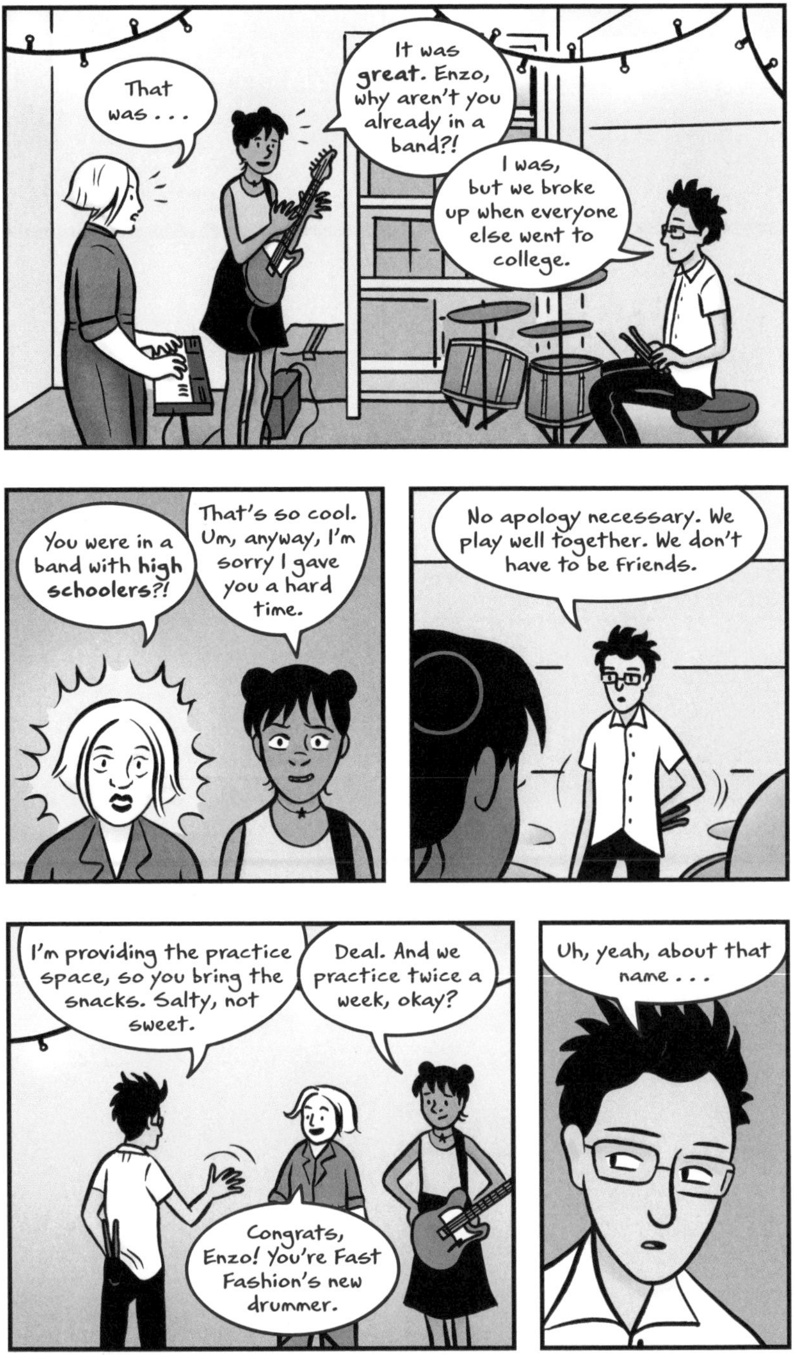
That was . . .
It was great. Enzo, why aren't you already in a band?!
I was, but we broke up when everyone else went to college.
You were in a band with high schoolers?!
That's so cool. Um, anyway, I'm sorry I gave you a hard time.
No apology necessary. We play well together. We don't have to be friends.
I'm providing the practice space, so you bring the snacks. Salty, not sweet.
Deal. And we practice twice a week, okay?
Congrats, Enzo! You're Fast Fashion's new drummer.
Uh, yeah, about that name . . .

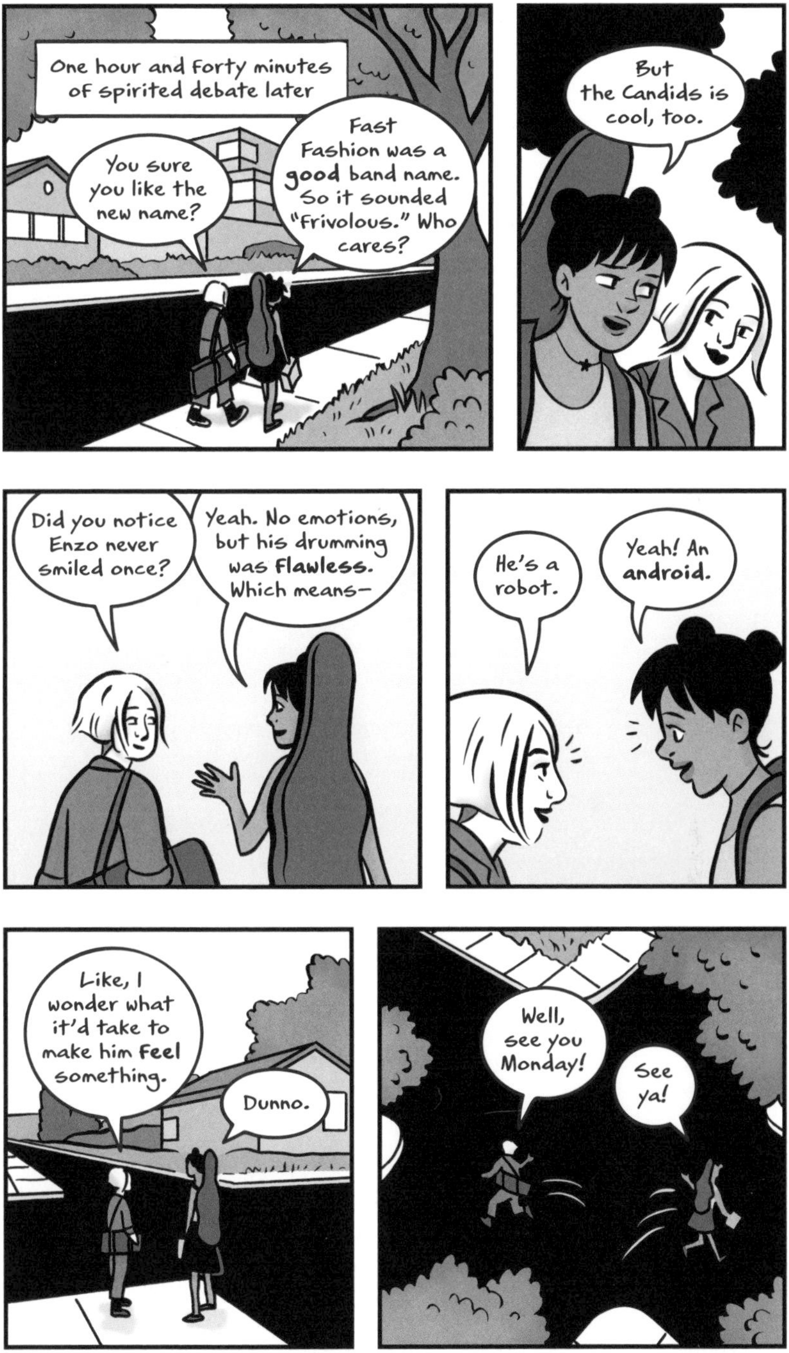
One hour and forty minutes of spirited debate later
You sure you like the new name?
Fast Fashion was a good band name. So it sounded "Frivolous." Who cares?
But the Candids is cool, too.
Did you notice Enzo never smiled once?
Yeah. No emotions, but his drumming was flawless. Which means—
He's a robot.
Yeah! An android.
Like, I wonder what it'd take to make him feel something.
Dunno.
Well, see you Monday!
See ya!

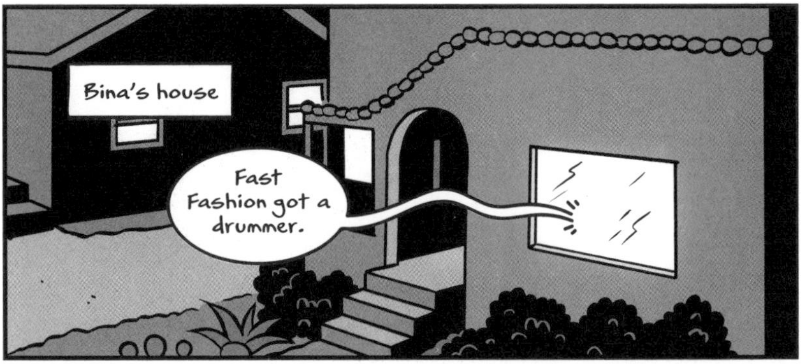
Bina's house
Fast Fashion got a drummer.

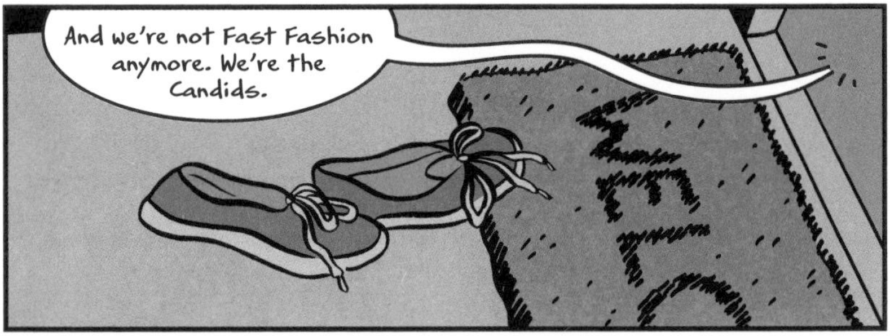
And we're not Fast Fashion anymore. We're the Candids.

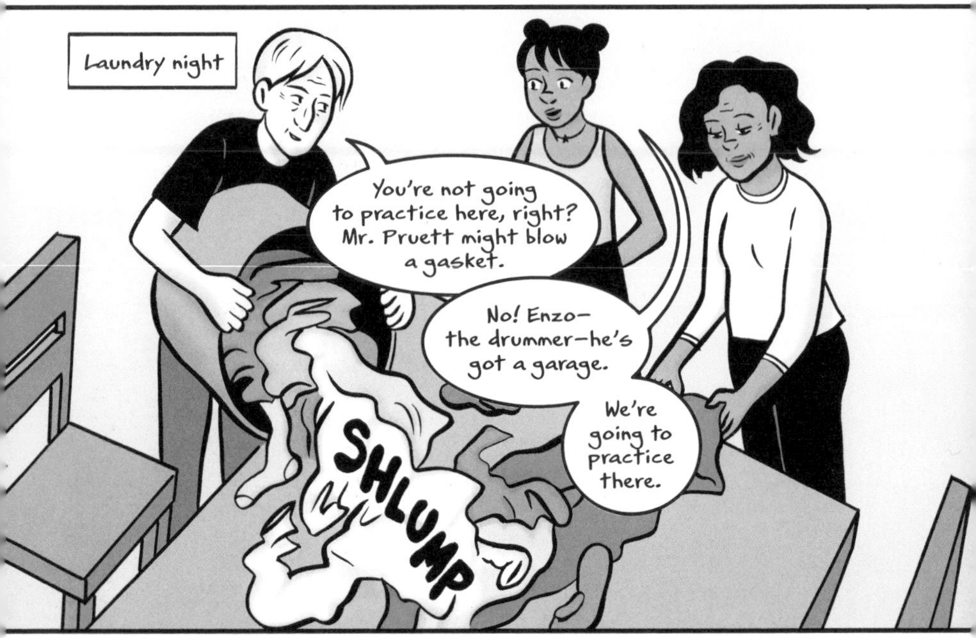
Laundry night
You're not going to practice here, right? Mr. Pruett might blow a gasket.
No! Enzo—the drummer—he's got a garage.
We're going to practice there.
SHLUMP

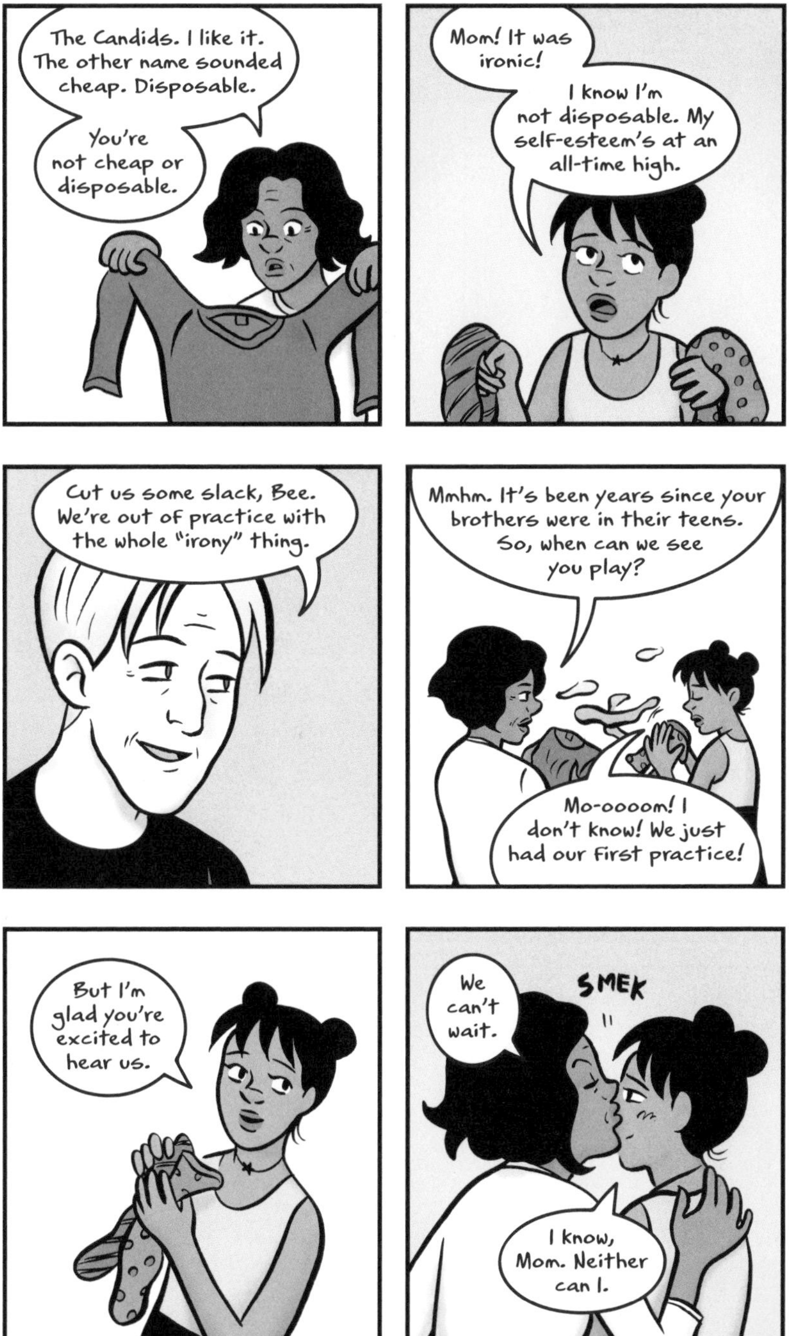
The Candids. I like it. The other name sounded cheap. Disposable.
You're not cheap or disposable.
Mom! It was ironic!
I know I'm not disposable. My self-esteem's at an all-time high.
Cut us some slack, Bee. We're out of practice with the whole "irony" thing.
Mmhm. It's been years since your brothers were in their teens. So, when can we see you play?
Mo-oooom! I don't know! We just had our first practice!
But I'm glad you're excited to hear us.
We can't wait.
SMEK
I know, Mom. Neither can I.

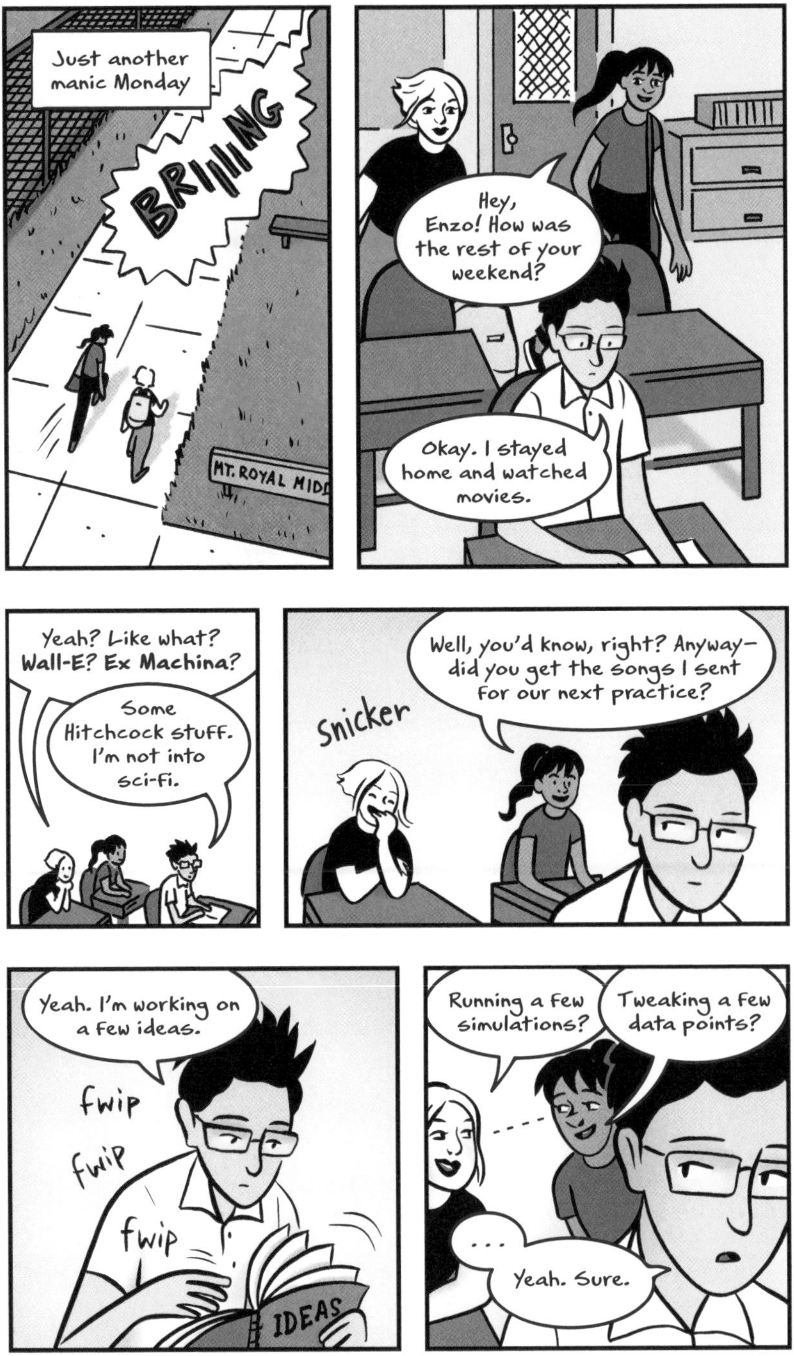
Just another manic Monday
BRIIIING
MT. ROYAL MIDD
Hey, Enzo! How was the rest of your weekend?
Okay. I stayed home and watched movies.
Yeah? Like what? Wall-E? Ex Machina?
Some Hitchcock stuff. I'm not into sci-fi.
Snicker
Well, you'd know, right? Anyway— did you get the songs I sent for our next practice?
Yeah. I'm working on a few ideas.
fwip
fwip
fwip
IDEAS
Running a few simulations?
Tweaking a few data points?
...
Yeah. Sure.

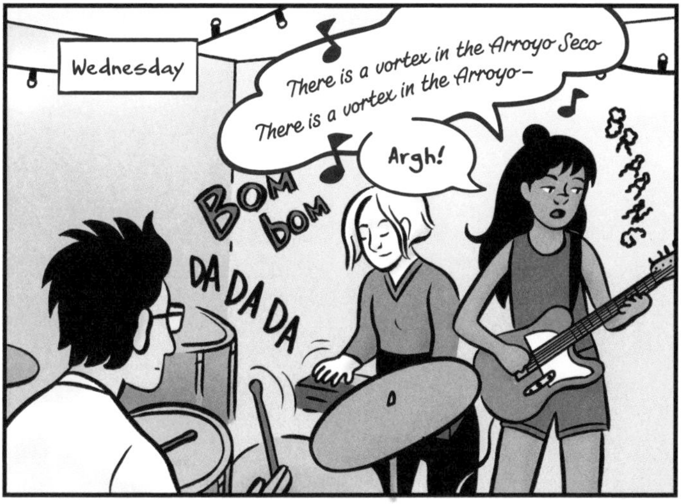
Wednesday
There is a vortex in the Arroyo Seco
There is a vortex in the Arroyo—
Argh!
BRRANG
BOM bom
DA DA DA DA

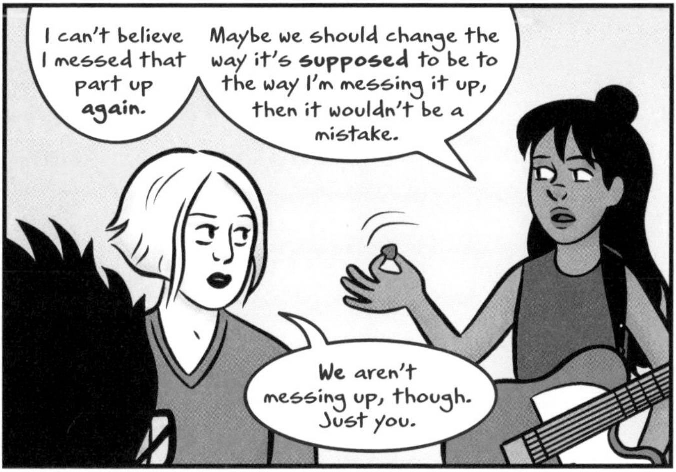
I can't believe I messed that part up again.
Maybe we should change the way it's **supposed** to be to the way I'm messing it up, then it wouldn't be a mistake.
We aren't messing up, though. Just you.

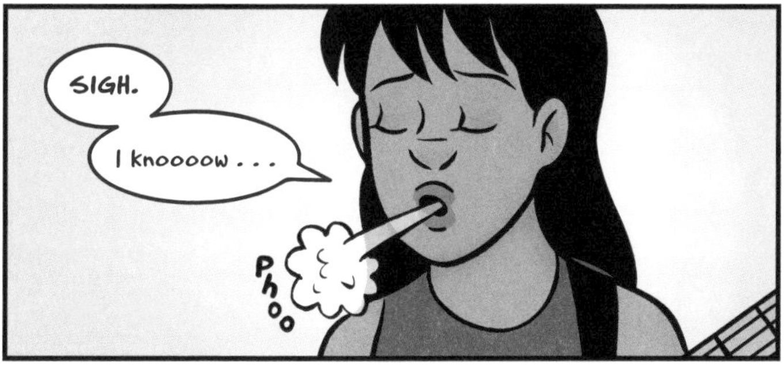
SIGH.
I knoooow . . .
Phoo

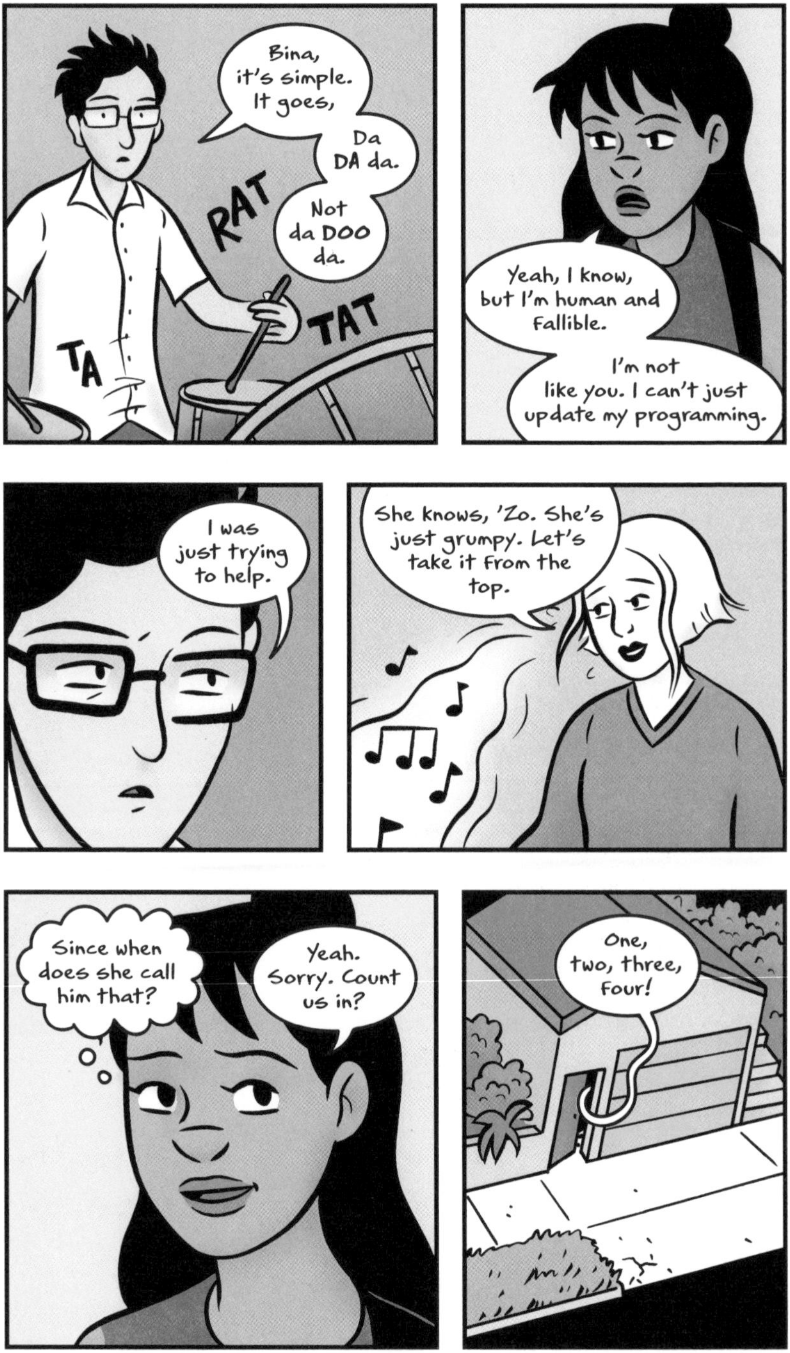
Bina, it's simple. It goes,
Da DA da.
Not da DOO da.
RAT
TAT
TA
Yeah, I know, but I'm human and fallible.
I'm not like you. I can't just update my programming.
I was just trying to help.
She knows, 'Zo. She's just grumpy. Let's take it from the top.
Since when does she call him that?
Yeah. Sorry. Count us in?
One, two, three, four!

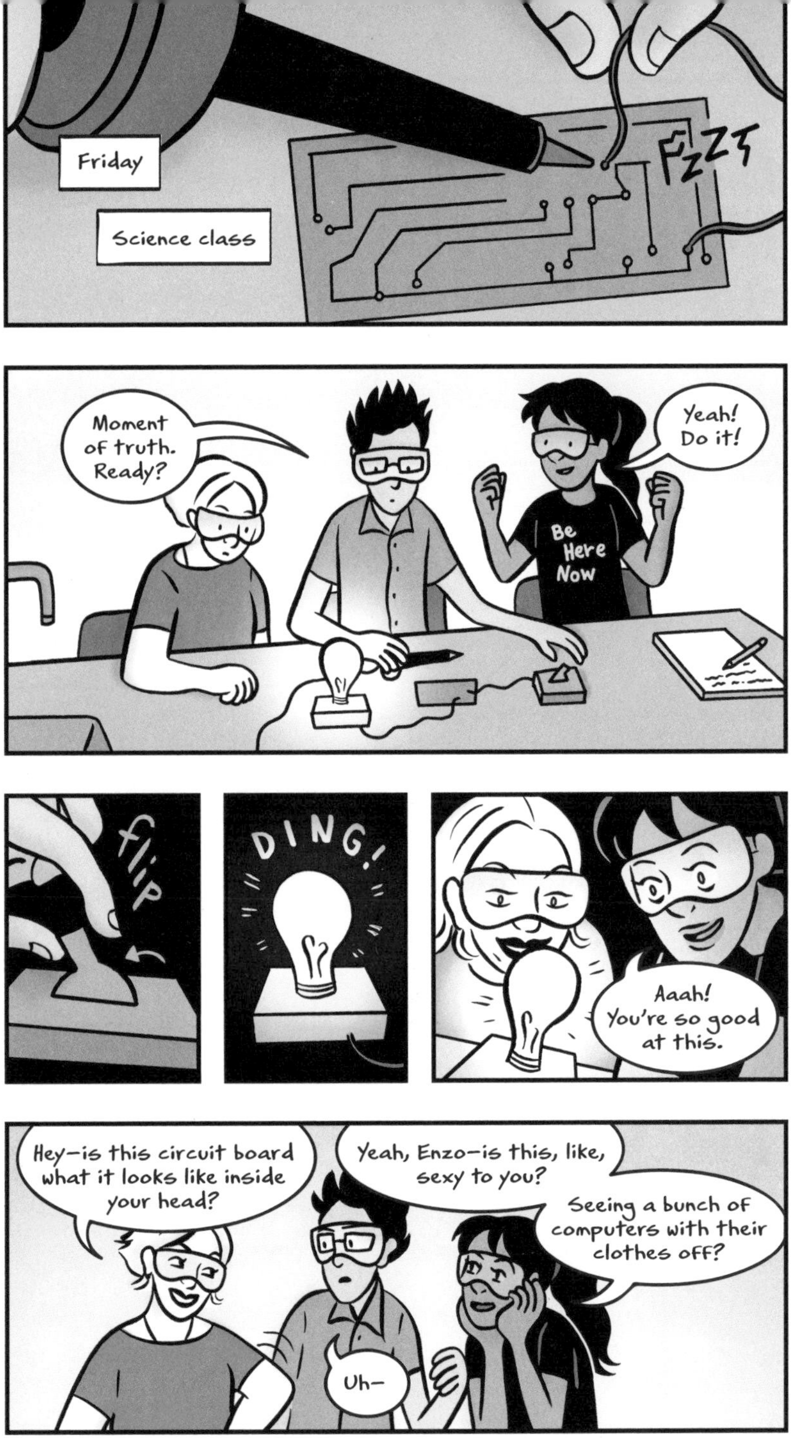

Friday
Science class
FZZZ
Moment of truth. Ready?
Yeah! Do it!
Be Here Now
flip
DING!
Aaah! You're so good at this.
Hey—is this circuit board what it looks like inside your head?
Yeah, Enzo—is this, like, sexy to you?
Seeing a bunch of computers with their clothes off?
Uh—

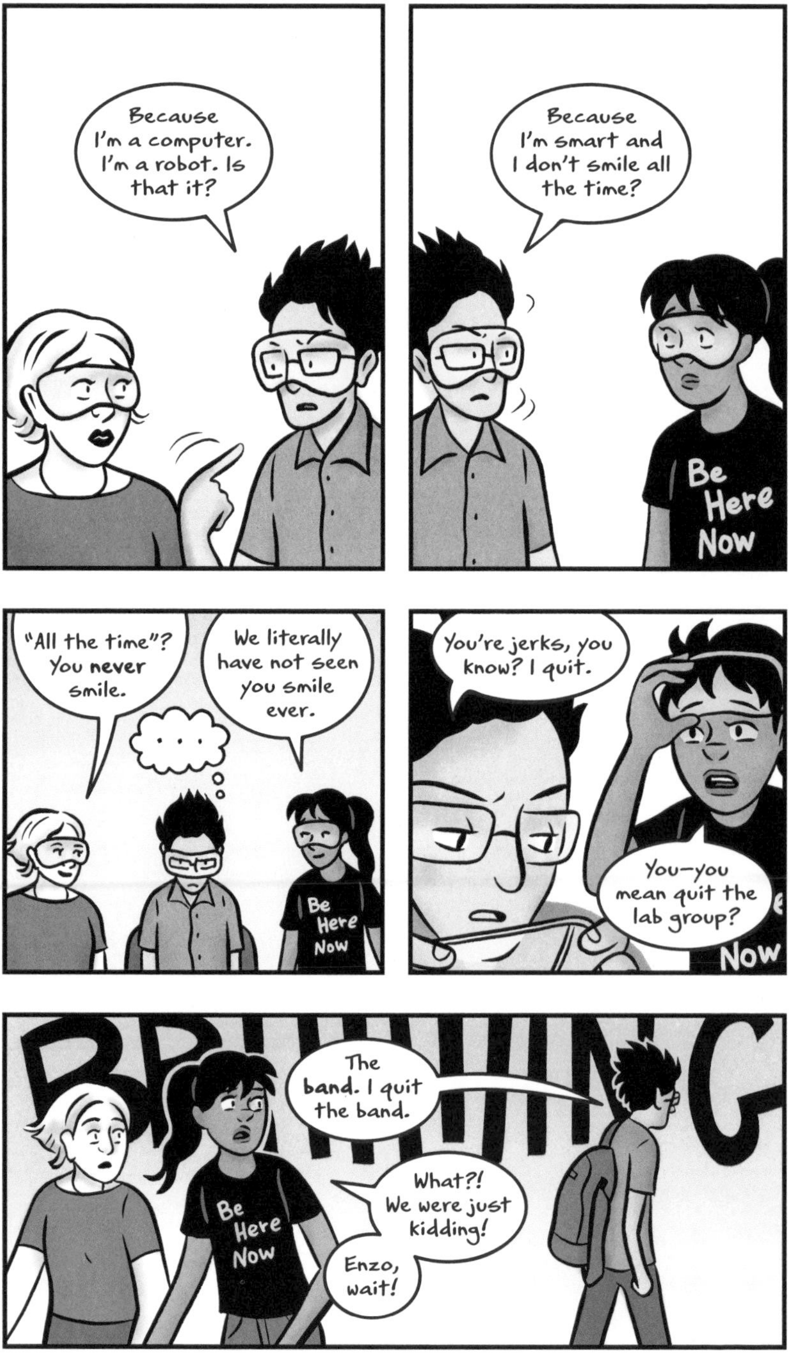
Because I'm a computer. I'm a robot. Is that it?
Because I'm smart and I don't smile all the time?
"All the time"? You never smile.
We literally have not seen you smile ever.
. . .
Be Here Now
You're jerks, you know? I quit.
You—you mean quit the lab group?
The band. I quit the band.
What?! We were just kidding!
Enzo, wait!

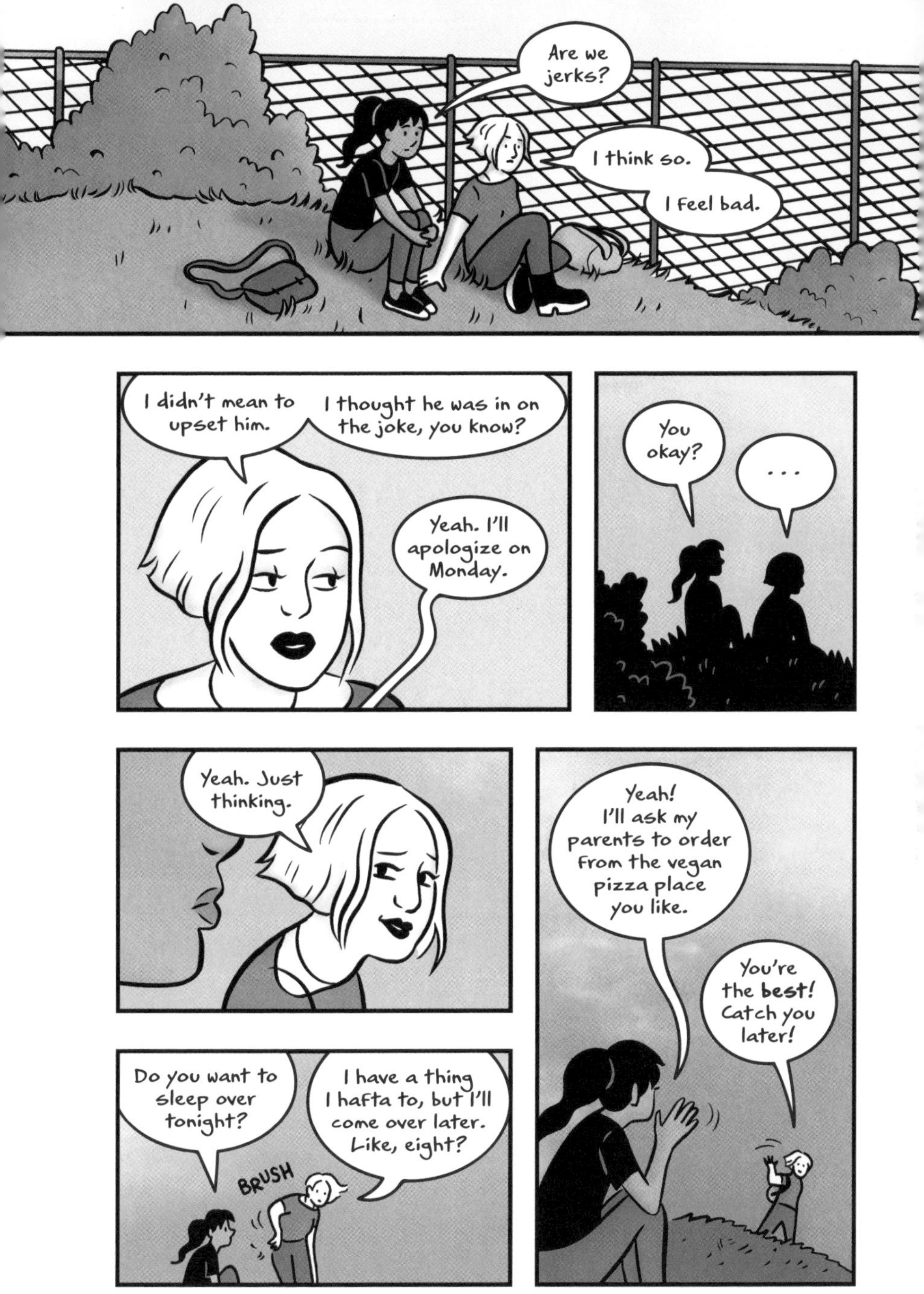
Are we jerks?
I think so.
I feel bad.
I didn't mean to upset him.
I thought he was in on the joke, you know?
Yeah. I'll apologize on Monday.
You okay?
...
Yeah. Just thinking.
Do you want to sleep over tonight?
BRUSH
I have a thing I hafta to, but I'll come over later. Like, eight?
Yeah! I'll ask my parents to order from the vegan pizza place you like.
You're the **best**! Catch you later!

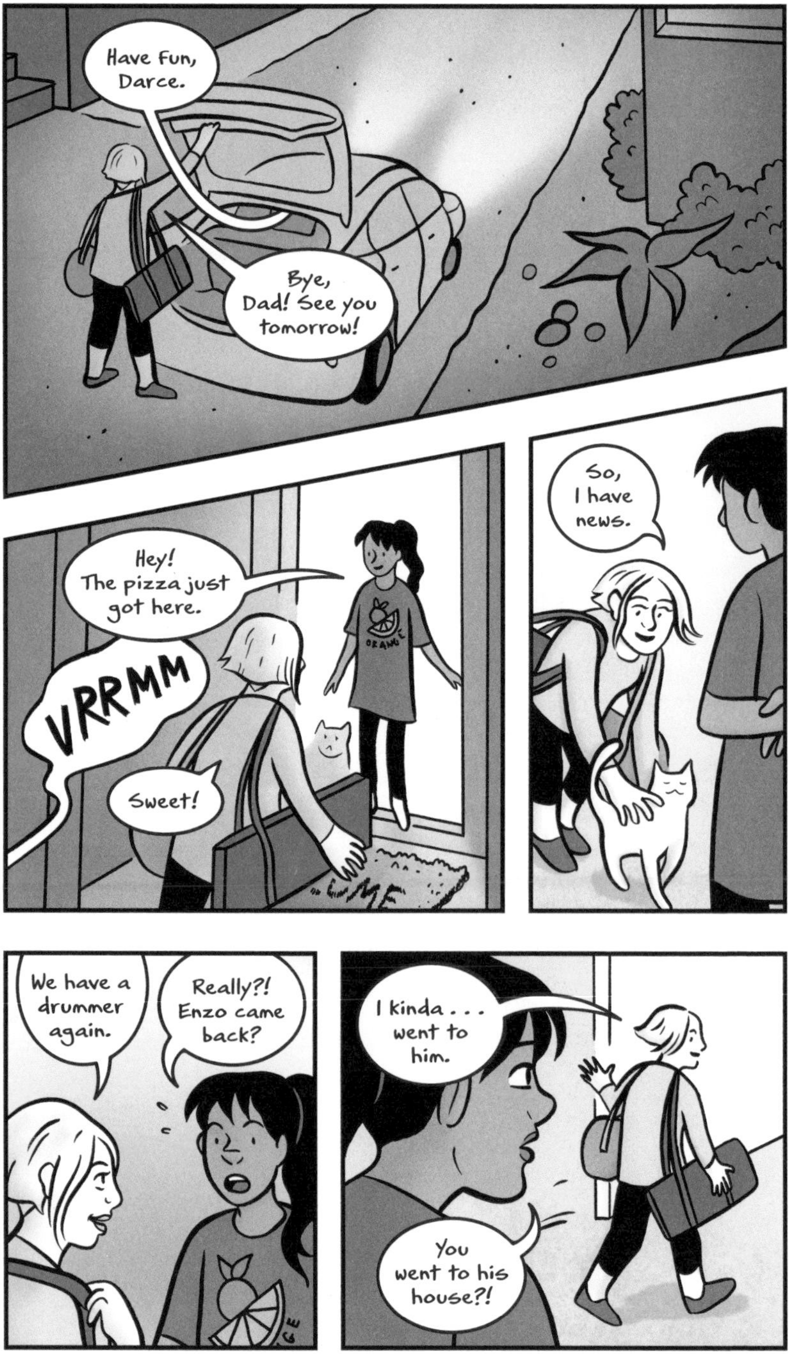
Have Fun, Darce.
Bye, Dad! See you tomorrow!
Hey! The pizza just got here.
VRRMM
Sweet!
So, I have news.
We have a drummer again.
Really?! Enzo came back?
I kinda . . . went to him.
You went to his house?!

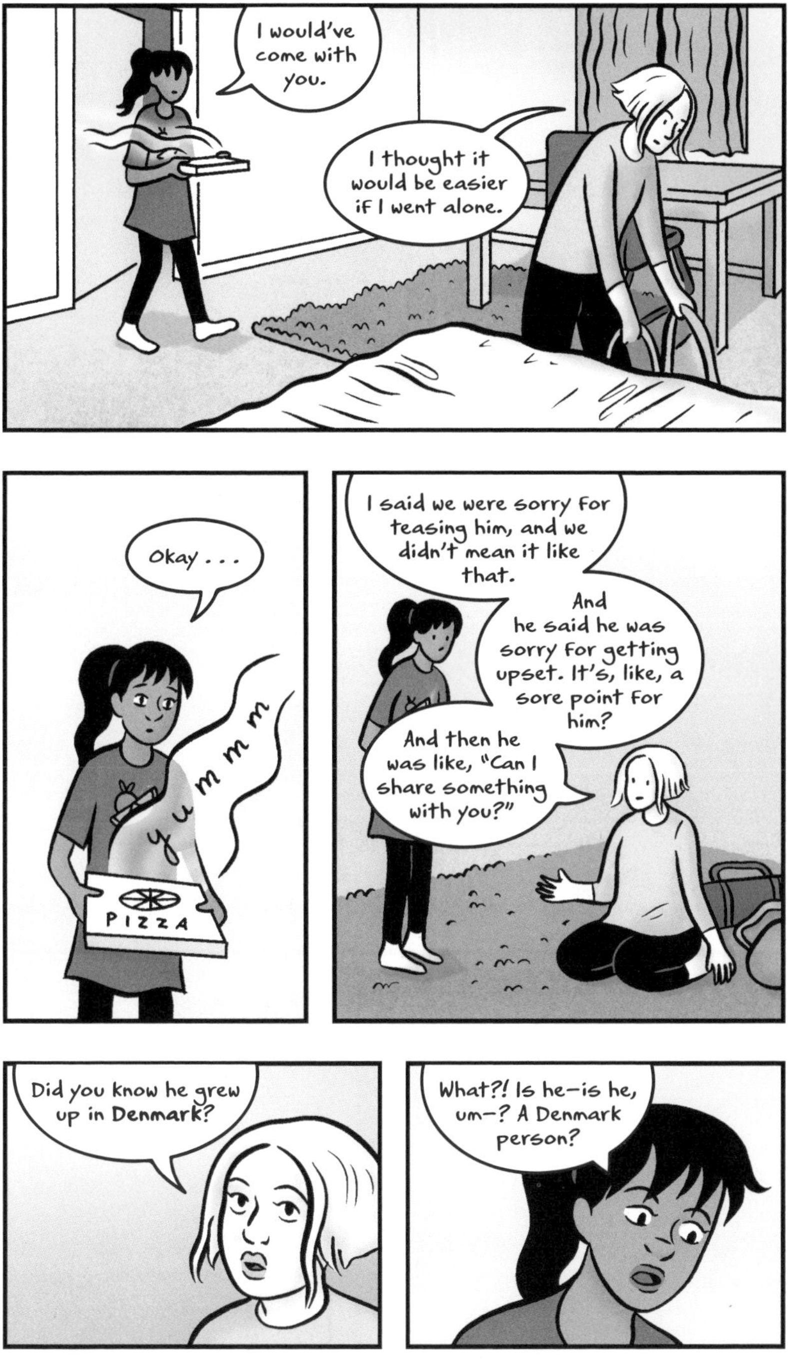
I would've come with you.
I thought it would be easier if I went alone.
Okay . . .
yummm
PIZZA
I said we were sorry for teasing him, and we didn't mean it like that.
And he said he was sorry for getting upset. It's, like, a sore point for him?
And then he was like, "Can I share something with you?"
Did you know he grew up in Denmark?
What?! Is he–is he, um–? A Denmark person?

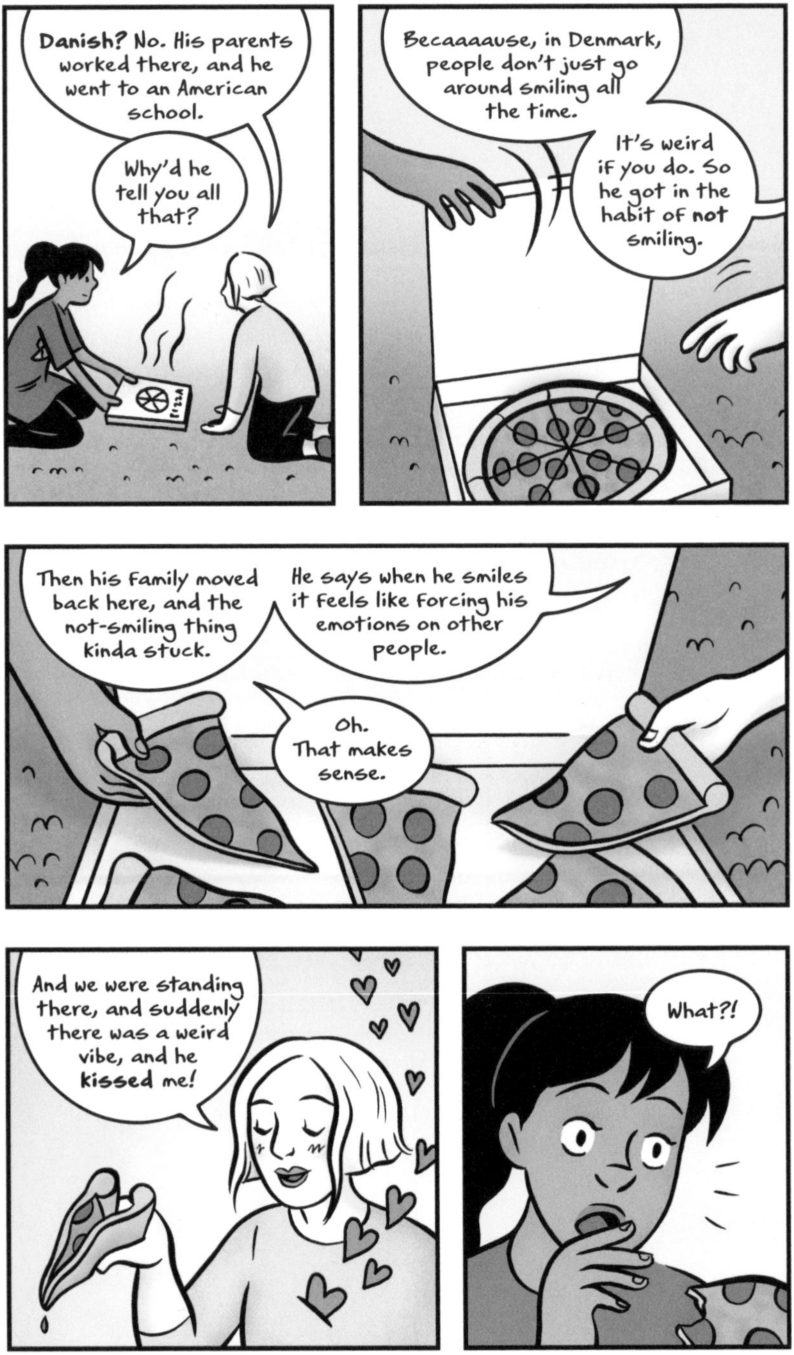
Danish? No. His parents worked there, and he went to an American school.
Why'd he tell you all that?
PIZZA
Becaaaause, in Denmark, people don't just go around smiling all the time.
It's weird if you do. So he got in the habit of not smiling.
Then his family moved back here, and the not-smiling thing kinda stuck.
He says when he smiles it feels like forcing his emotions on other people.
Oh. That makes sense.
And we were standing there, and suddenly there was a weird vibe, and he kissed me!
What?!

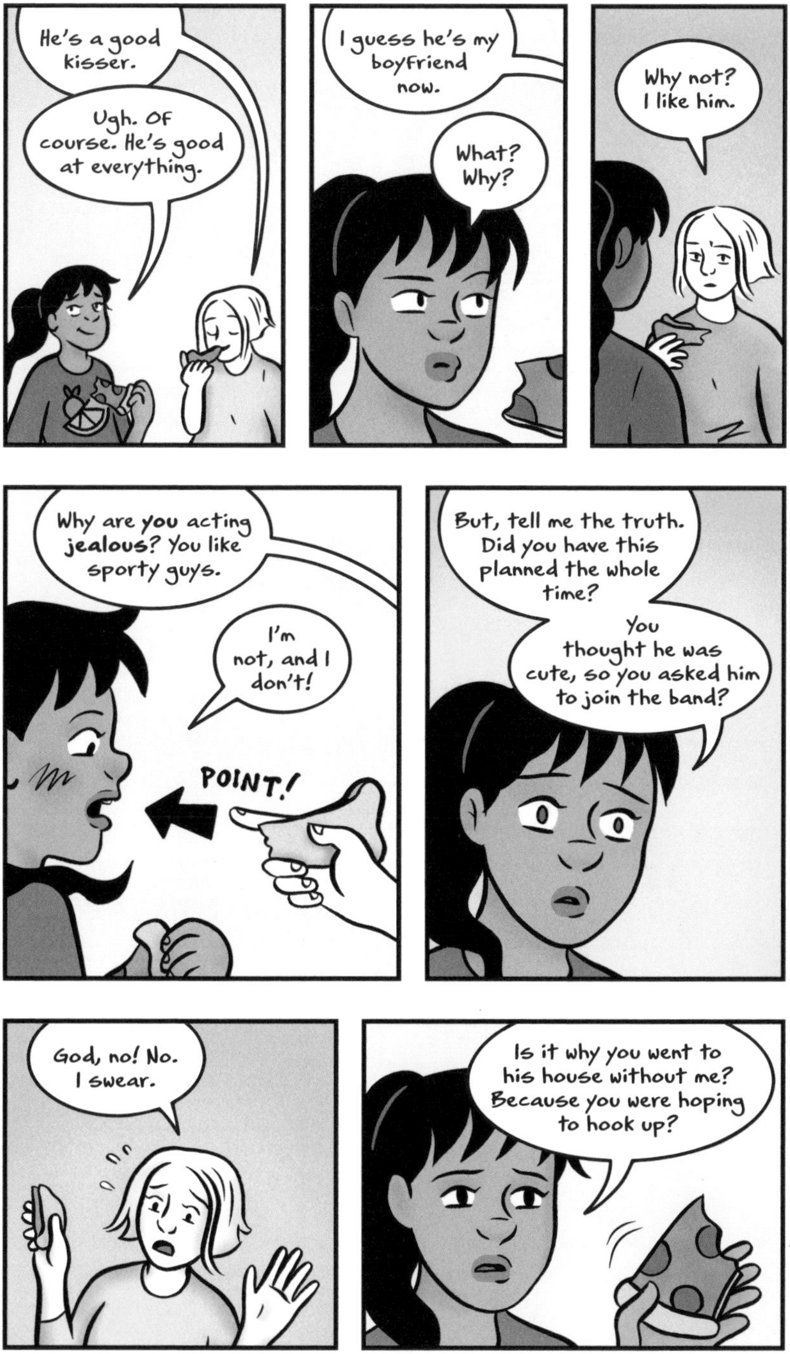
He's a good kisser.
Ugh. Of course. He's good at everything.
I guess he's my boyfriend now.
What? Why?
Why not? I like him.
Why are you acting jealous? You like sporty guys.
I'm not, and I don't!
POINT!
But, tell me the truth. Did you have this planned the whole time?
You thought he was cute, so you asked him to join the band?
God, no! No. I swear.
Is it why you went to his house without me? Because you were hoping to hook up?

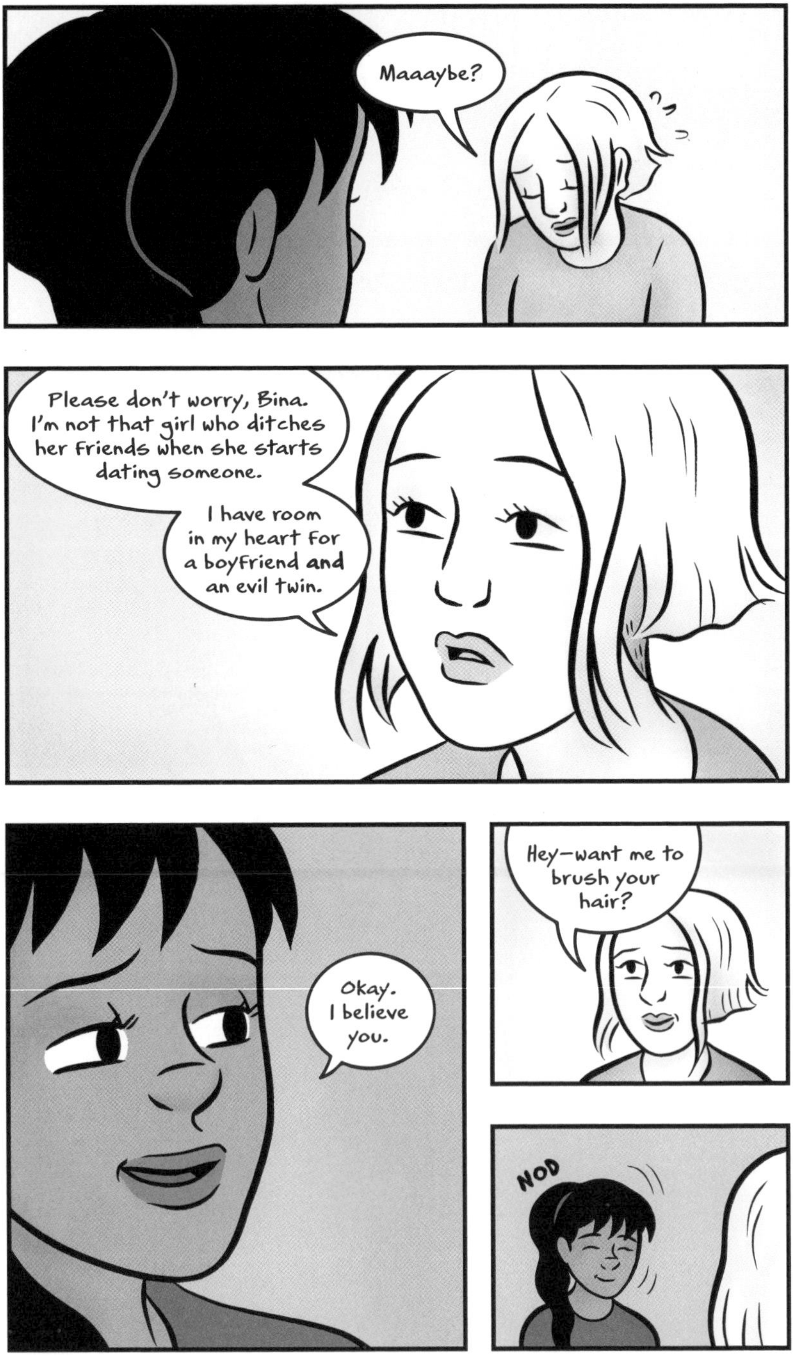
Maaaybe?
Please don't worry, Bina. I'm not that girl who ditches her friends when she starts dating someone.
I have room in my heart for a boyfriend and an evil twin.
Okay. I believe you.
Hey—want me to brush your hair?
NOD

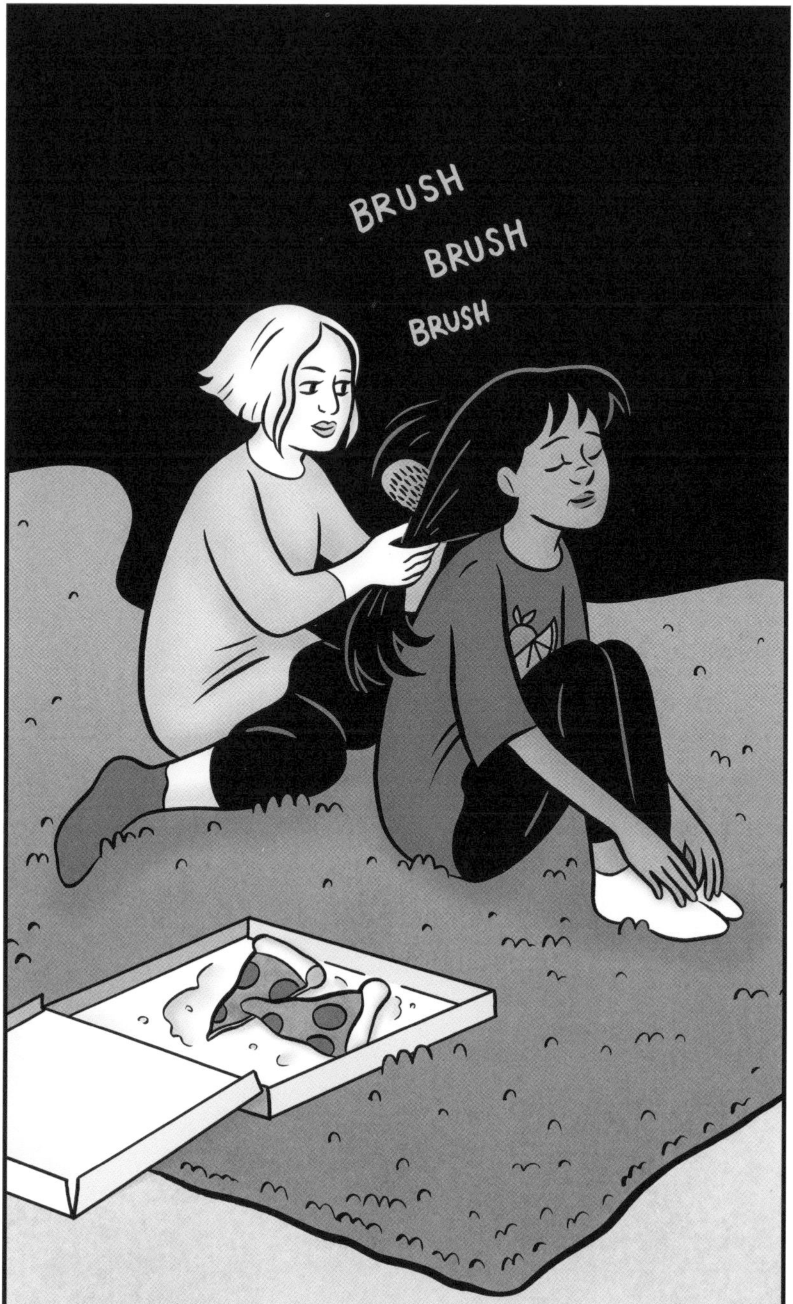
BRUSH
BRUSH
BRUSH

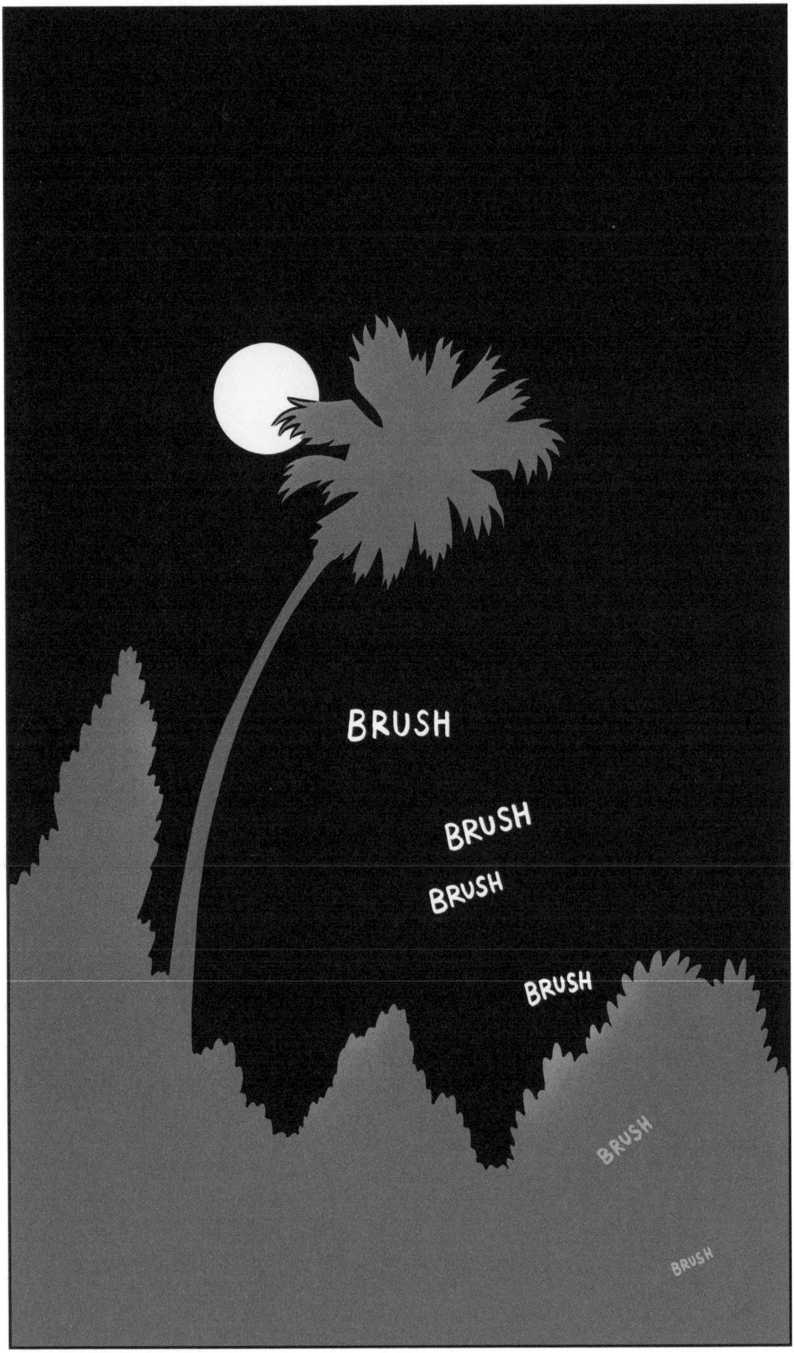
BRUSH
BRUSH
BRUSH
BRUSH
BRUSH
BRUSH

October

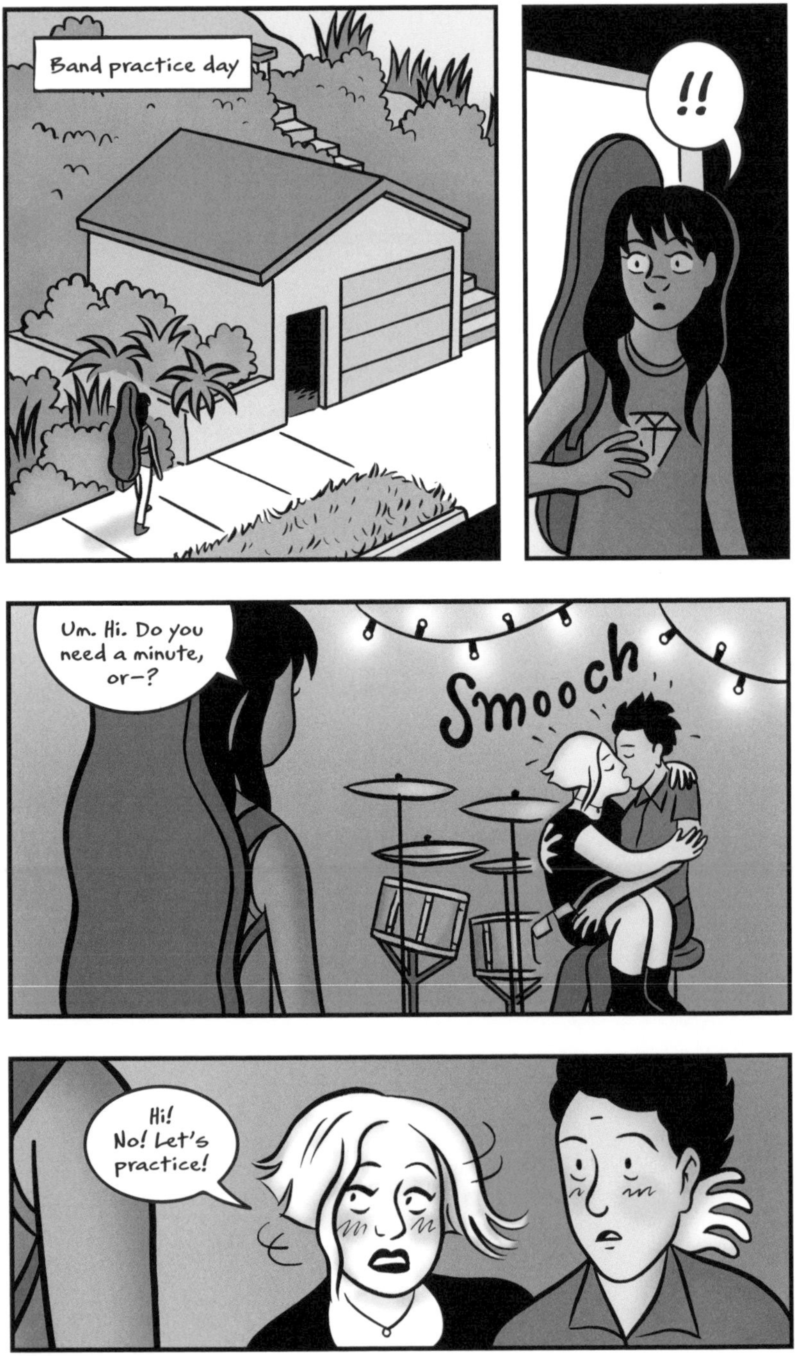
Band practice day
!!
Um. Hi. Do you need a minute, or–?
Smooch
Hi! No! Let's practice!

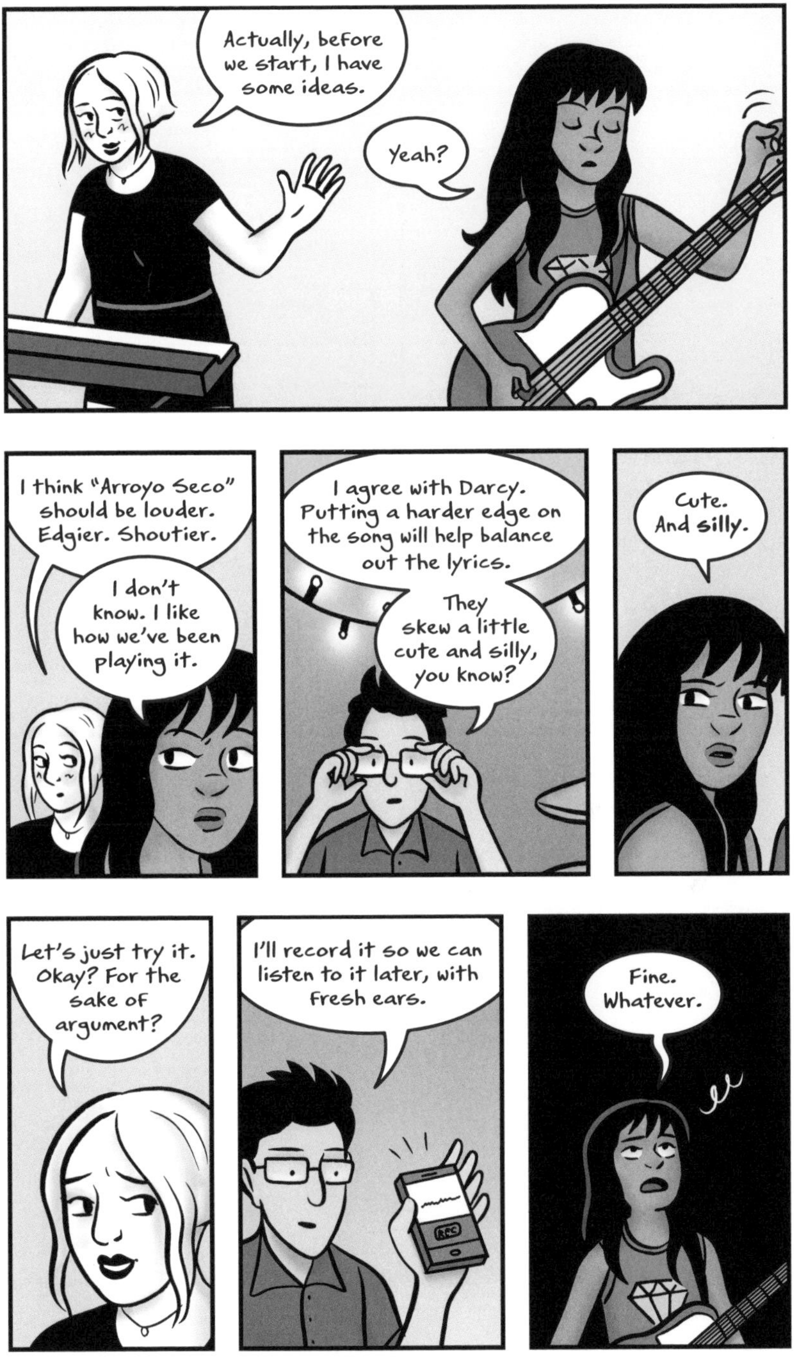
Actually, before we start, I have some ideas.
Yeah?
I think "Arroyo Seco" should be louder. Edgier. Shoutier.
I don't know. I like how we've been playing it.
I agree with Darcy. Putting a harder edge on the song will help balance out the lyrics.
They skew a little cute and silly, you know?
Cute. And silly.
Let's just try it. Okay? For the sake of argument?
I'll record it so we can listen to it later, with fresh ears.
REC
Fine. Whatever.

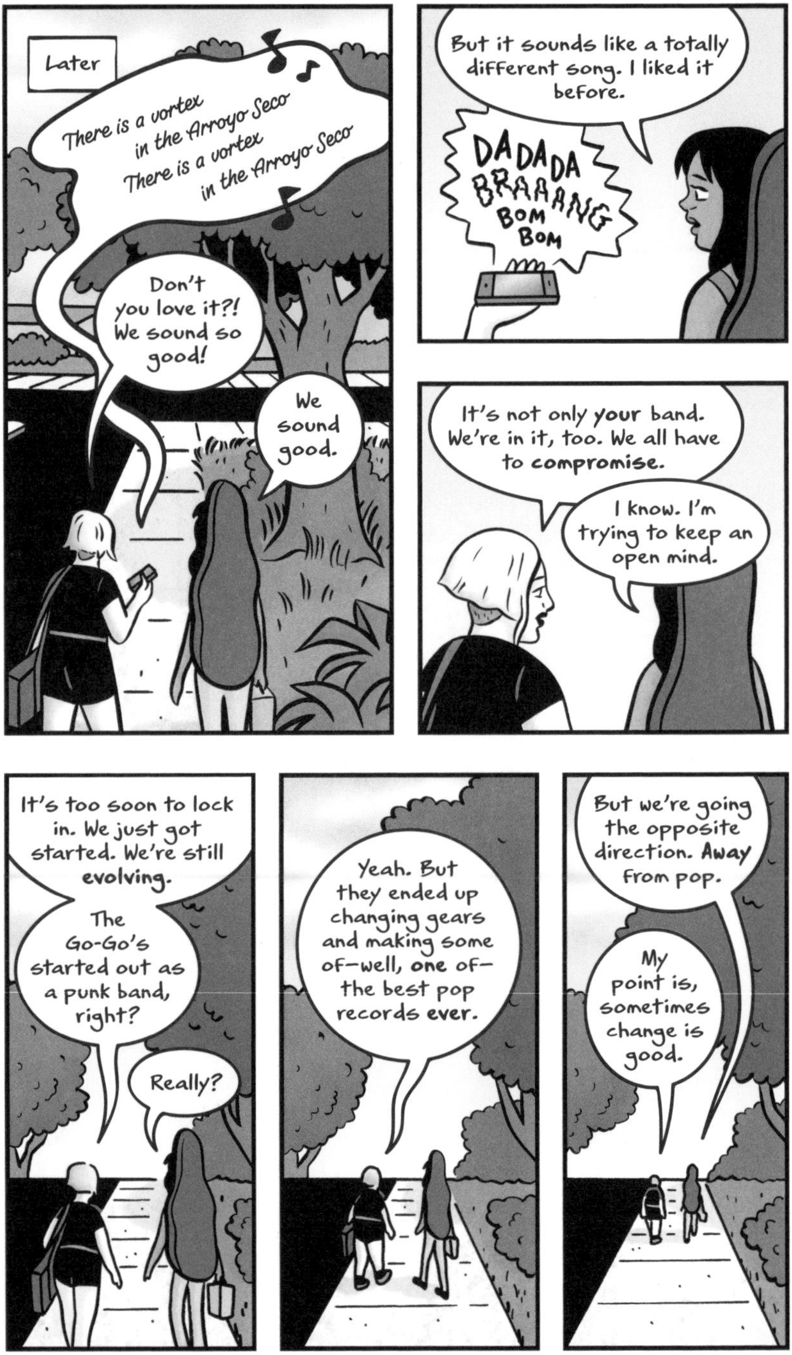
Later
There is a vortex in the Arroyo Seco There is a vortex in the Arroyo Seco
Don't you love it?! We sound so good!
We sound good.
But it sounds like a totally different song. I liked it before.
DADADA BRAAAANG BOM BOM
It's not only your band. We're in it, too. We all have to compromise.
I know. I'm trying to keep an open mind.
It's too soon to lock in. We just got started. We're still evolving.
The Go-Go's started out as a punk band, right?
Really?
Yeah. But they ended up changing gears and making some of—well, one of—the best pop records ever.
But we're going the opposite direction. Away from pop.
My point is, sometimes change is good.

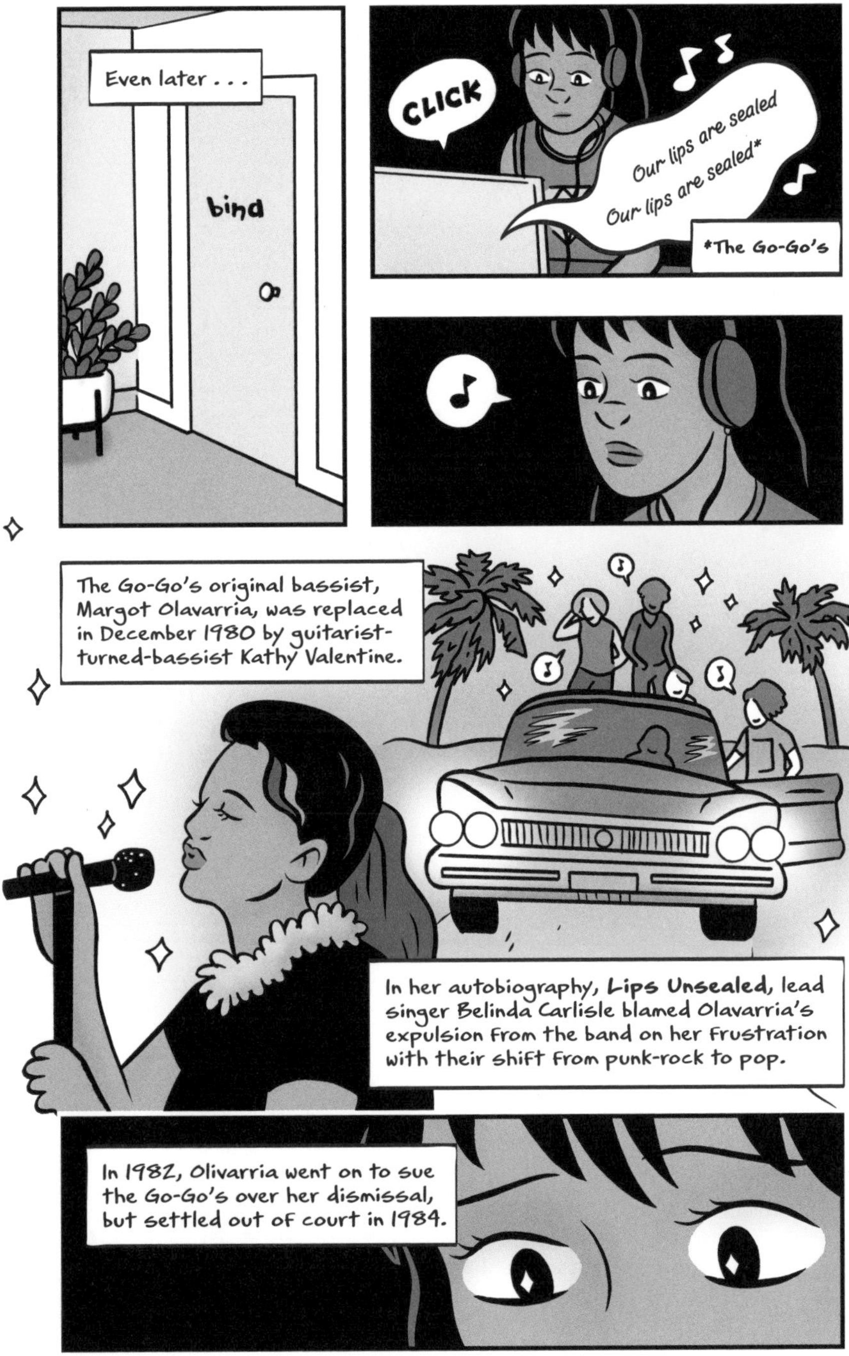

Even later . . .
bina
CLICK
Our lips are sealed
Our lips are sealed*
*The Go-Go's
The Go-Go's original bassist, Margot Olavarria, was replaced in December 1980 by guitarist-turned-bassist Kathy Valentine.
In her autobiography, **Lips Unsealed**, lead singer Belinda Carlisle blamed Olavarria's expulsion from the band on her frustration with their shift from punk-rock to pop.
In 1982, Olivarria went on to sue the Go-Go's over her dismissal, but settled out of court in 1984.

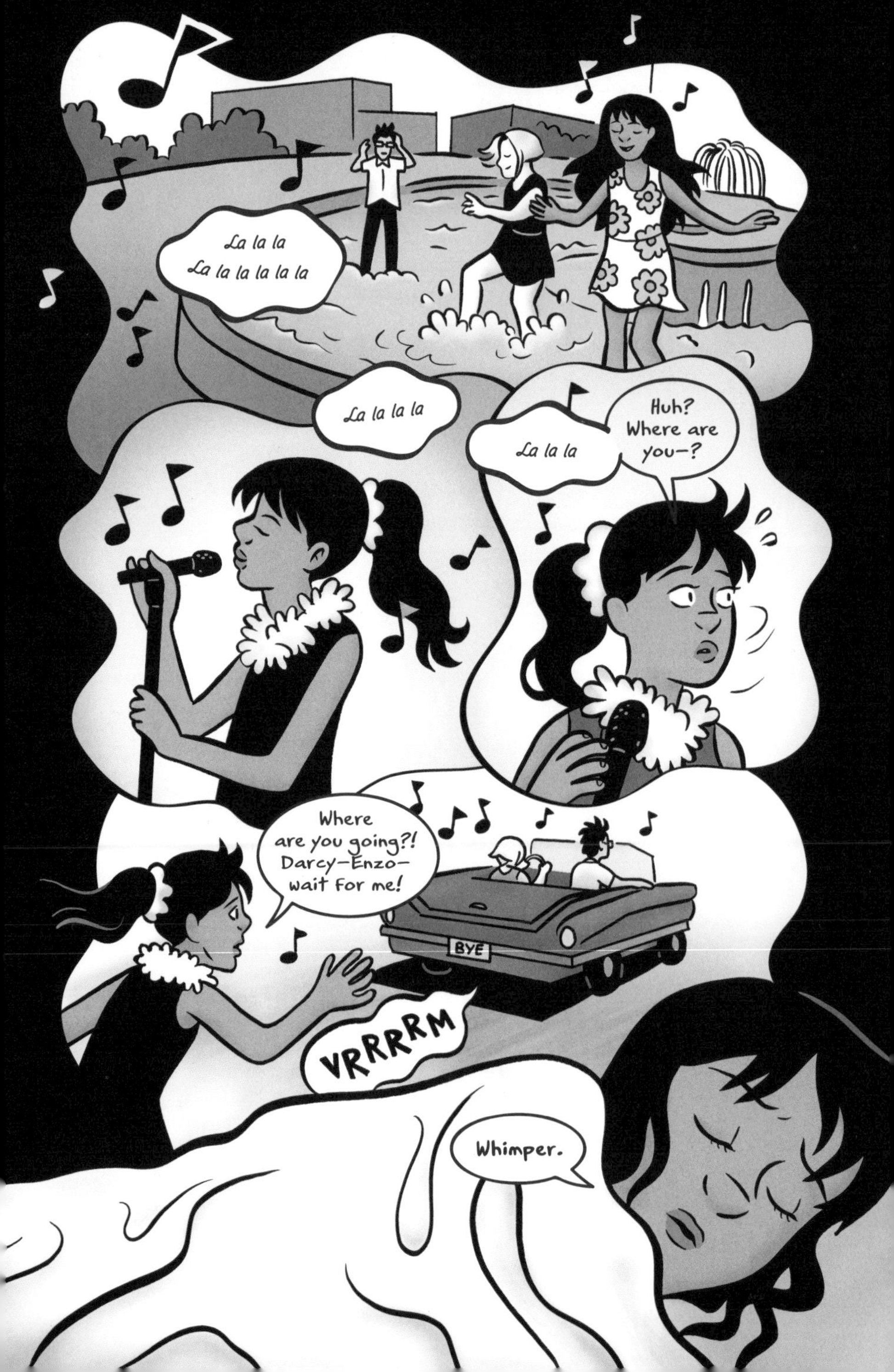
La la la
La la la la la la
La la la la
La la la
Huh? Where are you–?
Where are you going?! Darcy–Enzo–wait for me!
BYE
VRRRRM
Whimper.

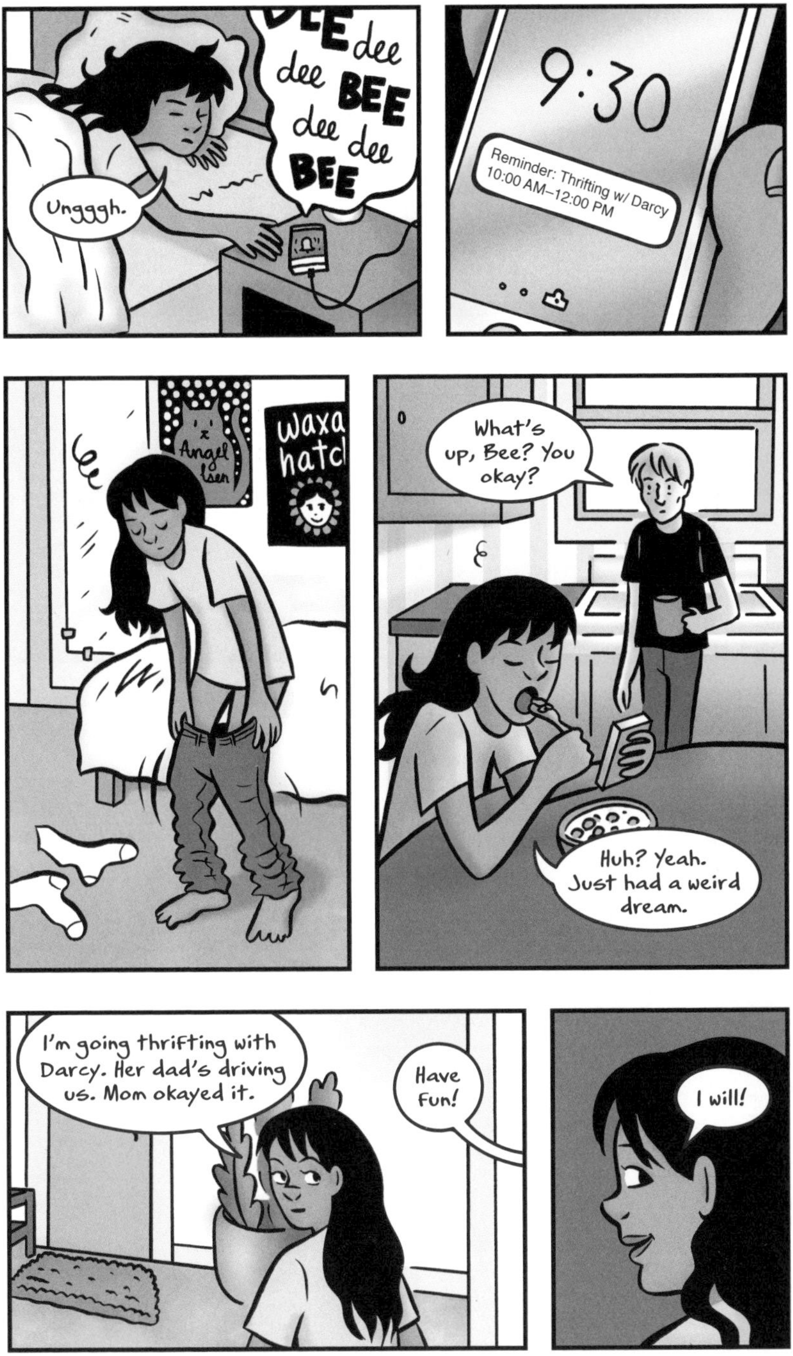
DEE dee dee BEE dee dee BEE
Ungggh.
9:30
Reminder: Thrifting w/ Darcy 10:00 AM–12:00 PM
Waxa hatc
What's up, Bee? You okay?
Huh? Yeah. Just had a weird dream.
I'm going thrifting with Darcy. Her dad's driving us. Mom okayed it.
Have fun!
I will!

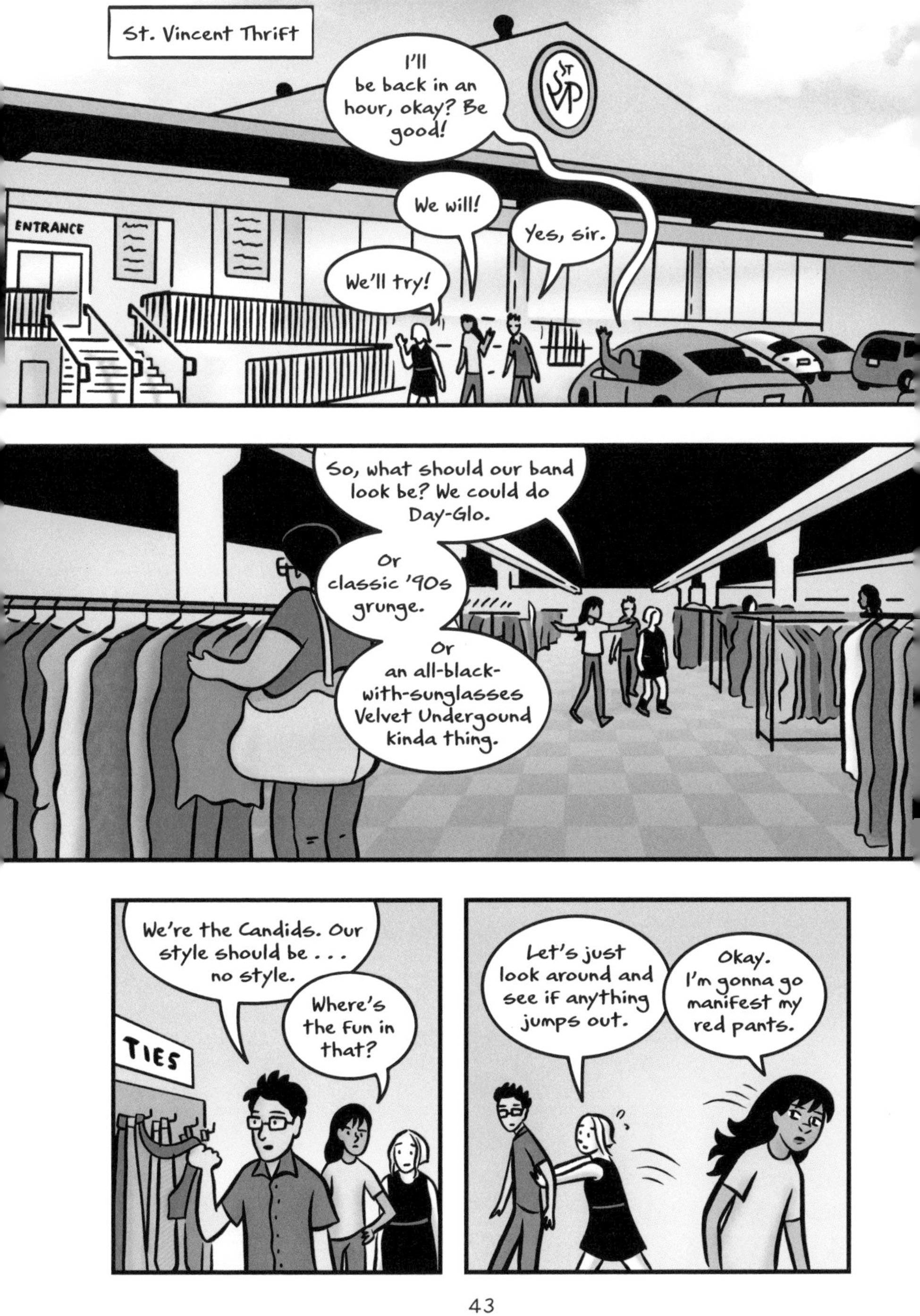
St. Vincent Thrift
I'll be back in an hour, okay? Be good!
We will!
Yes, sir.
We'll try!
ENTRANCE
So, what should our band look be? We could do Day-Glo.
Or classic '90s grunge.
Or an all-black-with-sunglasses Velvet Undergound kinda thing.
We're the Candids. Our style should be . . . no style.
Where's the fun in that?
TIES
Let's just look around and see if anything jumps out.
Okay. I'm gonna go manifest my red pants.

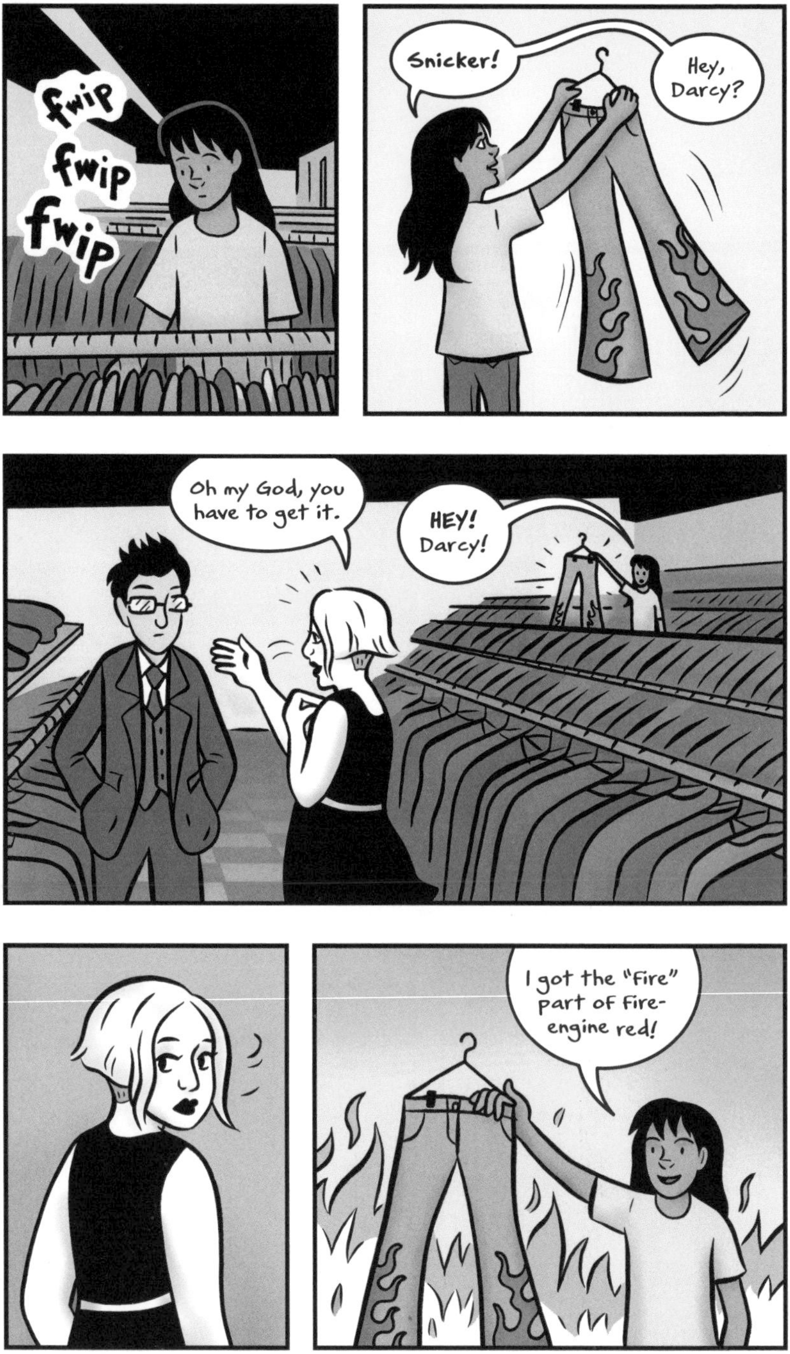
fwip
fwip
fwip
Snicker!
Hey, Darcy?
Oh my God, you have to get it.
HEY! Darcy!
I got the "Fire" part of Fire-engine red!

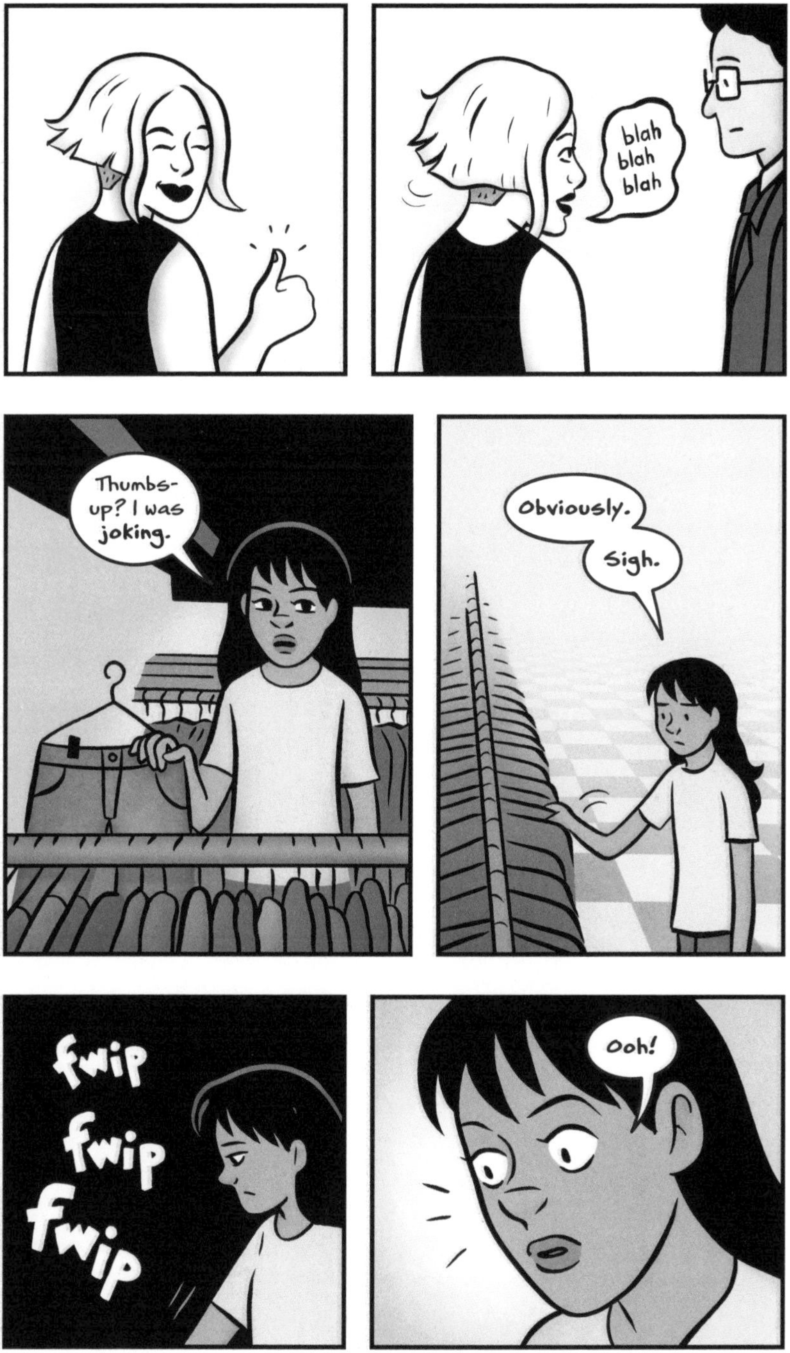
blah
blah
blah
Thumbs-up? I was joking.
Obviously.
Sigh.
fwip
fwip
fwip
Ooh!

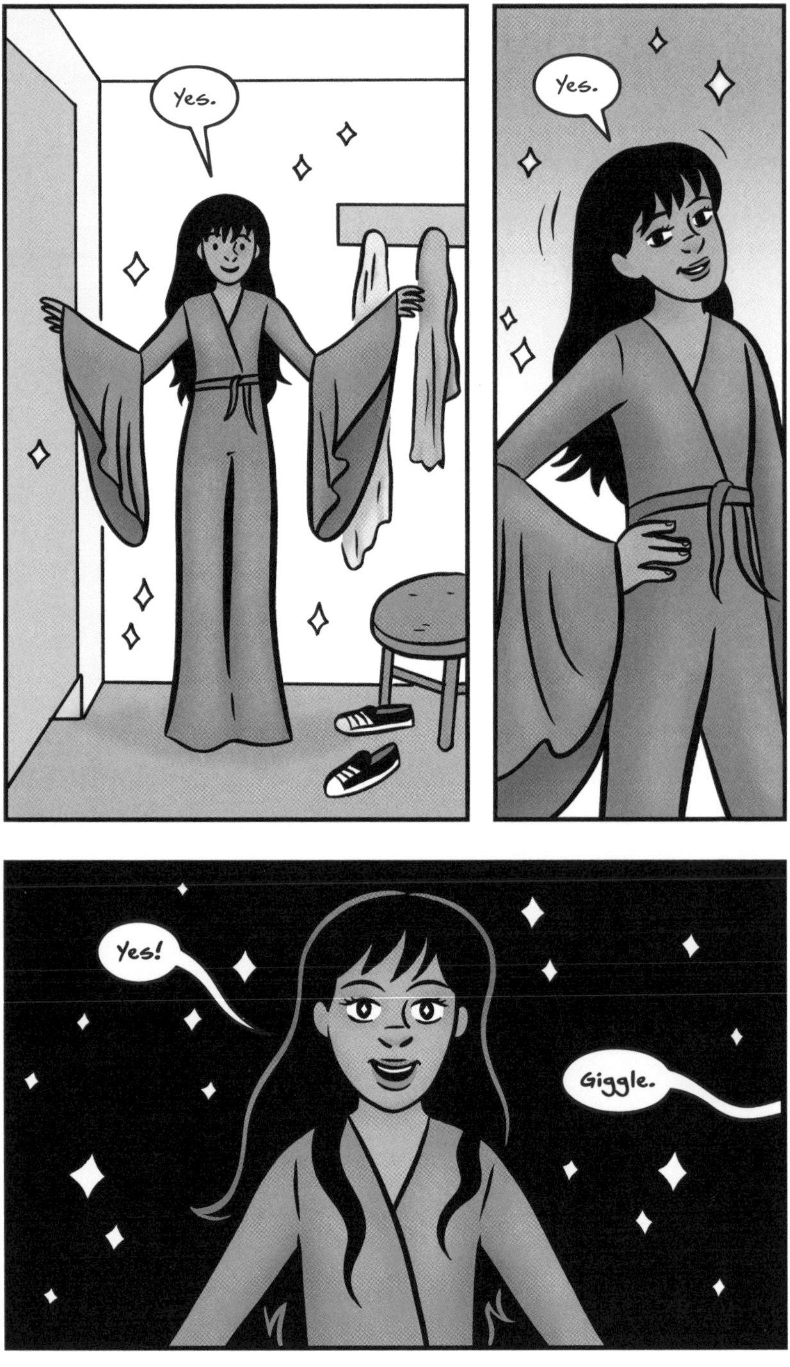
Yes.
Yes.
Yes!
Giggle.

48

49

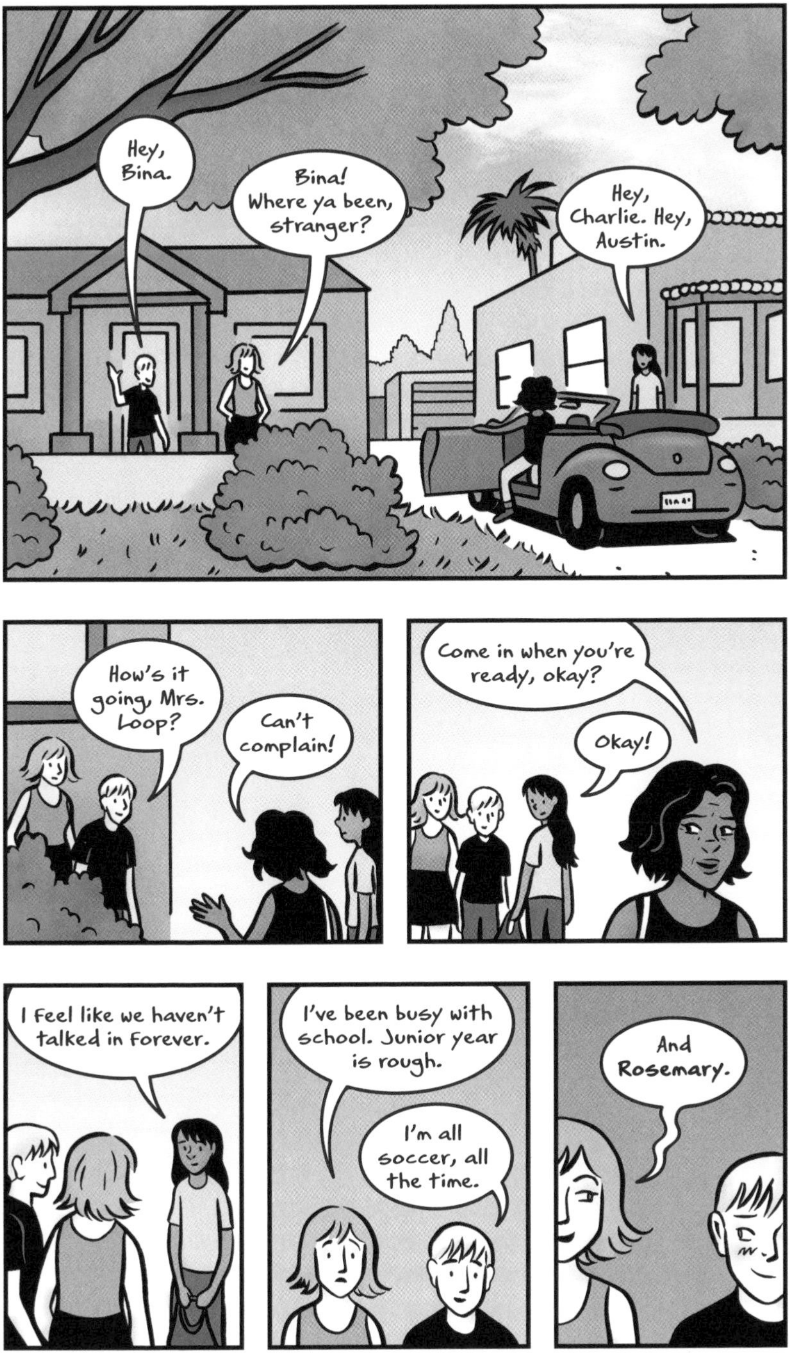
Hey, Bina.
Bina! Where ya been, stranger?
Hey, Charlie. Hey, Austin.
How's it going, Mrs. Loop?
Can't complain!
Come in when you're ready, okay?
Okay!
I feel like we haven't talked in forever.
I've been busy with school. Junior year is rough.
I'm all soccer, all the time.
And Rosemary.

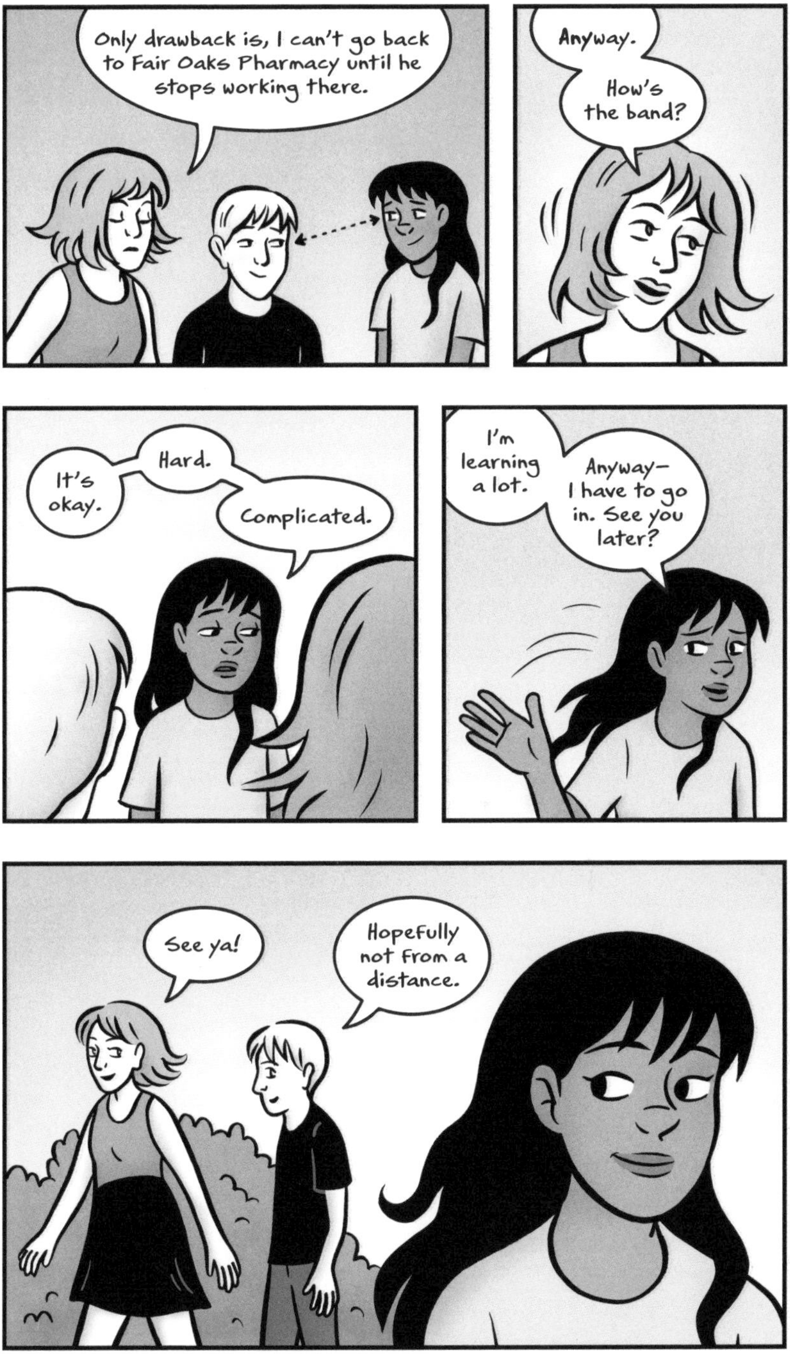
Only drawback is, I can't go back to Fair Oaks Pharmacy until he stops working there.
Anyway.
How's the band?
It's okay.
Hard.
Complicated.
I'm learning a lot.
Anyway— I have to go in. See you later?
See ya!
Hopefully not from a distance.

Bzzzt!

Hey. Enzo and I talked.

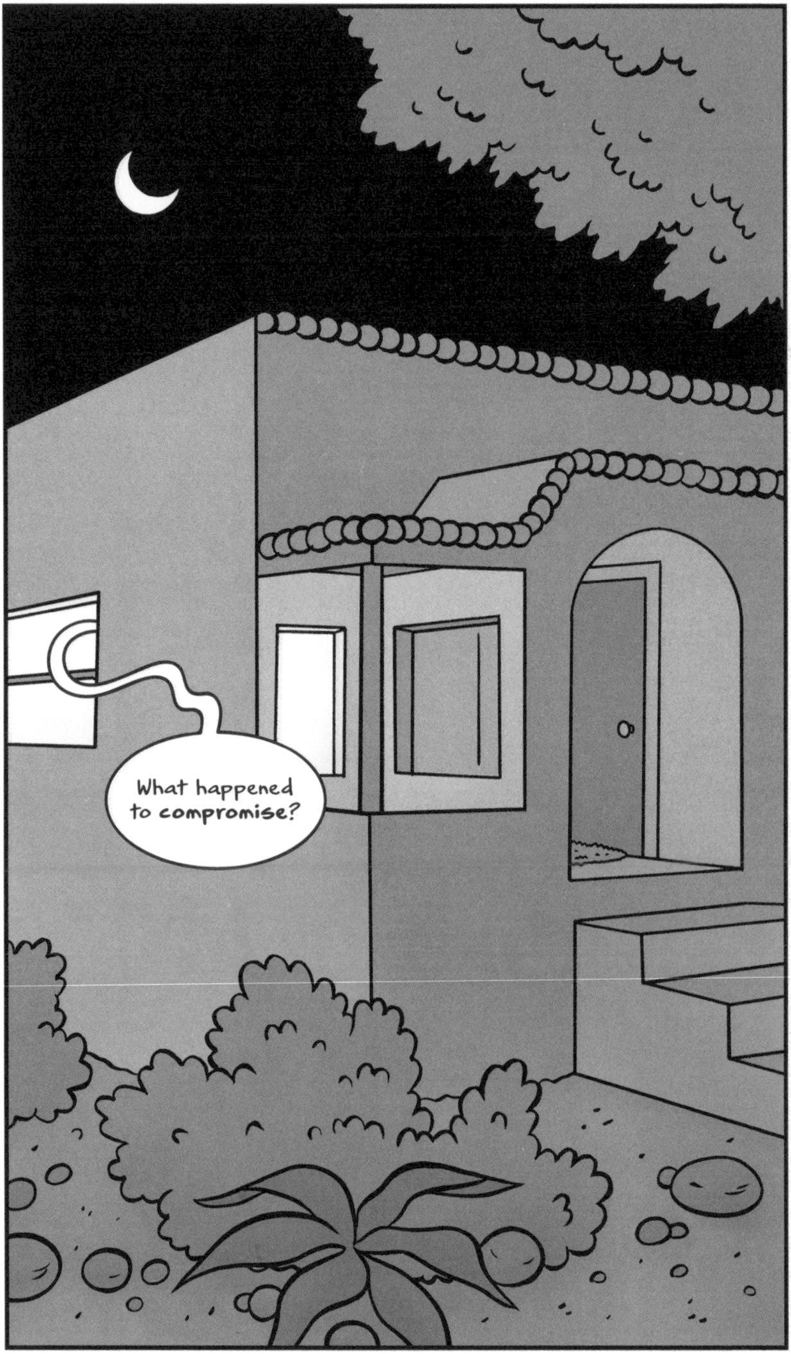
What happened to compromise?

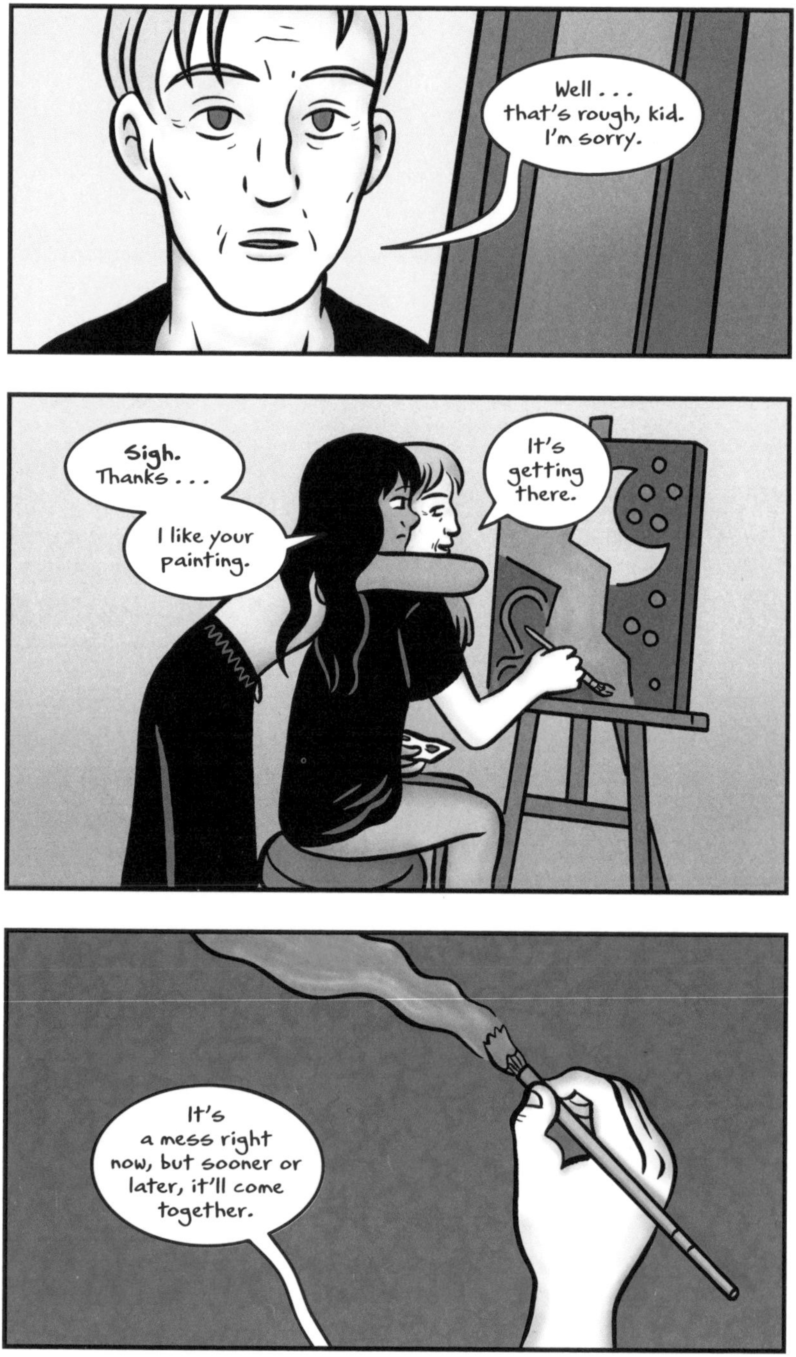
Well . . . that's rough, kid. I'm sorry.
Sigh. Thanks . . .
I like your painting.
It's getting there.
It's a mess right now, but sooner or later, it'll come together.

November

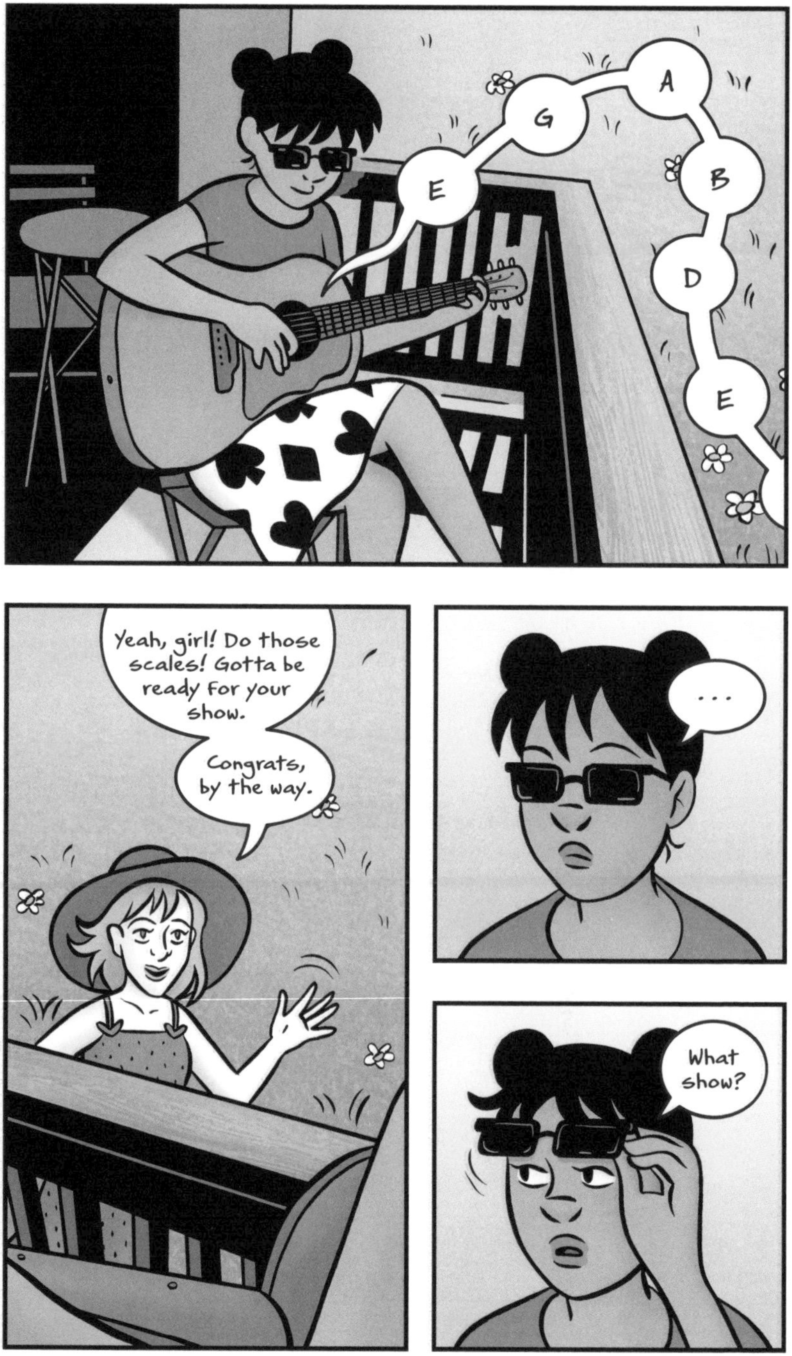
E
G
A
B
D
E
Yeah, girl! Do those scales! Gotta be ready for your show.
Congrats, by the way.
...
What show?

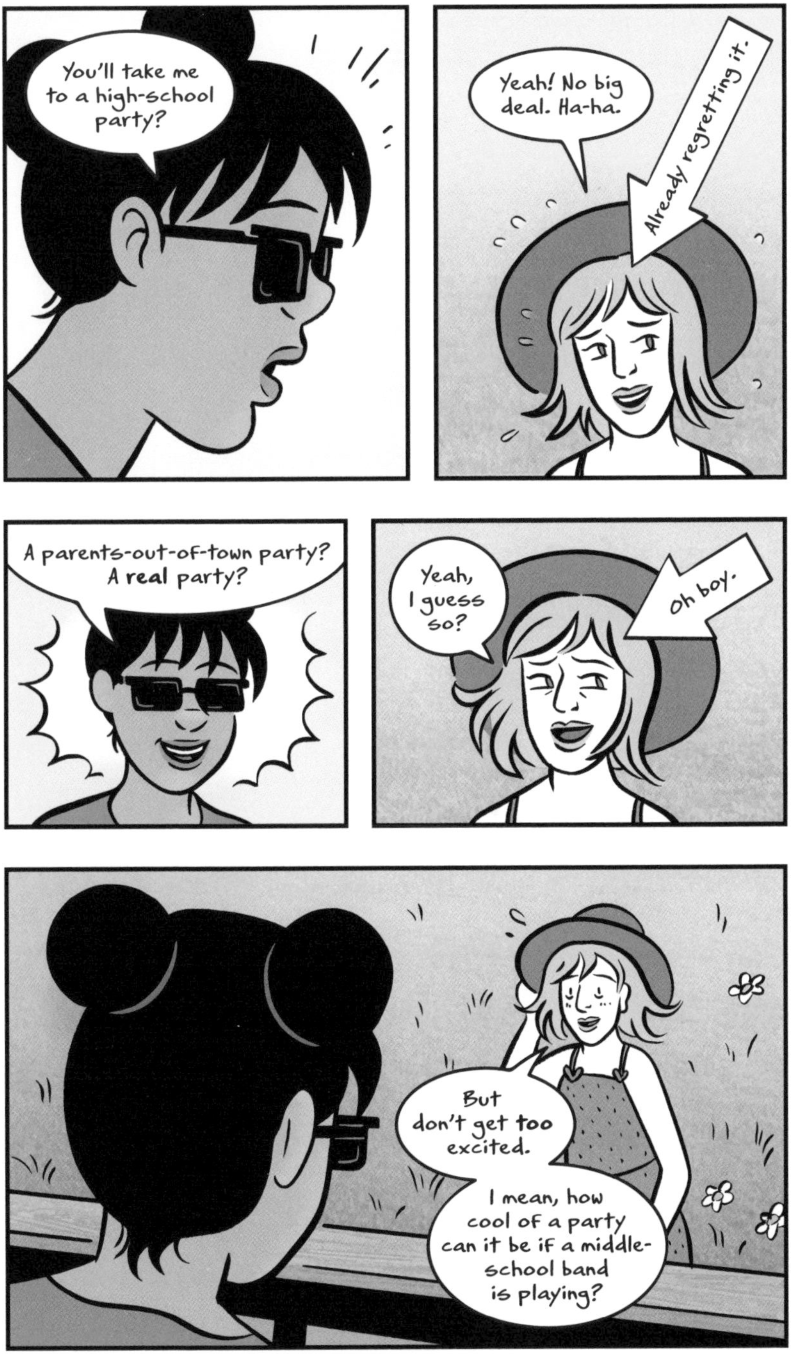
You'll take me to a high-school party?
Yeah! No big deal. Ha-ha.
Already regretting it.
A parents-out-of-town party? A real party?
Yeah, I guess so?
Oh boy.
But don't get too excited.
I mean, how cool of a party can it be if a middle-school band is playing?

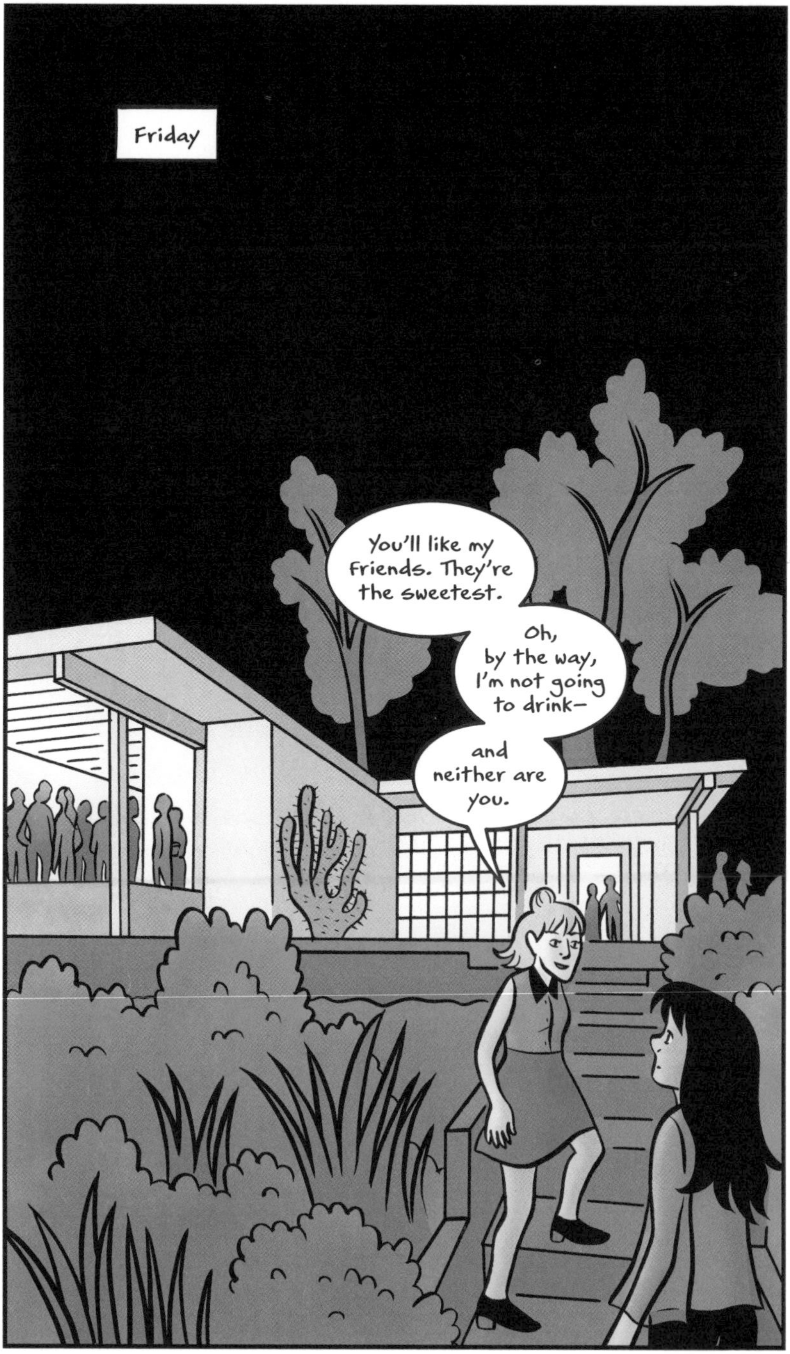
Friday
You'll like my friends. They're the sweetest.
Oh, by the way, I'm not going to drink–
and neither are you.

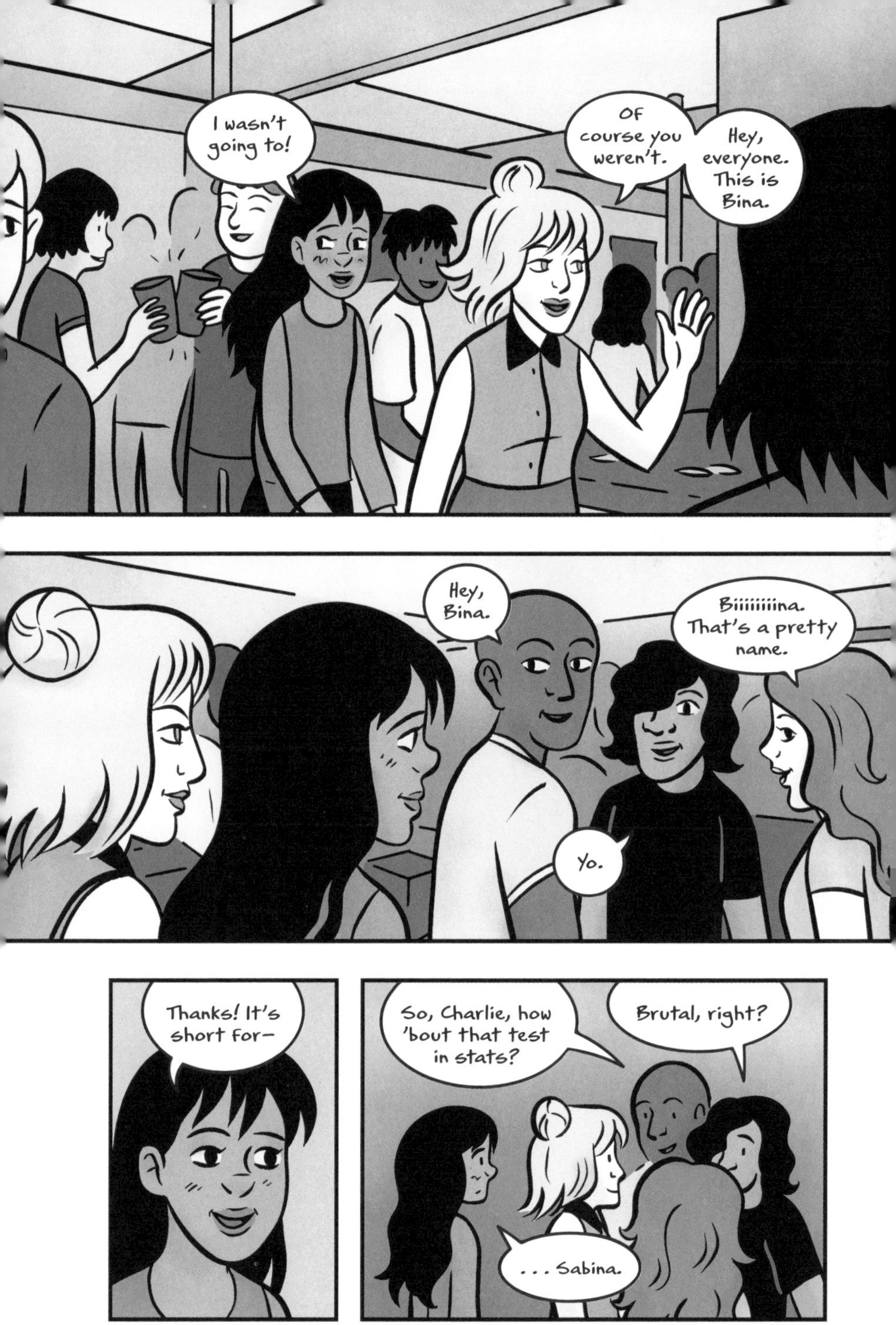
I wasn't going to!
Of course you weren't.
Hey, everyone. This is Bina.
Hey, Bina.
Biiiiiiiiina. That's a pretty name.
Yo.
Thanks! It's short for—
So, Charlie, how 'bout that test in stats?
Brutal, right?
. . . Sabina.

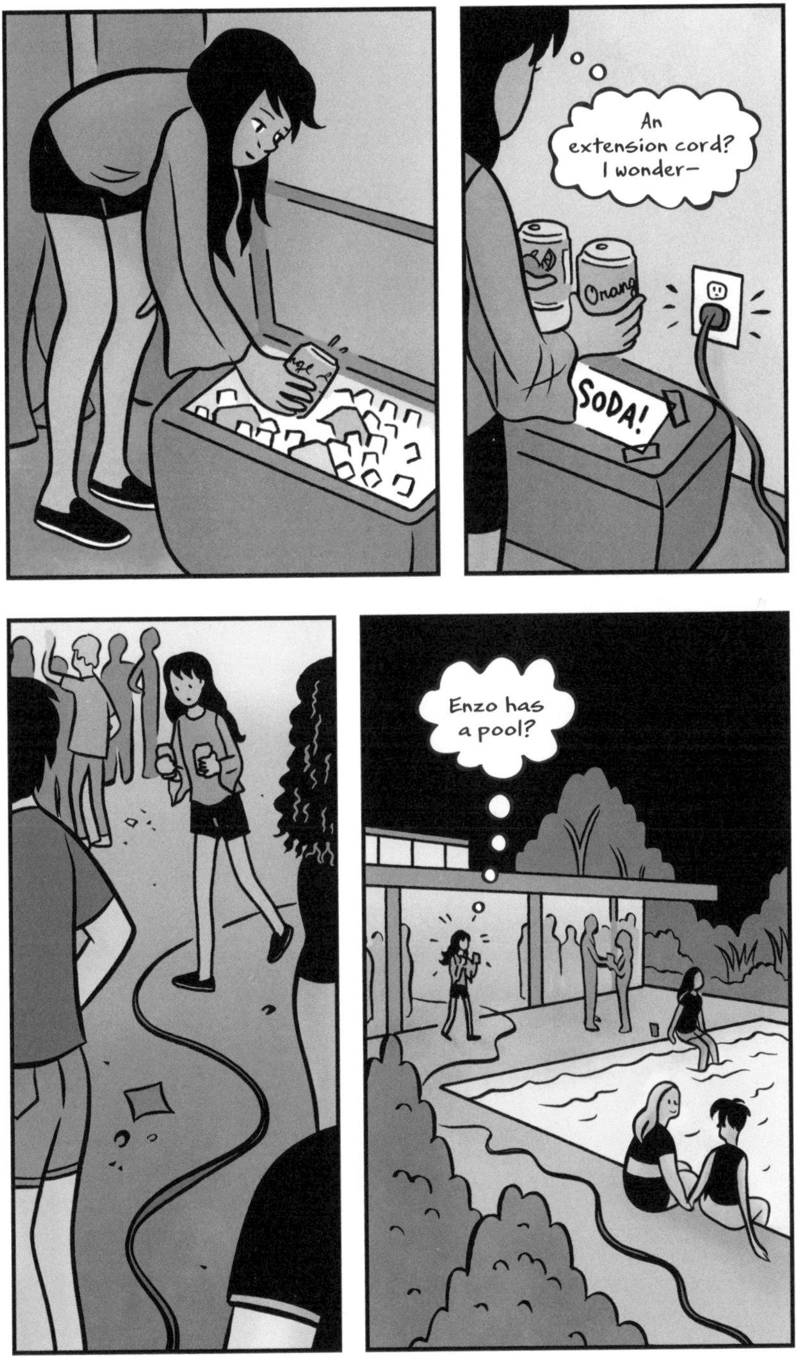
An extension cord? I wonder–
Orang
SODA!
Enzo has a pool?

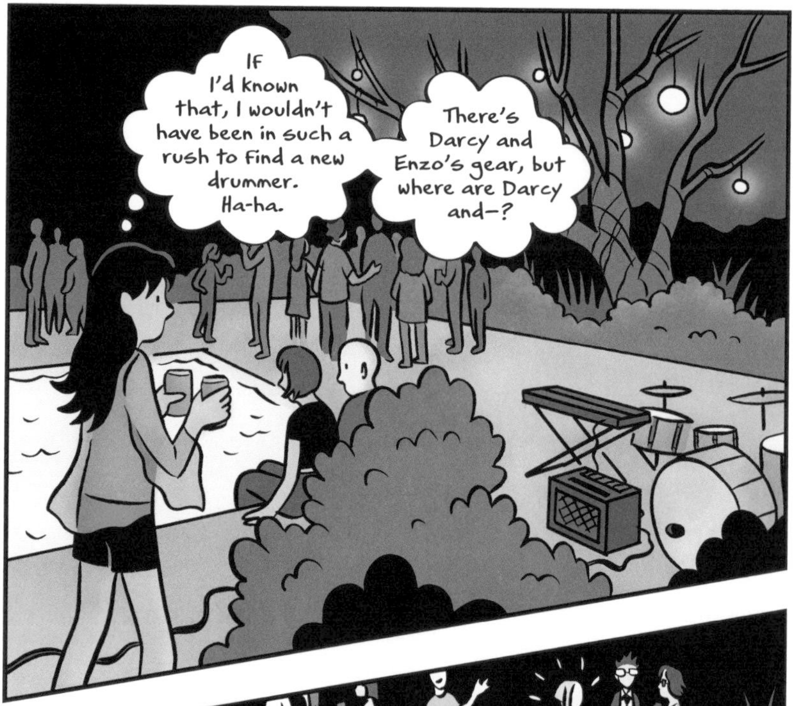
If I'd known that, I wouldn't have been in such a rush to find a new drummer. Ha-ha.
There's Darcy and Enzo's gear, but where are Darcy and–?

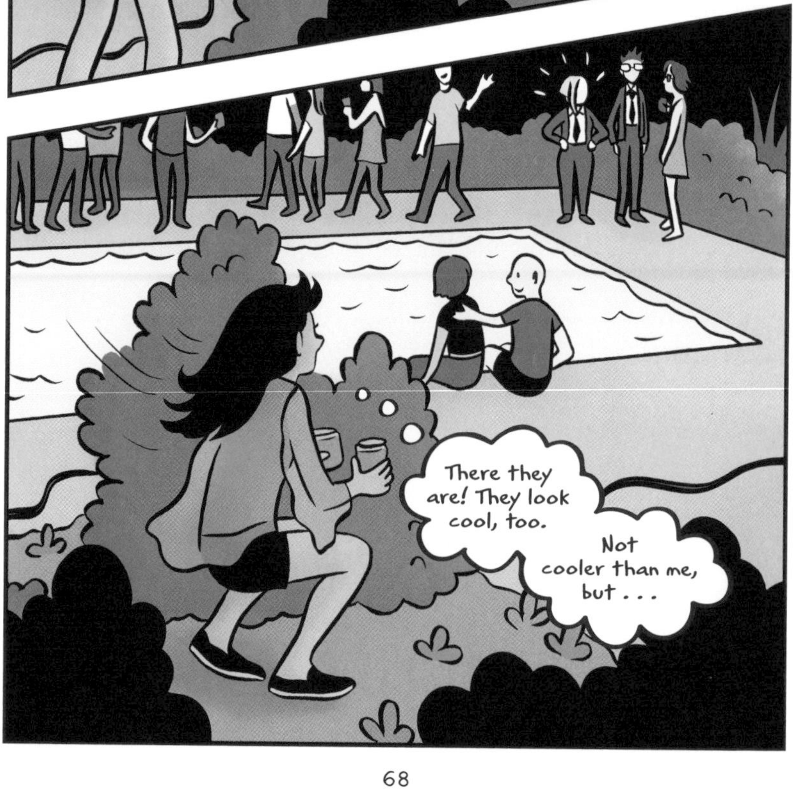
There they are! They look cool, too.
Not cooler than me, but . . .

71

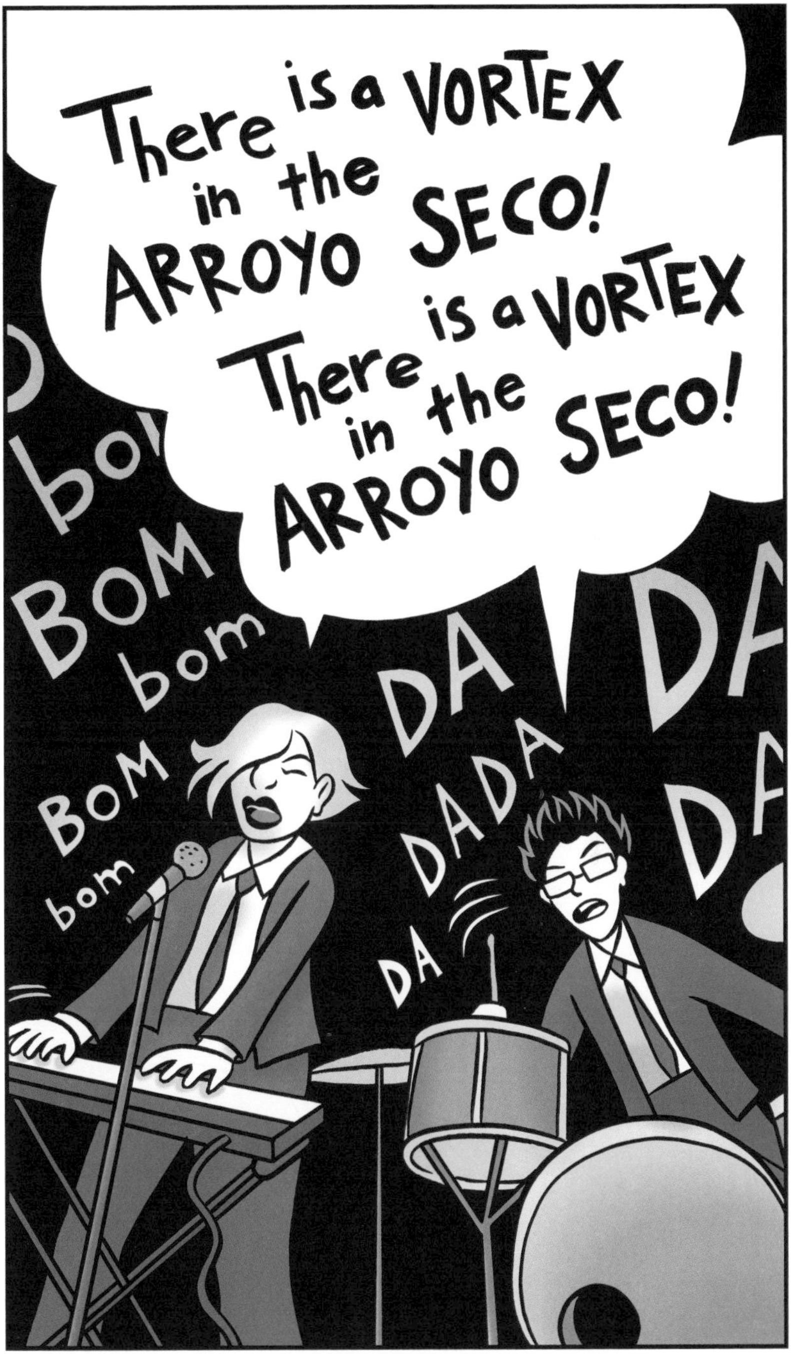
There is a VORTEX in the ARROYO SECO! There is a VORTEX in the ARROYO SECO!
BOM
bom
BOM
bom
DA
DADA
DA
DA
DA
DA

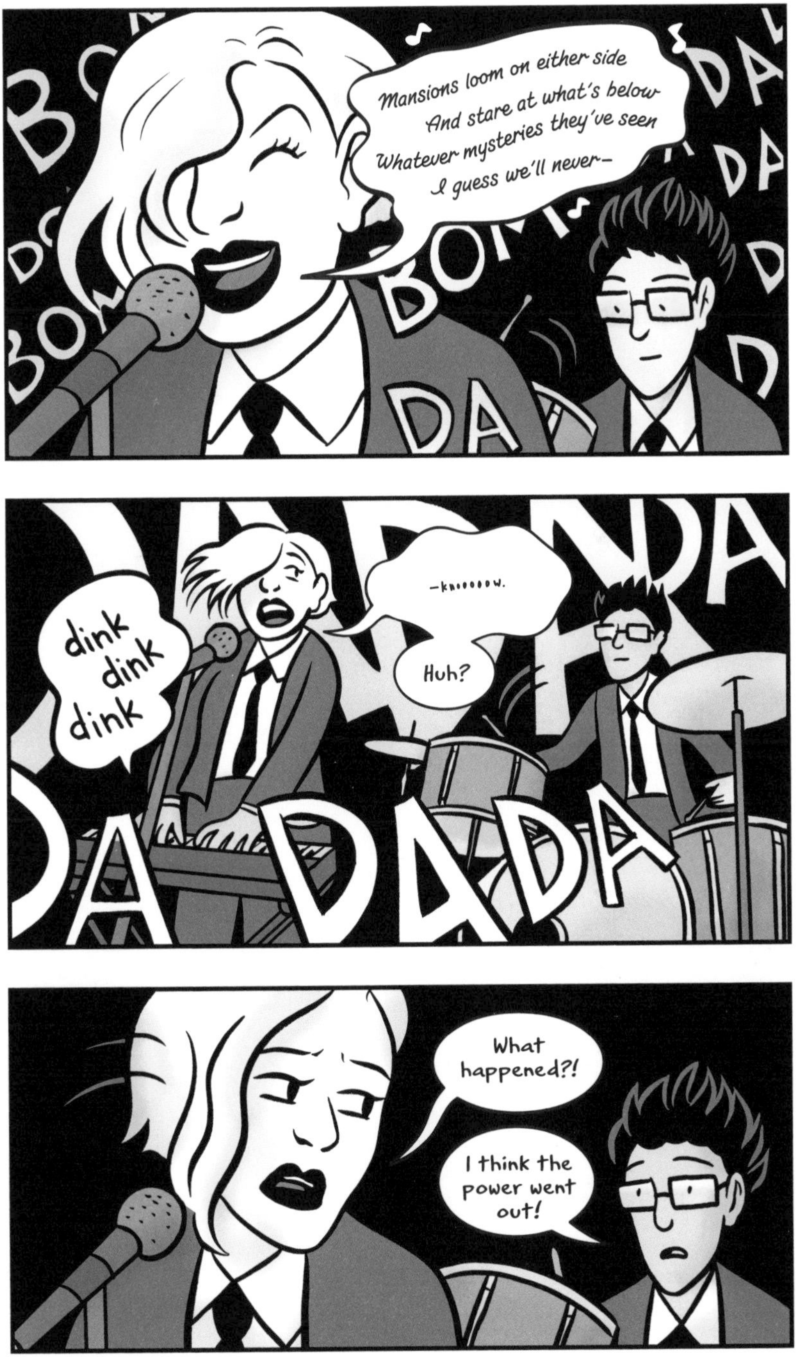
Mansions loom on either side
And stare at what's below
Whatever mysteries they've seen
I guess we'll never—
BOM
BOM
DA
DA
dink dink dink
—knoooooow.
Huh?
DADA
What happened?!
I think the power went out!

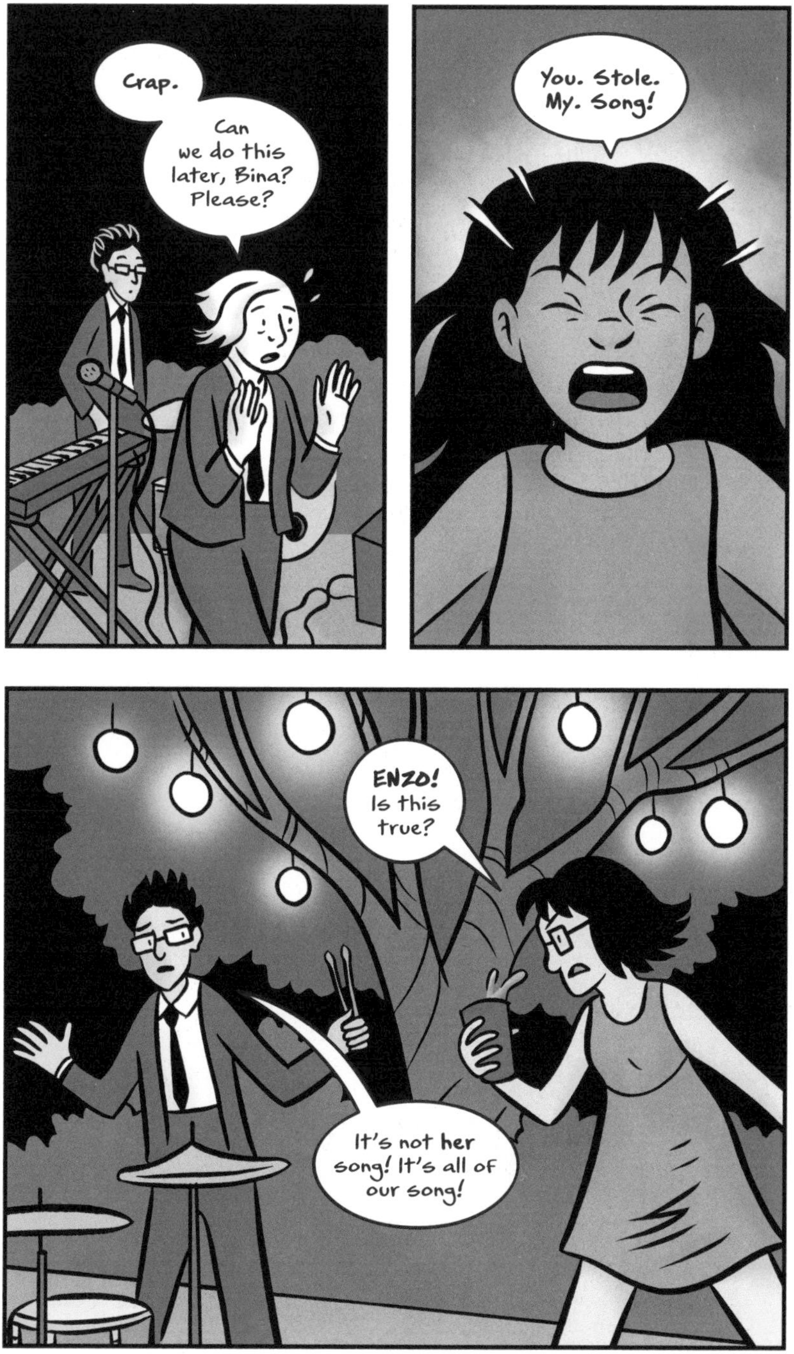
Crap.
Can we do this later, Bina? Please?
You. Stole. My. Song!
ENZO! Is this true?
It's not her song! It's all of our song!

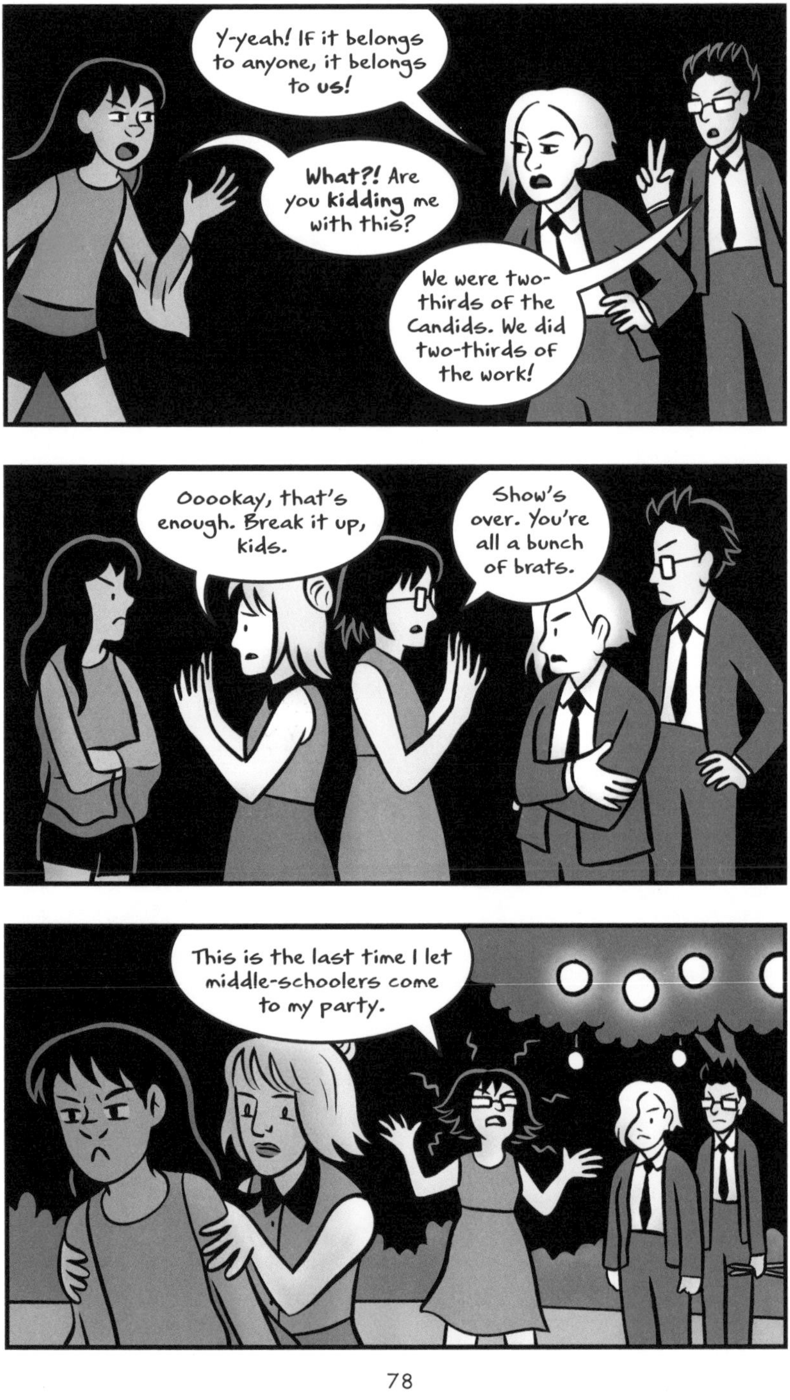

Y-yeah! If it belongs to anyone, it belongs to us!
What?! Are you **kidding** me with this?
We were two-thirds of the Candids. We did two-thirds of the work!
Ooookay, that's enough. Break it up, kids.
Show's over. You're all a bunch of brats.
This is the last time I let middle-schoolers come to my party.

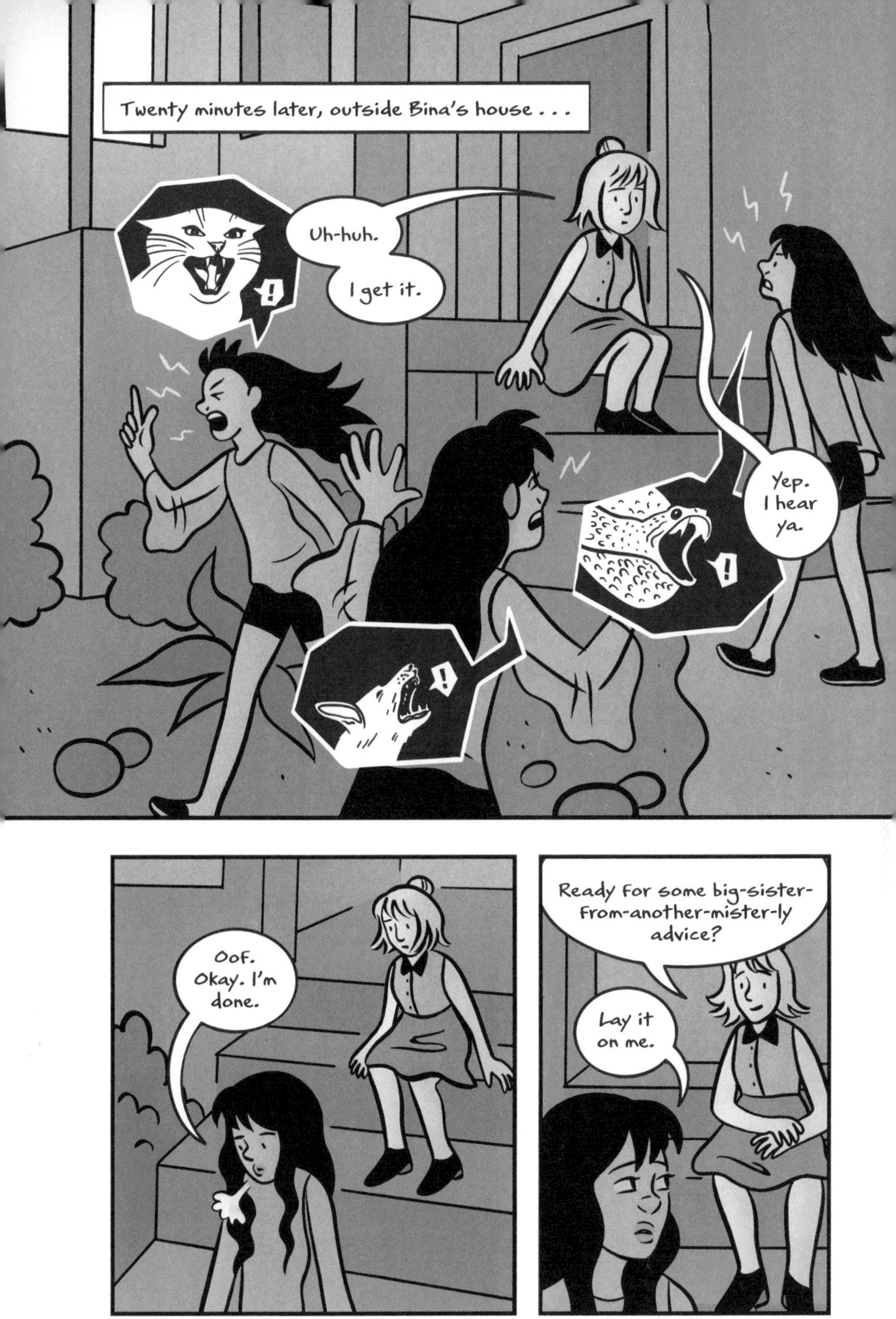
Twenty minutes later, outside Bina's house . . .
!
Uh-huh.
I get it.
Yep.
I hear ya.
!
!
Oof. Okay. I'm done.
Ready for some big-sister-from-another-mister-ly advice?
Lay it on me.

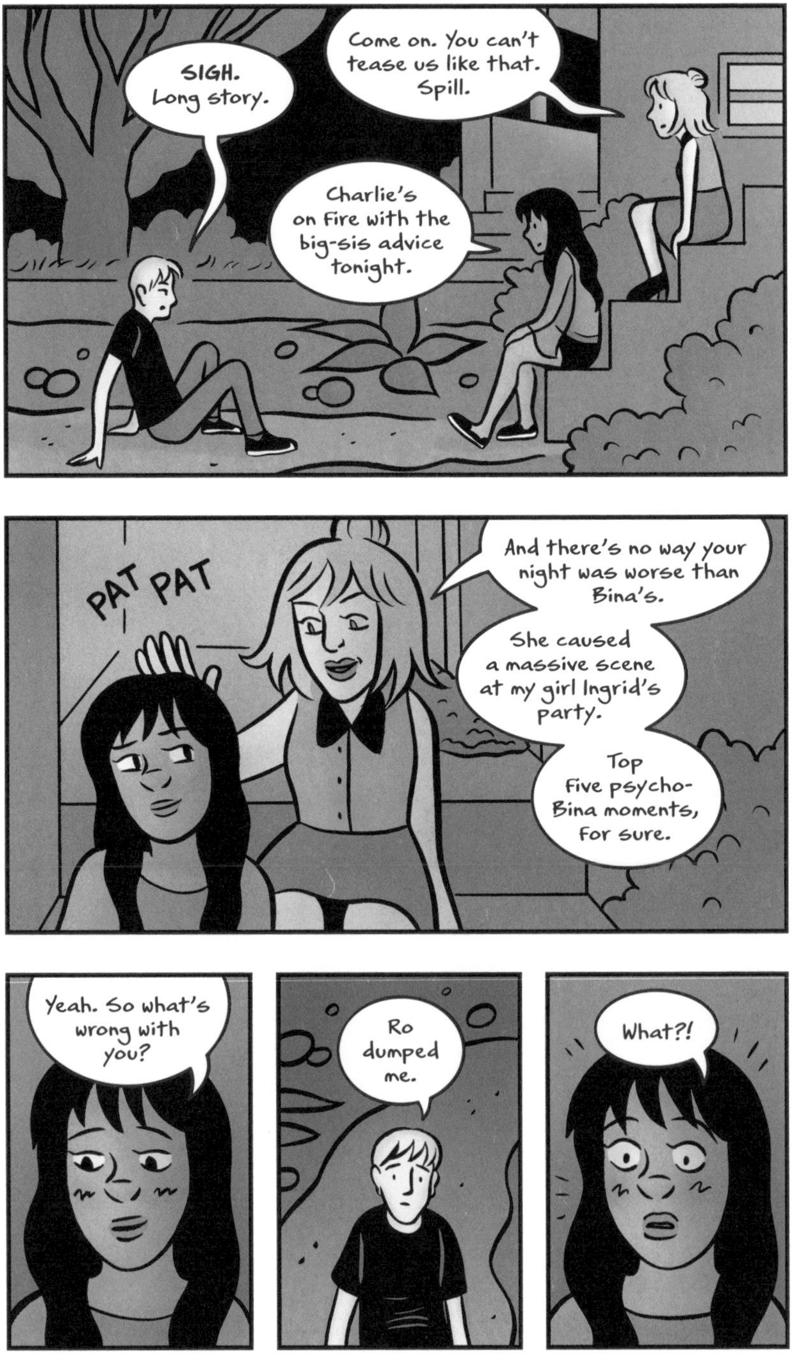
SIGH.
Long story.
Come on. You can't tease us like that. Spill.
Charlie's on fire with the big-sis advice tonight.
PAT PAT
And there's no way your night was worse than Bina's.
She caused a massive scene at my girl Ingrid's party.
Top five psycho-Bina moments, for sure.
Yeah. So what's wrong with you?
Ro dumped me.
What?!

84

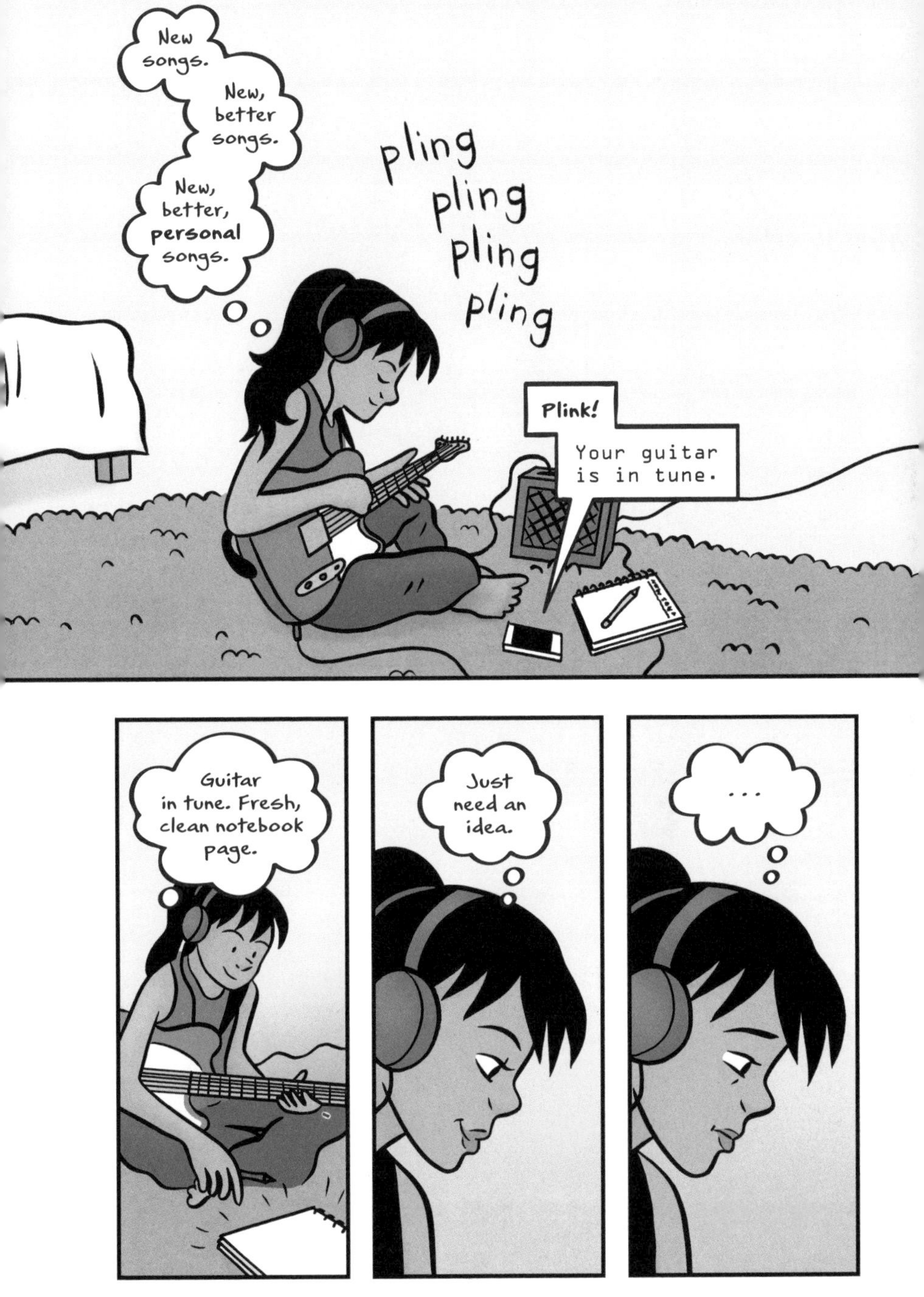
New songs.
New, better songs.
New, better, **personal** songs.
pling pling pling pling
Plink!
Your guitar is in tune.
Guitar in tune. Fresh, clean notebook page.
Just need an idea.
. . .

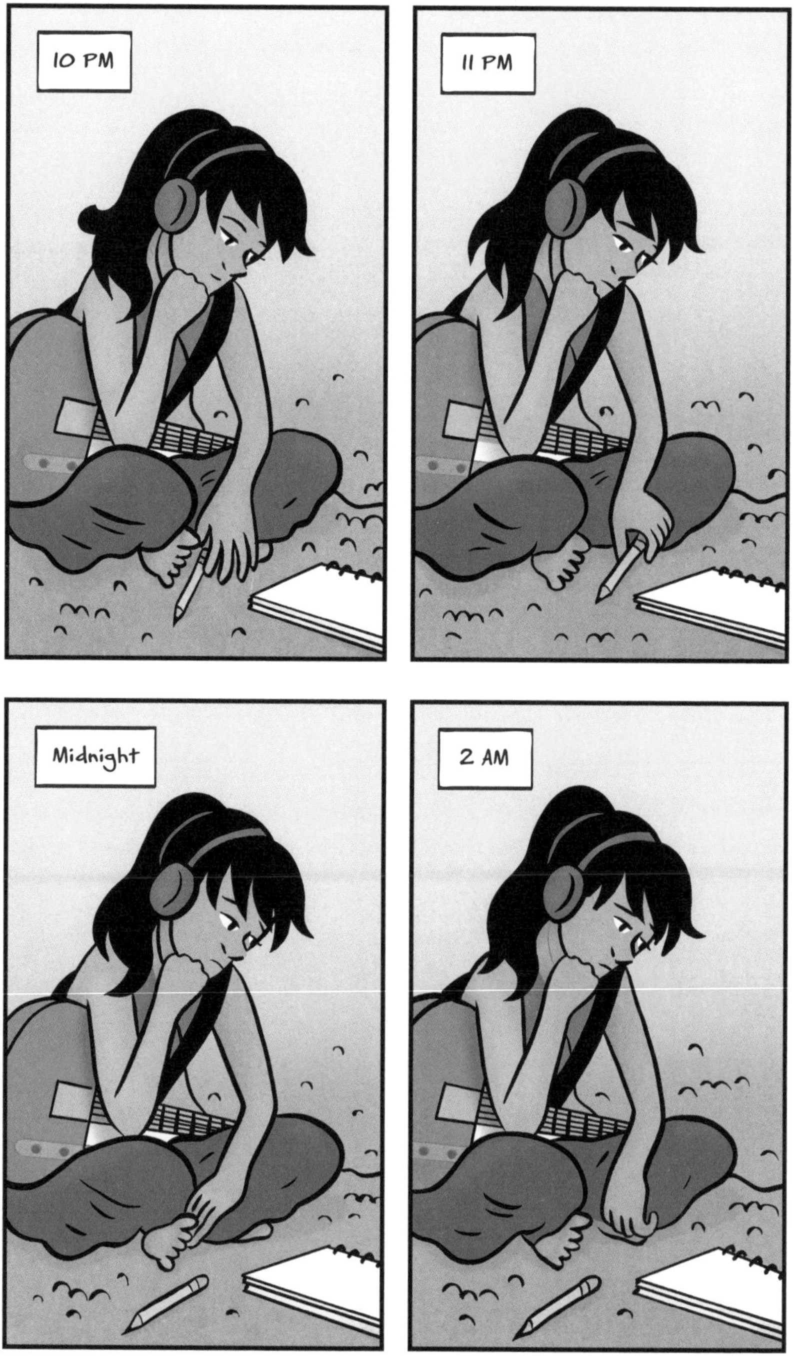
10 PM
11 PM
Midnight
2 AM

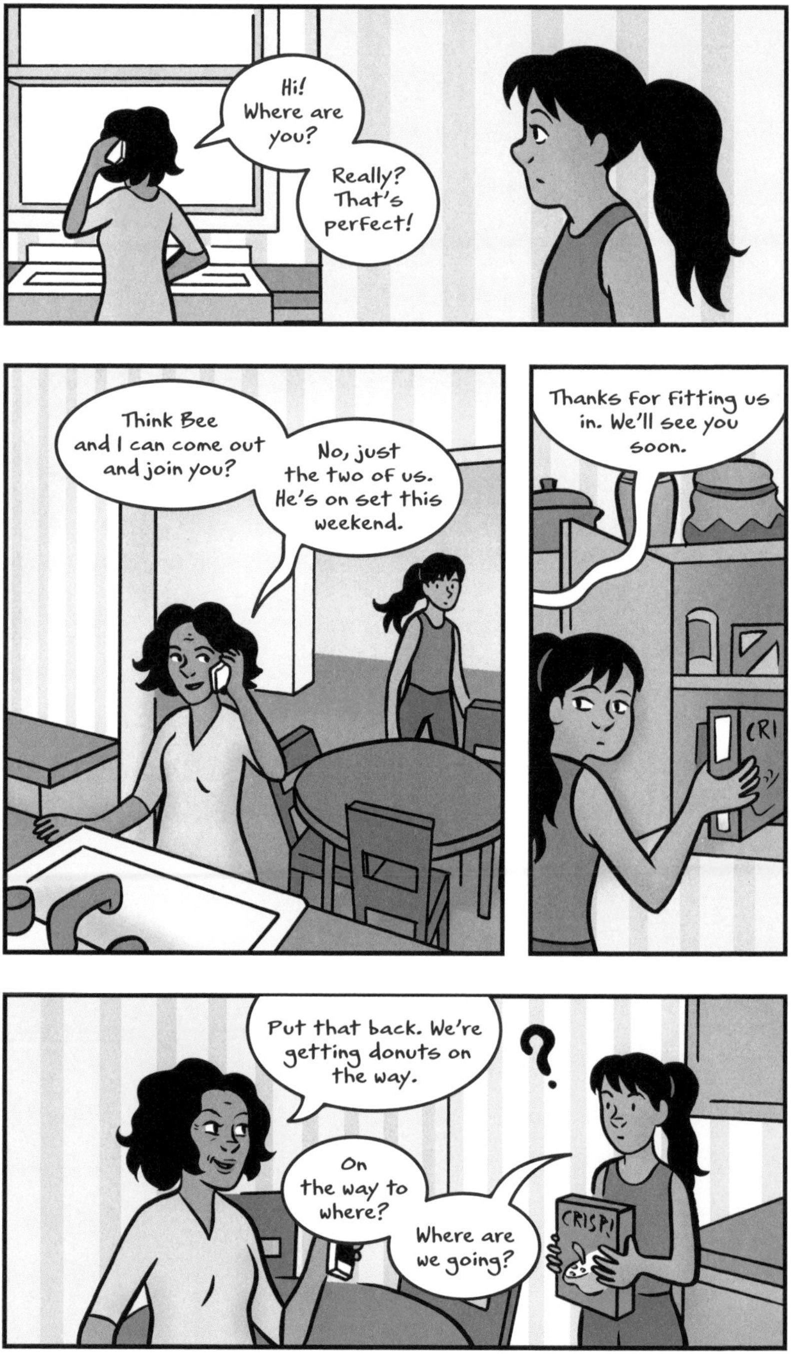
Hi! Where are you?
Really? That's perfect!
Think Bee and I can come out and join you?
No, just the two of us. He's on set this weekend.
Thanks for fitting us in. We'll see you soon.
CRI
Put that back. We're getting donuts on the way.
?
On the way to where?
Where are we going?
CRISP!

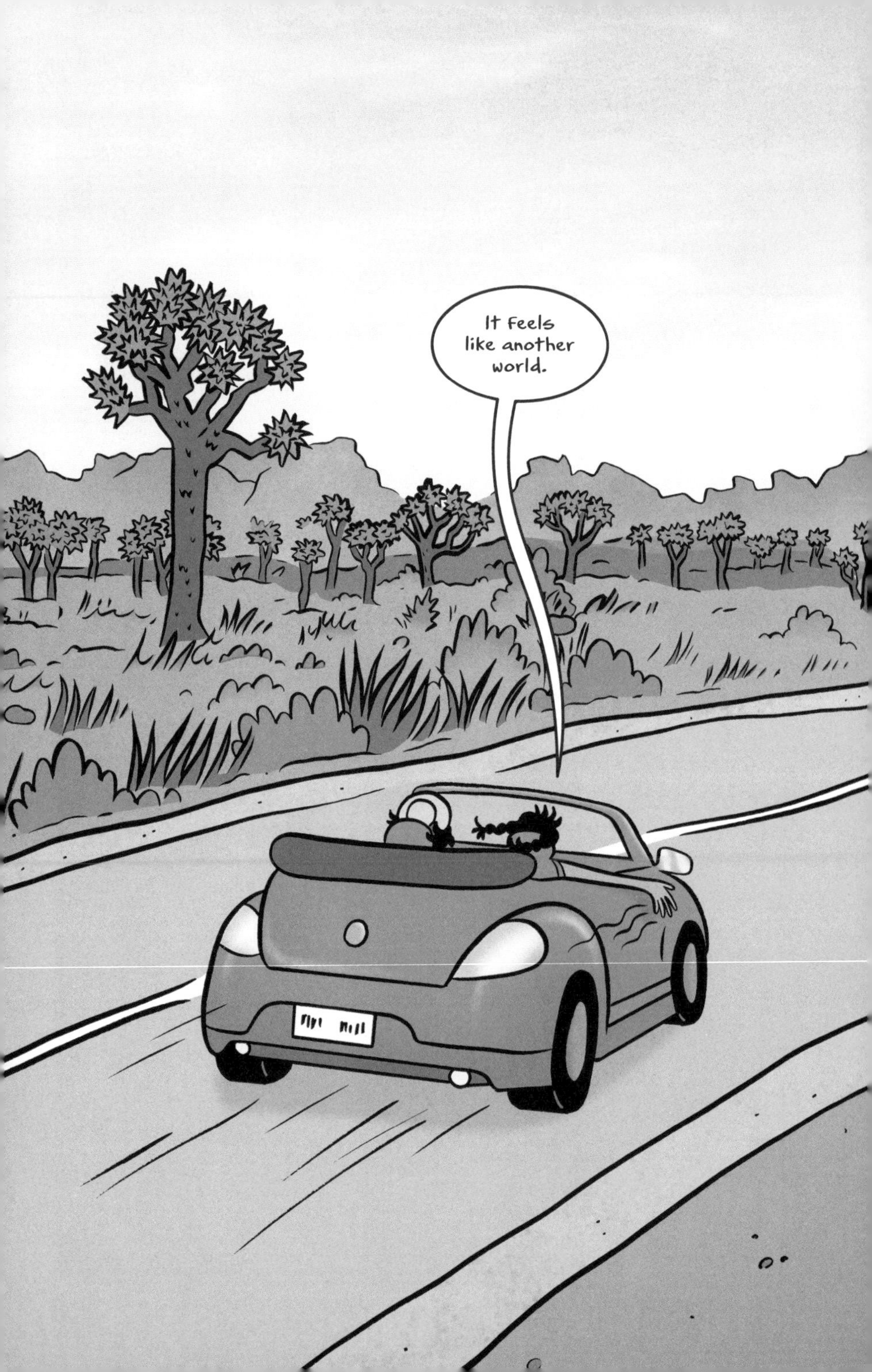
It feels like another world.

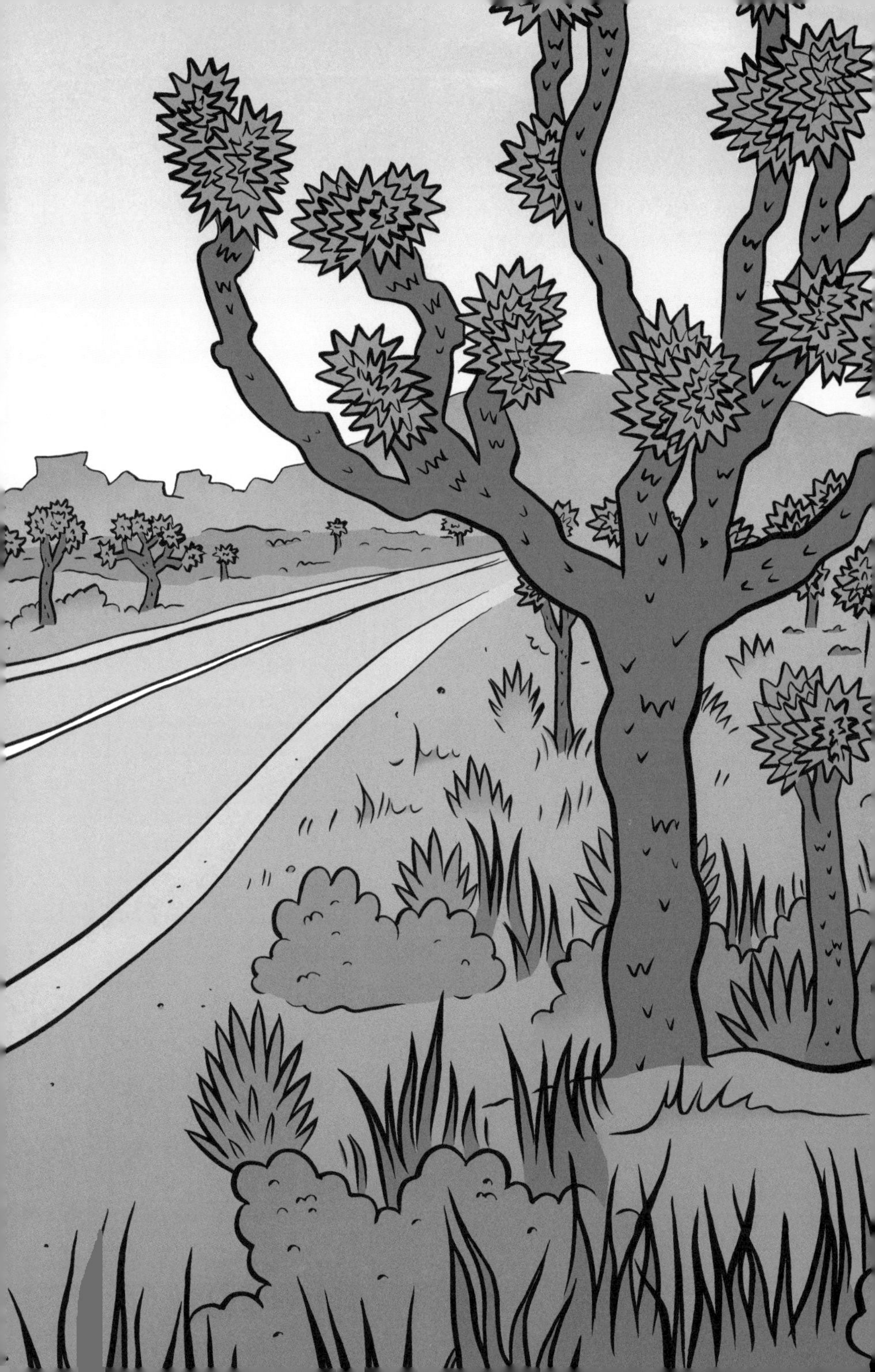

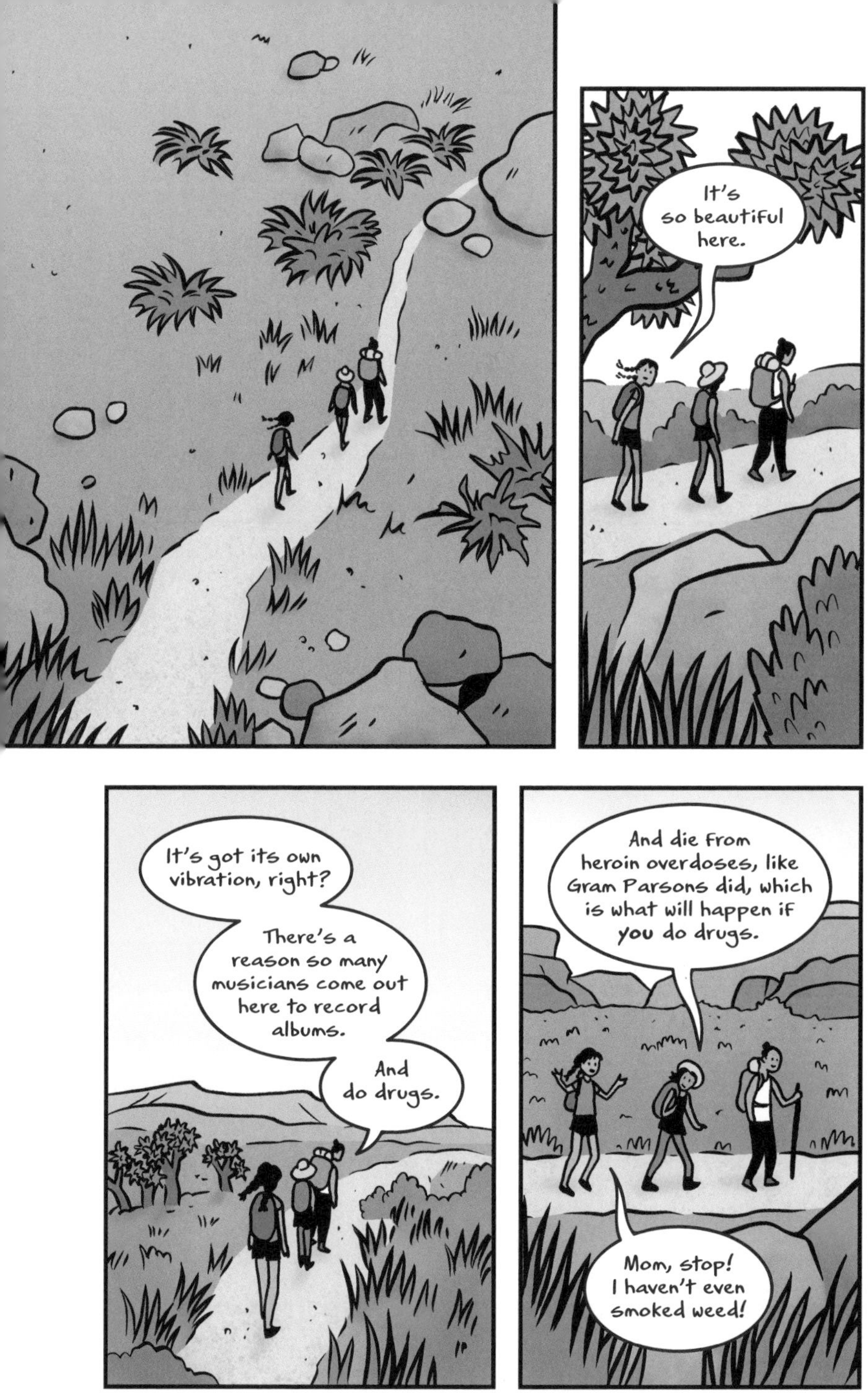
It's so beautiful here.
It's got its own vibration, right?
There's a reason so many musicians come out here to record albums.
And do drugs.
And die from heroin overdoses, like Gram Parsons did, which is what will happen if you do drugs.
Mom, stop! I haven't even smoked weed!

"Joshua Tree's the best place on Earth to connect with the universe."
Why would anyone do drugs if they could see stars like this?
We can hardly see any in LA.
At least, not these kinds of stars.
Feeling inspired yet?
No.
But I'm not feeling uninspired.

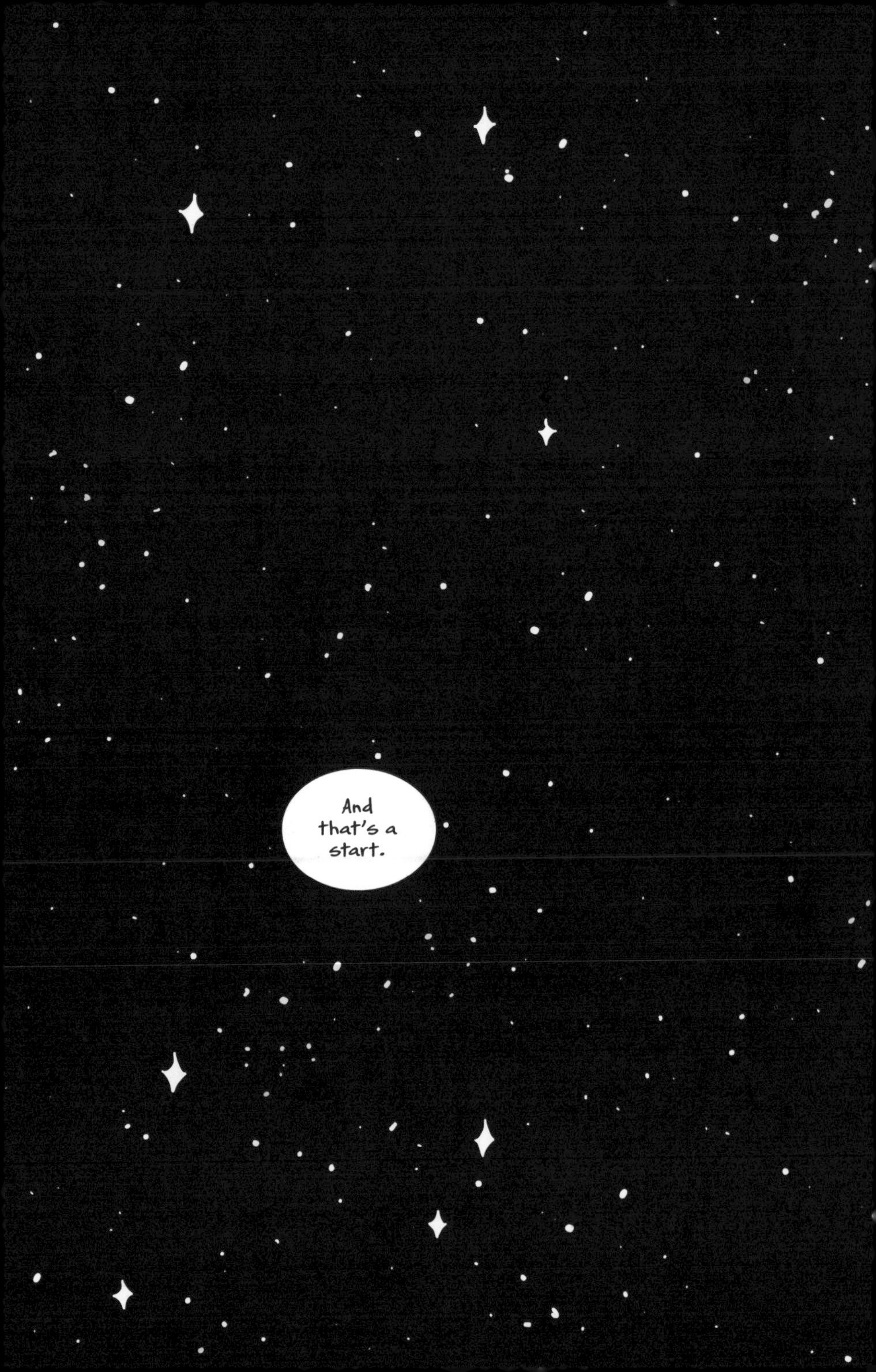
And that's a start.

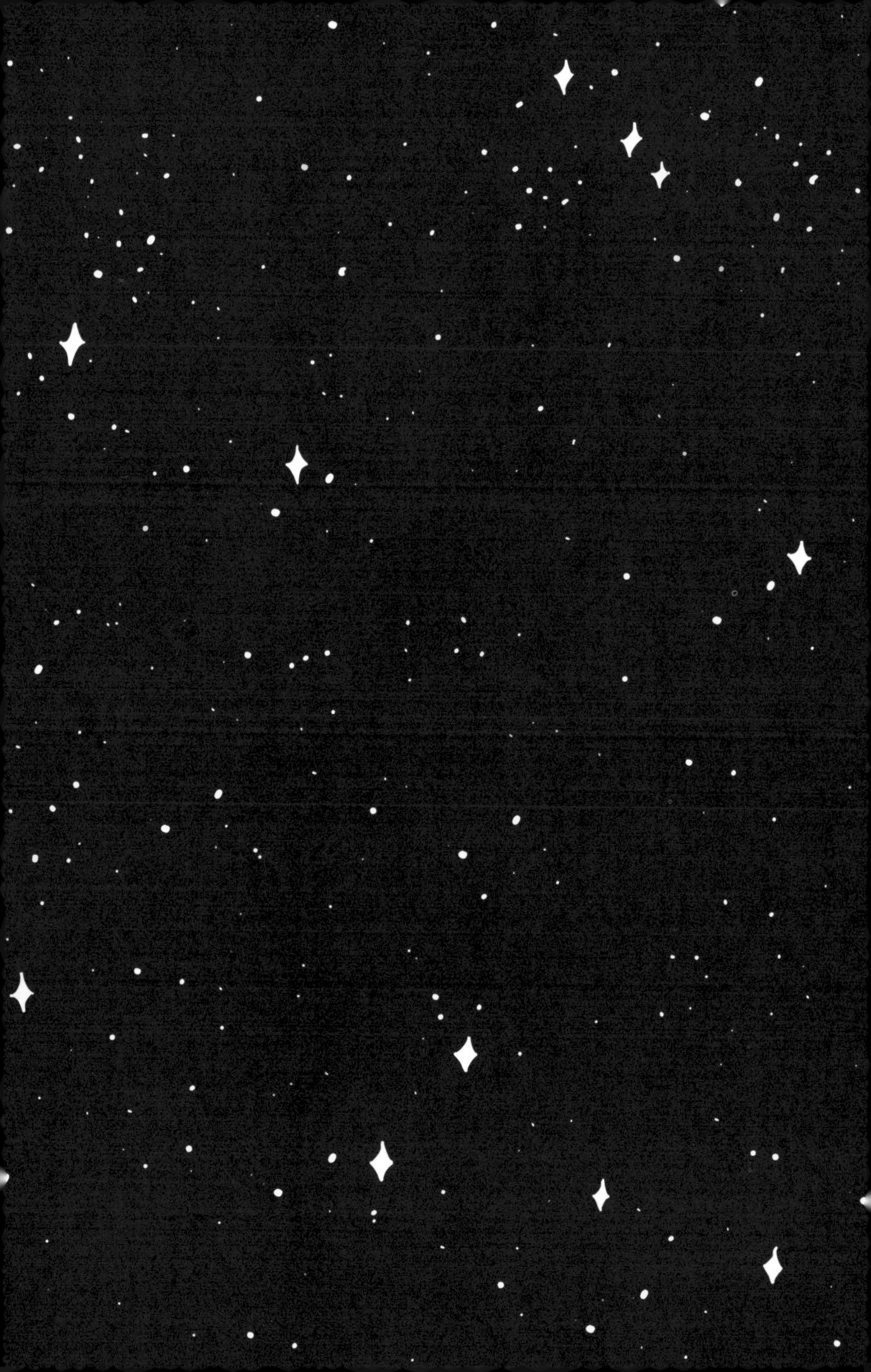

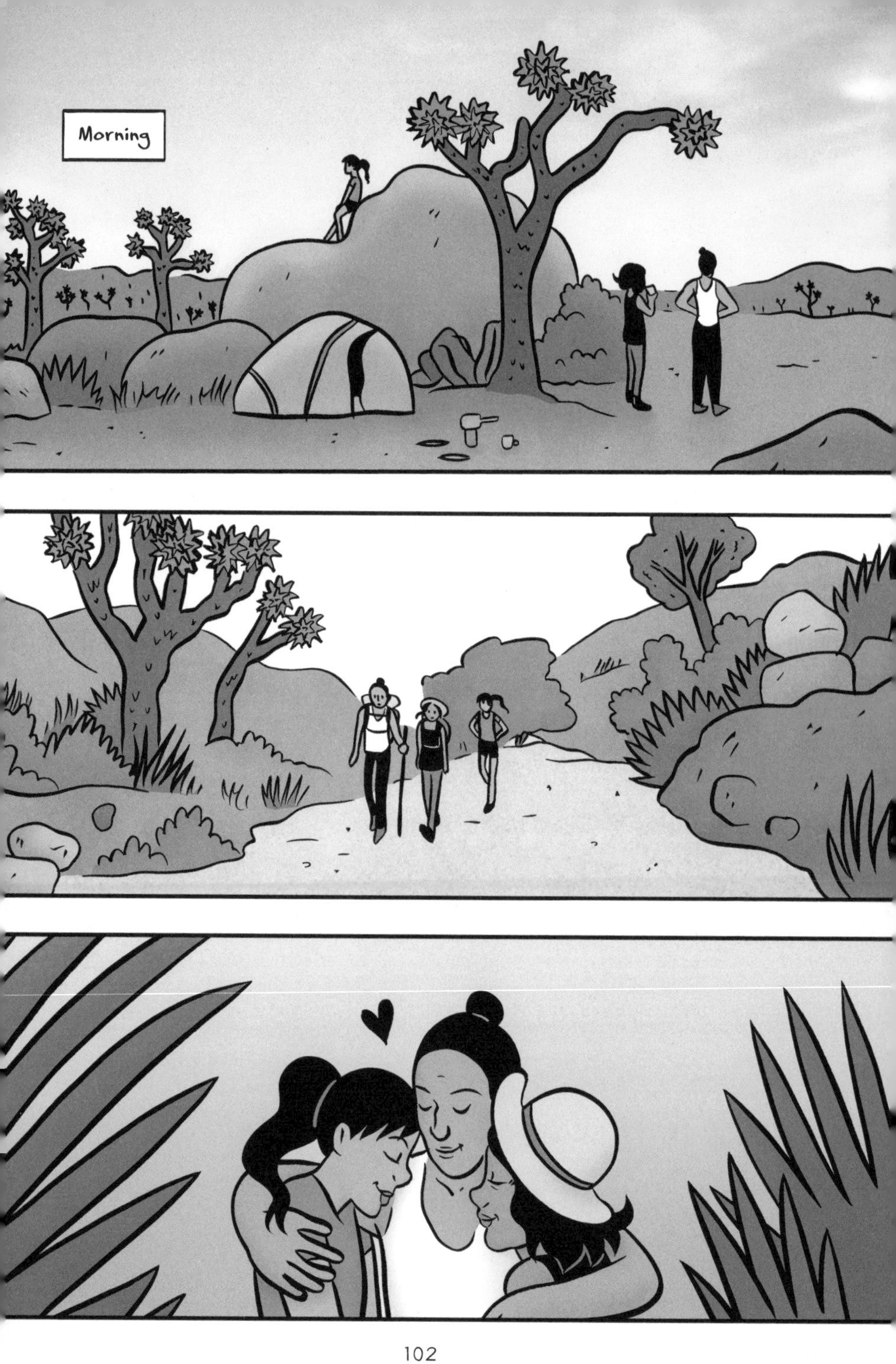
Morning

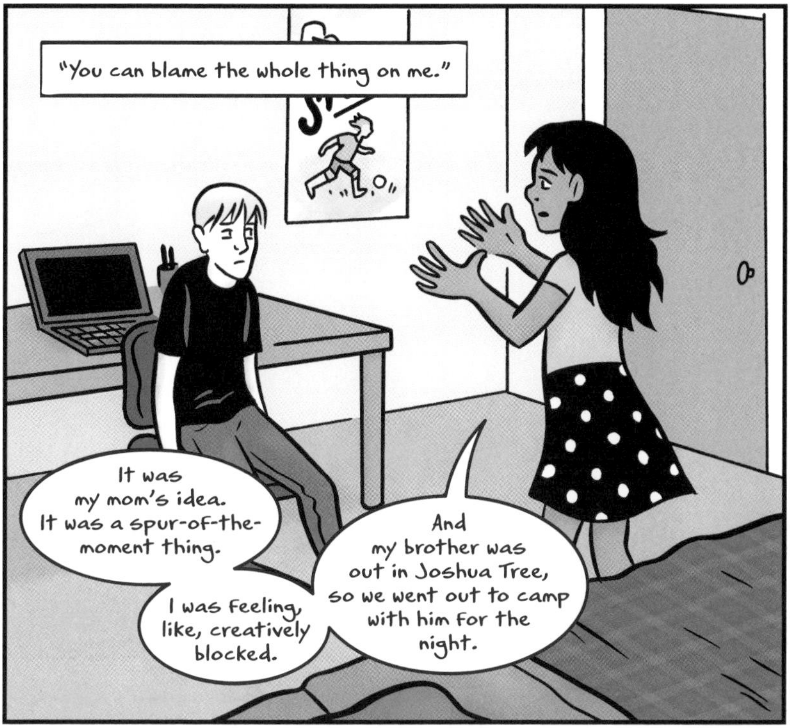
"You can blame the whole thing on me."
It was my mom's idea. It was a spur-of-the-moment thing.
I was feeling, like, creatively blocked.
And my brother was out in Joshua Tree, so we went out to camp with him for the night.

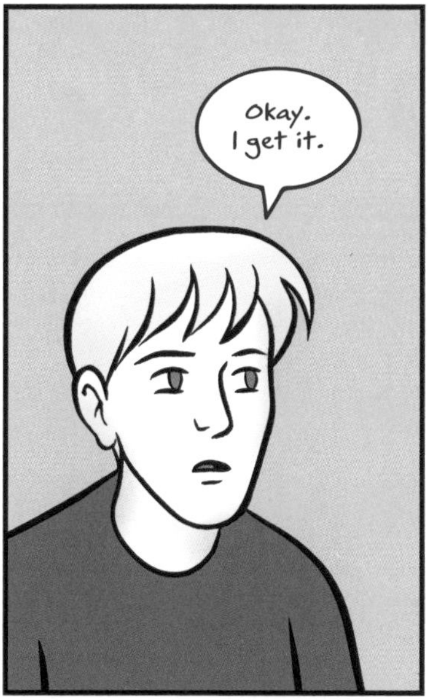
Okay. I get it.

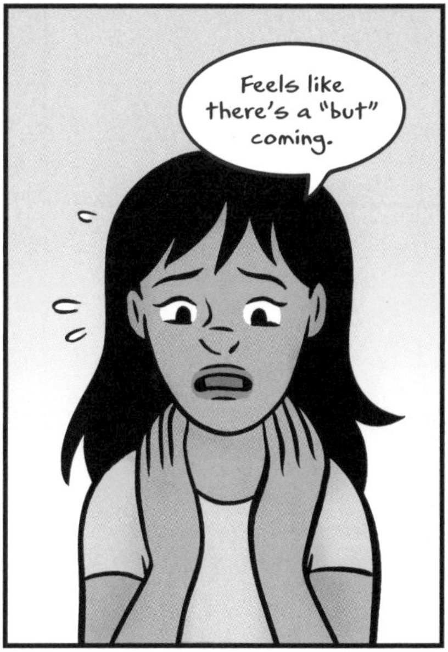
Feels like there's a "but" coming.

But I had this whole thing planned, and you forgot we were hanging out.
I'm sorry. Really sorry.
Can we do your plan now?
Nah. It's too late.
Can we do something else? Make a new plan?
SHRUG
C'mon, Austin—
TUG

Okay. Enough. What's wrong? Are you mad at me? Or upset about Rosemary? Or–
Sorry. I'm trying to cheer up. I just . . .
Ughhh. Charlie told me to be careful.
Huh? About what?
I wanted to do something special.
Why? Dude, what are you talking about?

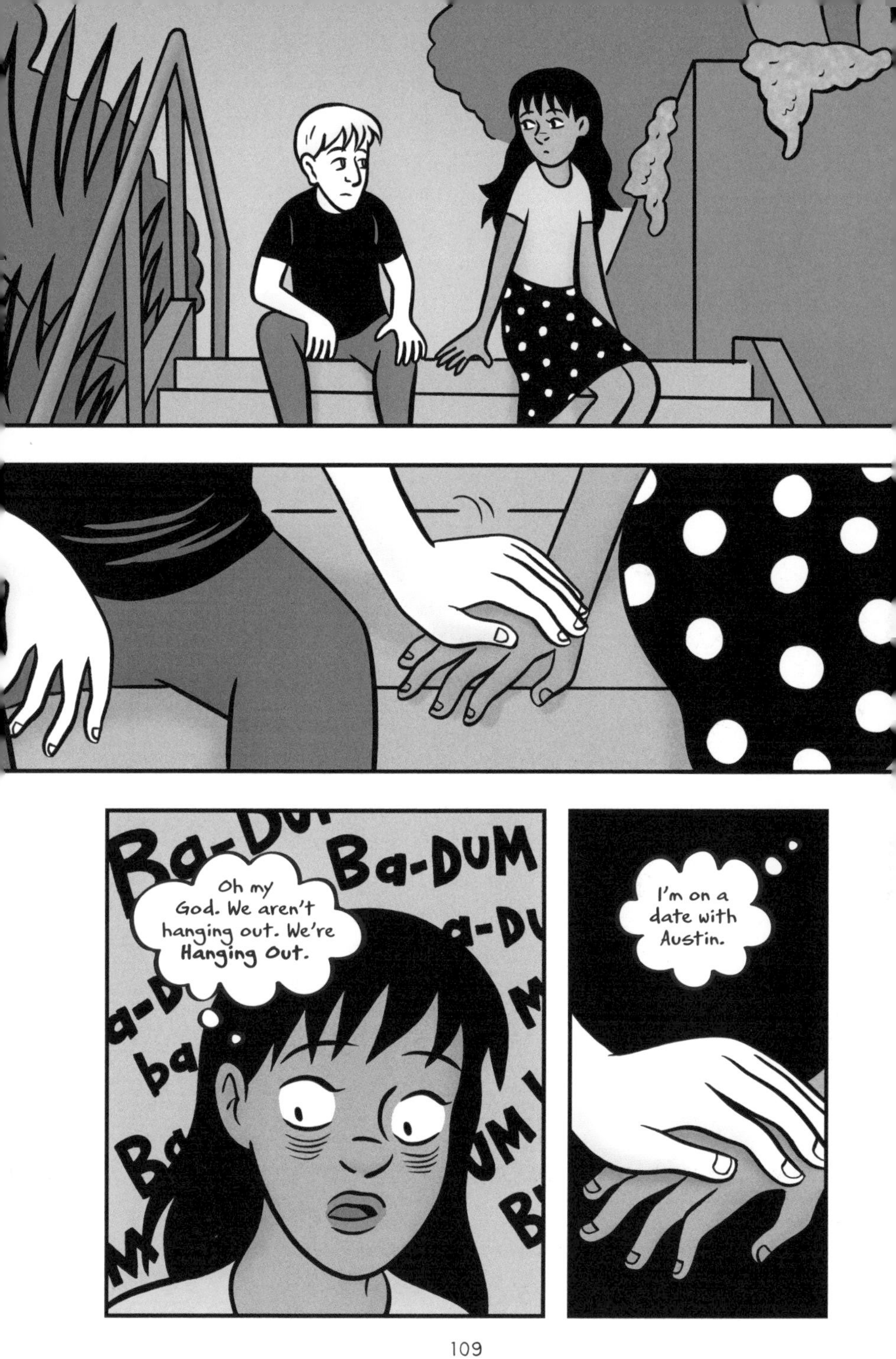
Ba-DUM
Oh my God. We aren't hanging out. We're Hanging Out.
I'm on a date with Austin.

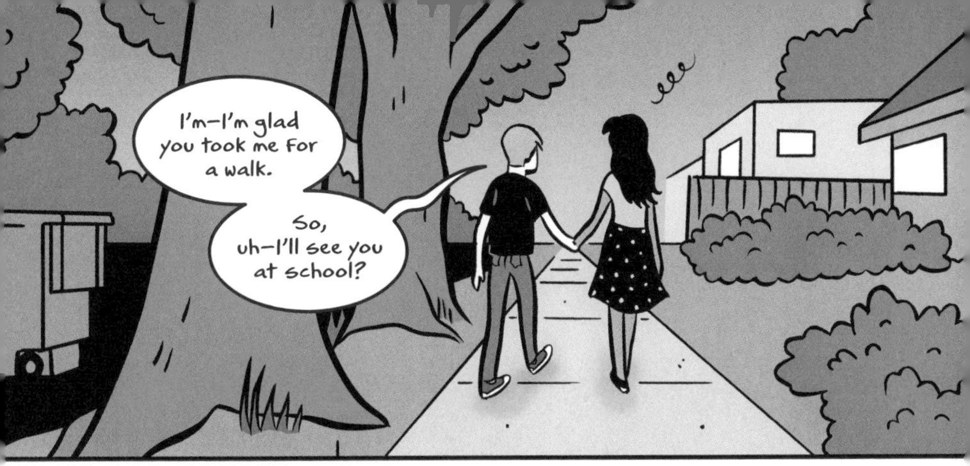
I'm—I'm glad you took me for a walk.
So, uh—I'll see you at school?

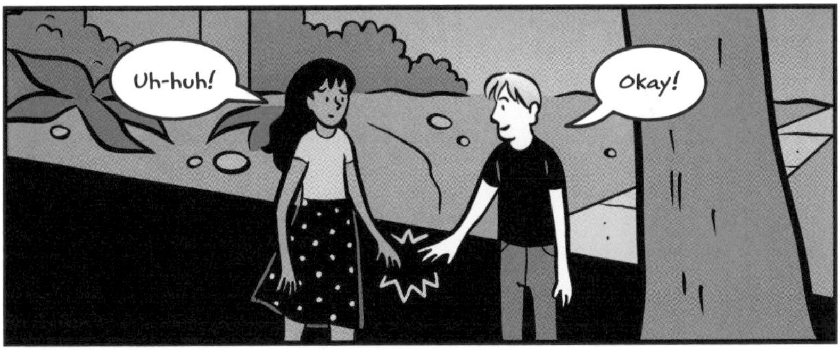
Uh-huh!
Okay!

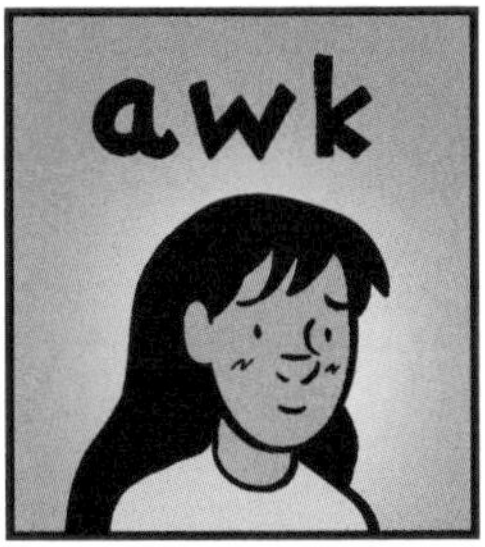
awk

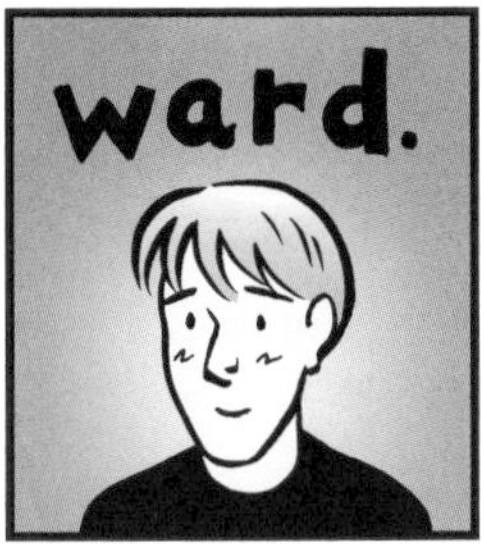
ward.

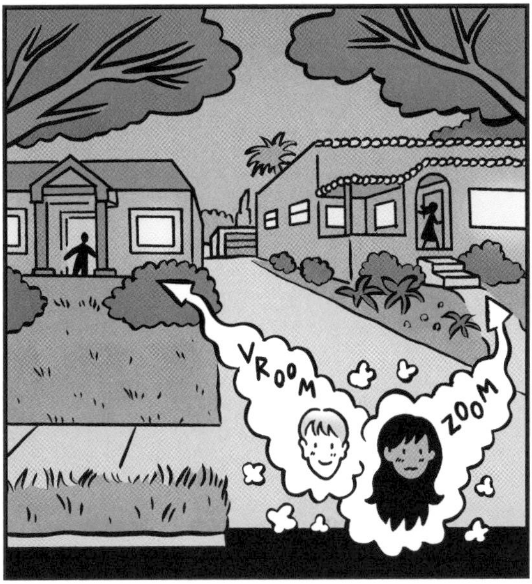
VROOM
ZOOM

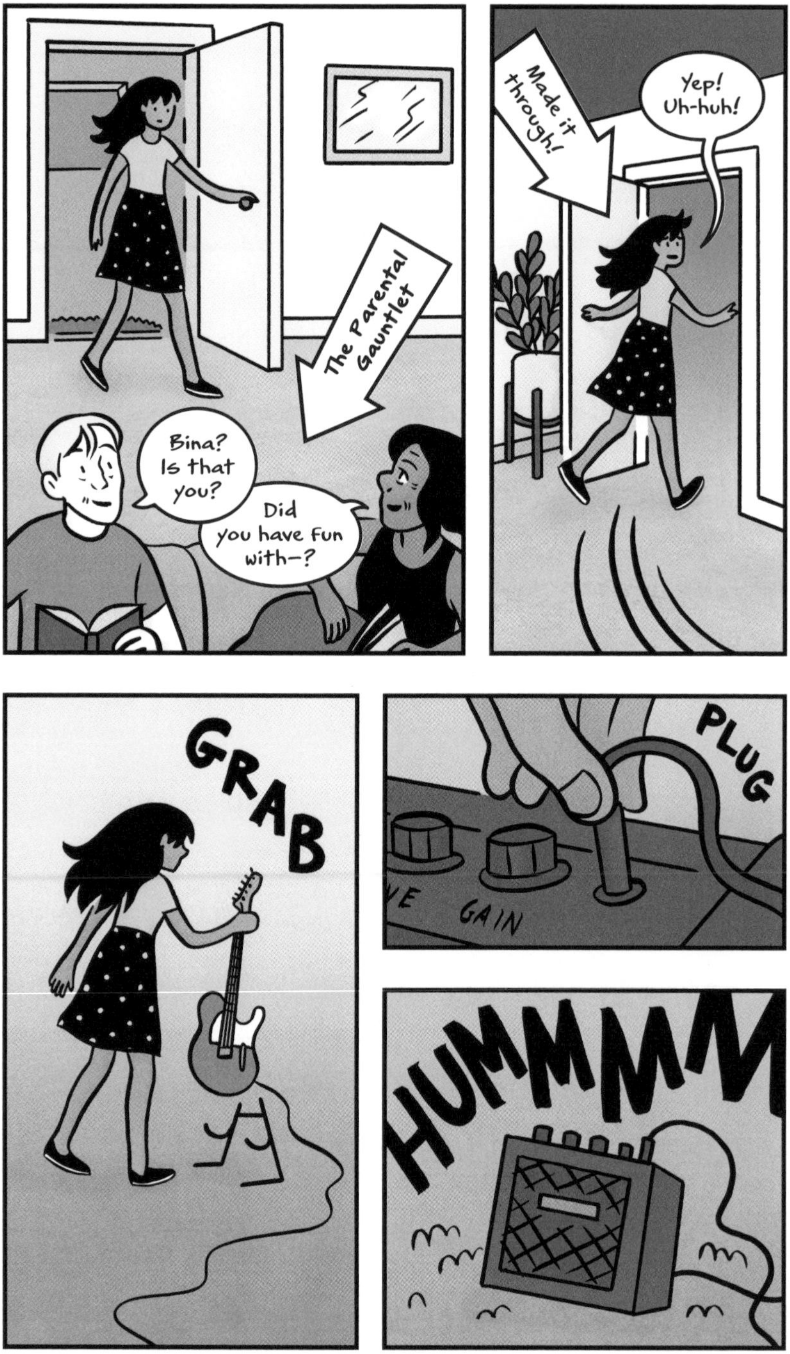
The Parental Gauntlet
Bina? Is that you?
Did you have fun with–?
Made it through!
Yep! Uh-huh!
GRAB
PLUG
GAIN
HUMMMM

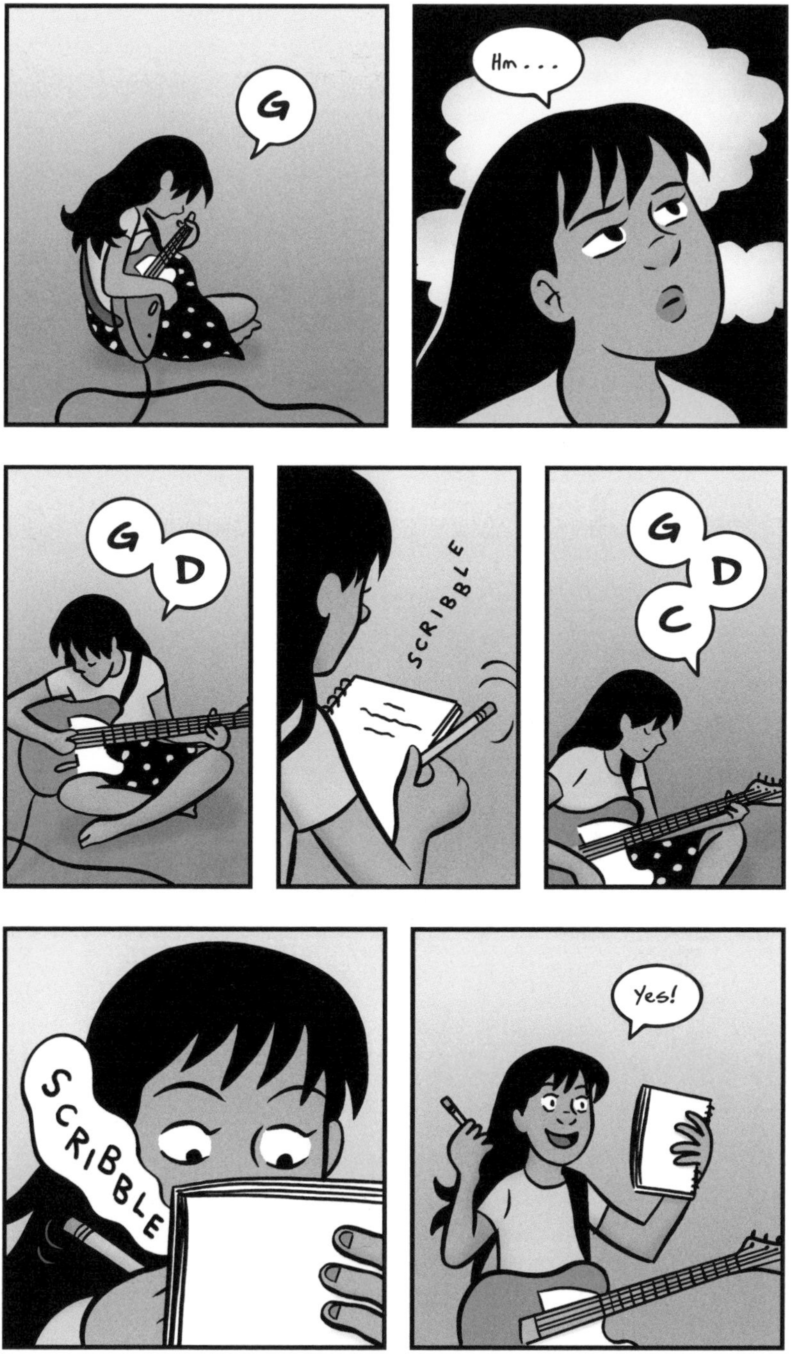
G
Hm...
G
D
SCRIBBLE
G
D
C
SCRIBBLE
Yes!

114

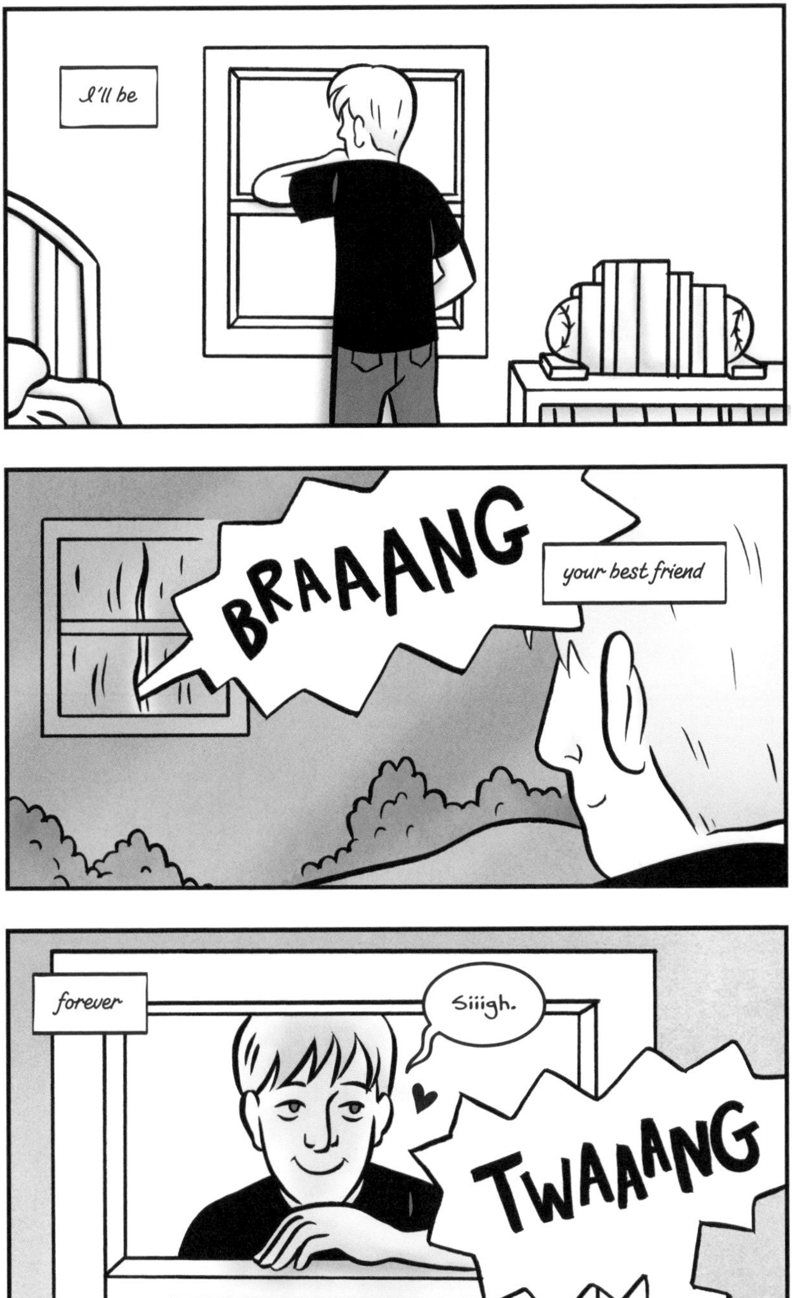
I'll be
BRAAANG
your best friend
forever
Siiigh.
TWAAANG

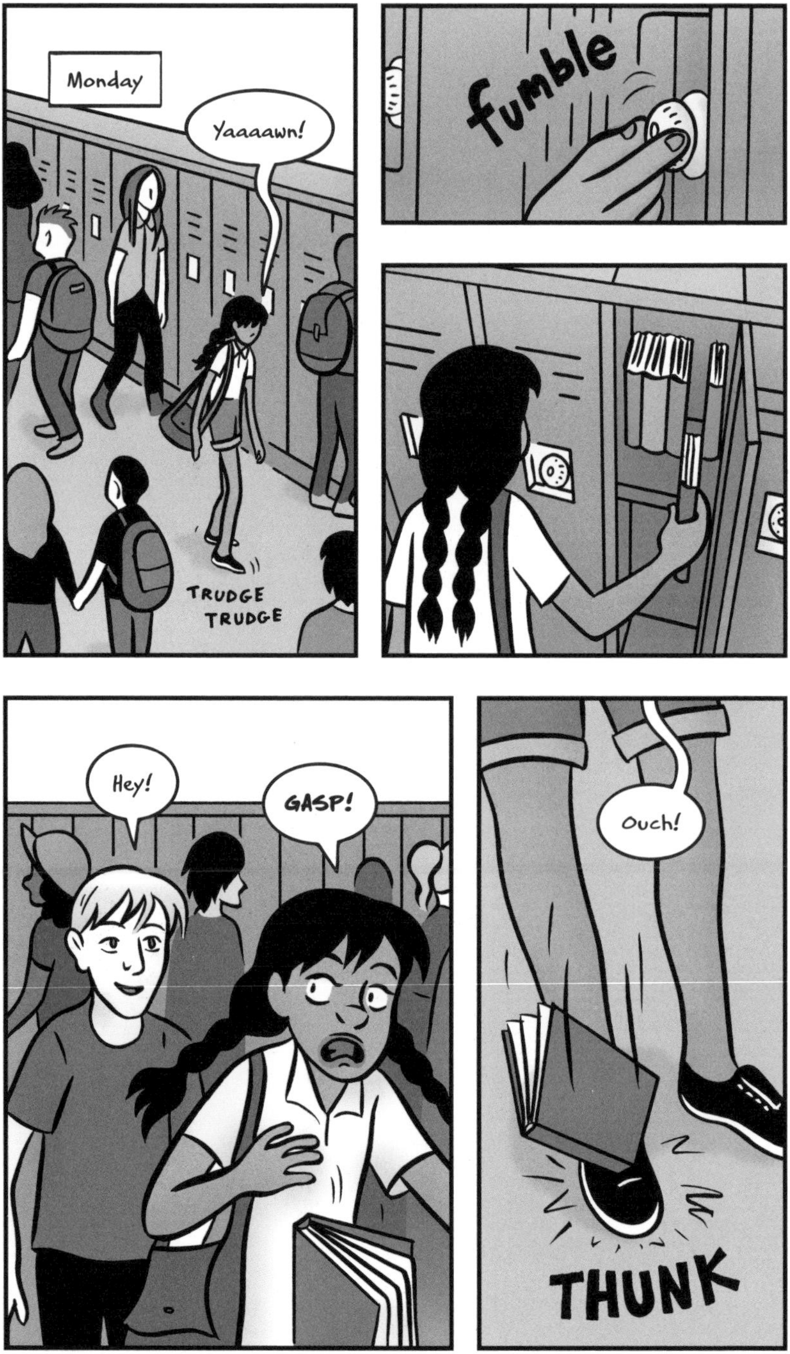

Monday
Yaaaawn!
TRUDGE
TRUDGE
fumble
Hey!
GASP!
Ouch!
THUNK

Sorry, Bee. I didn't mean to scare you. Is your foot okay?
Yeah, it's fine. I knew I should've worn my Docs today.
Good. I just wanted to say that, uh, I heard you playing music yesterday!
What?! What did you hear?! I'm still working on the lyrics!
What does he know? Does he know I feel weird about dating him?
What was I thinking, making my music personal?!
Everything I do these days is a terrible mistake! A terrible, terrible—
I, uh, couldn't hear the lyrics. Just the guitar. But it sounded good.
Oh! Ha-ha-ha! Whew!
Since when are you shy about your music?

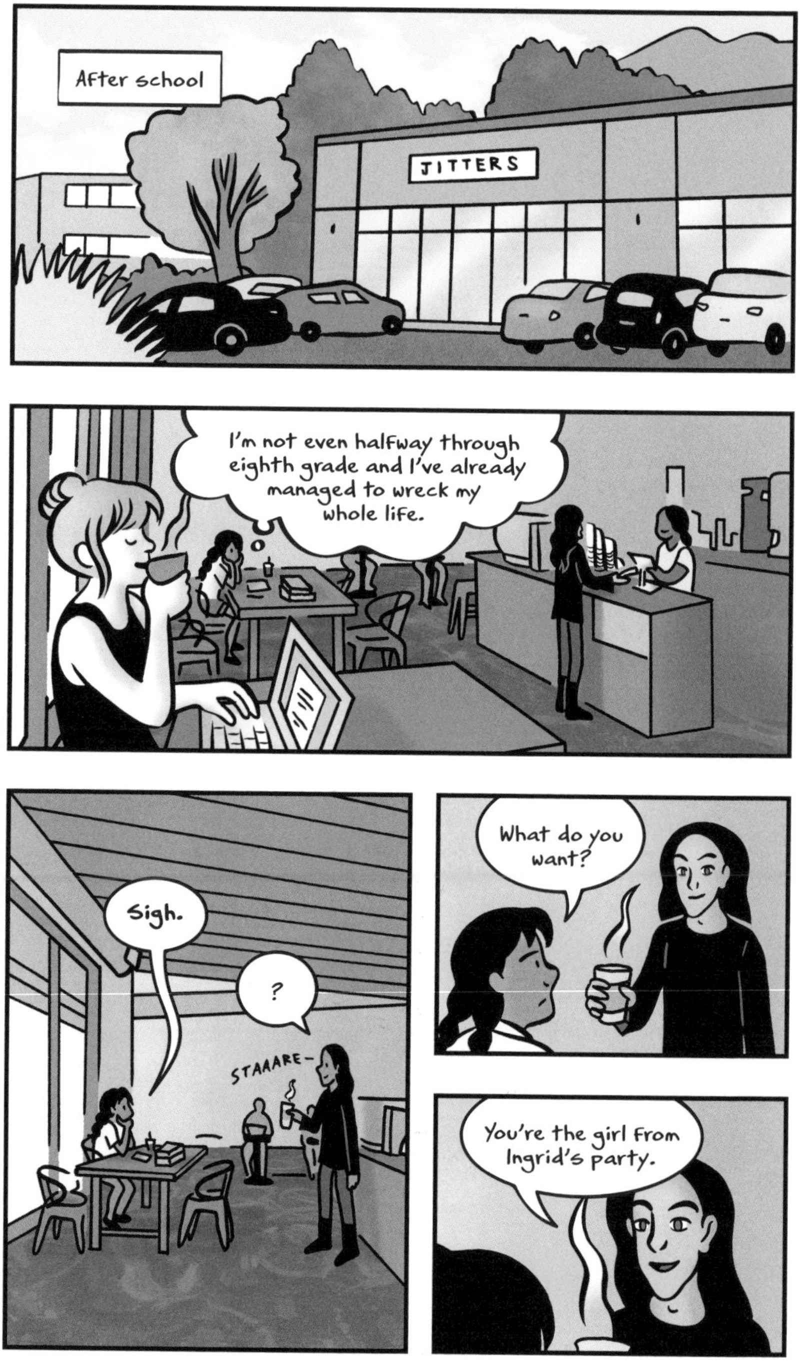
After school
JITTERS
I'm not even halfway through eighth grade and I've already managed to wreck my whole life.
Sigh.
?
STAAARE-
What do you want?
You're the girl from Ingrid's party.

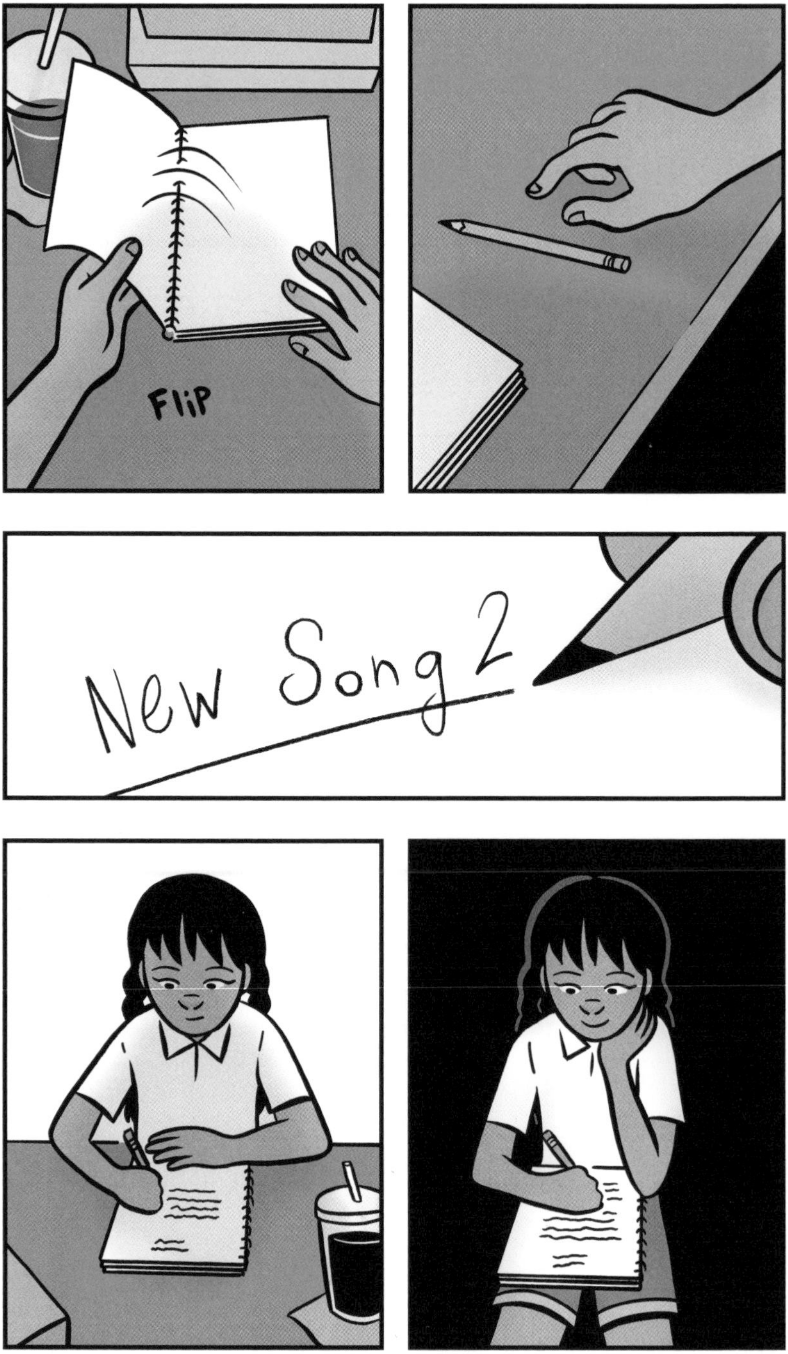
FliP
New Song 2

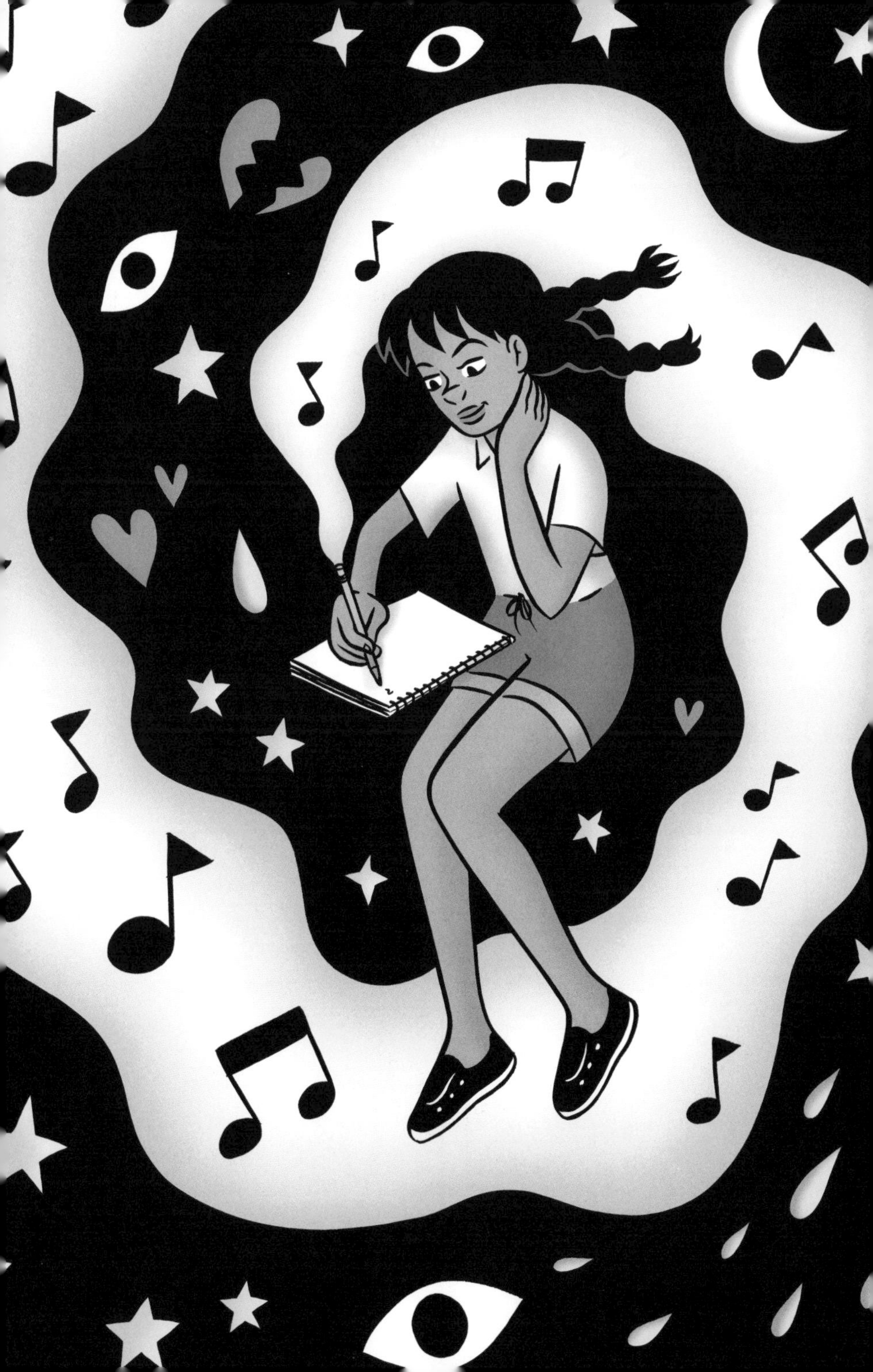

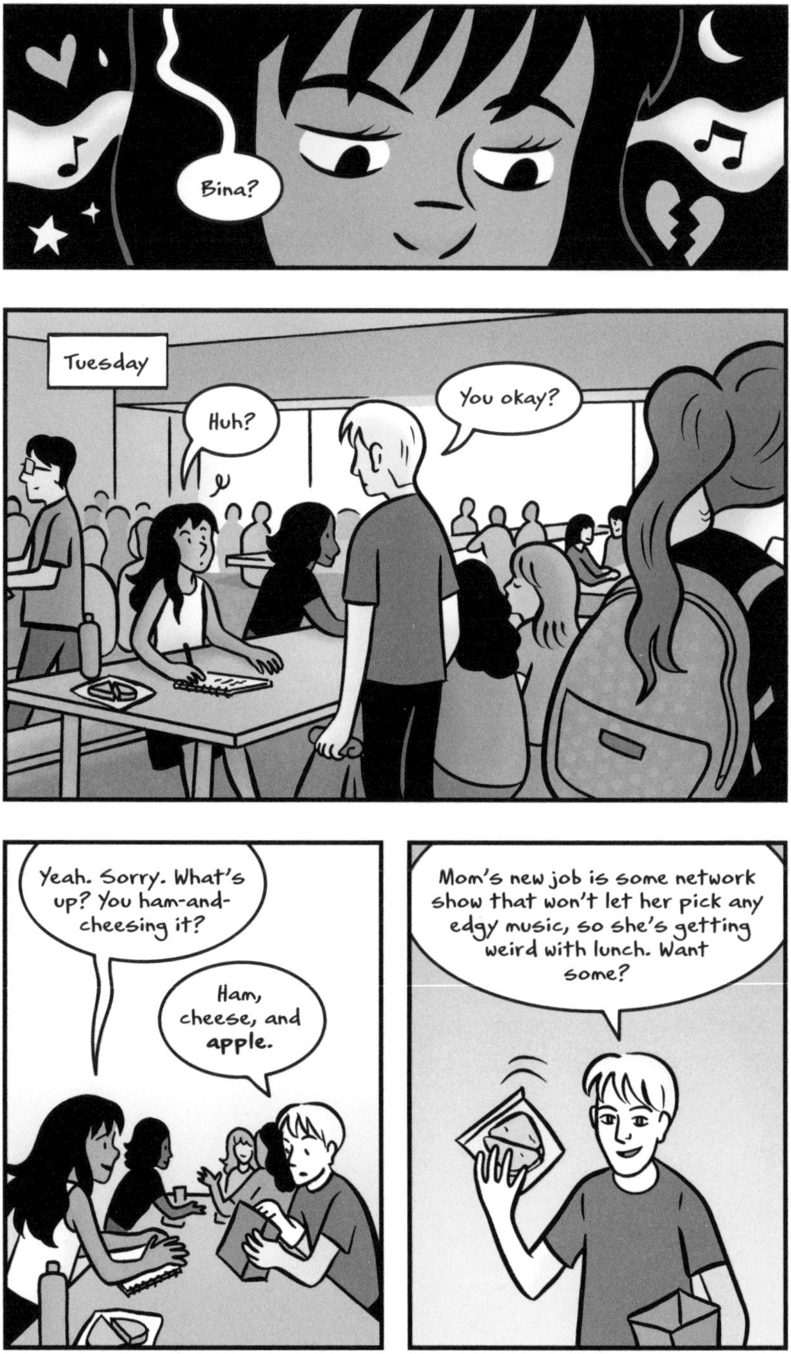
Bina?
Tuesday
Huh?
You okay?
Yeah. Sorry. What's up? You ham-and-cheesing it?
Ham, cheese, and apple.
Mom's new job is some network show that won't let her pick any edgy music, so she's getting weird with lunch. Want some?

IF he comes to the show, he'll hear the songs.
IF he hears the songs, he'll know I'm not sure about us being an **us**.
THUNK
This sucks. IF my songs aren't personal enough, they aren't good enough.
IF they're **too** personal, someone gets hurt.
I wish I could just be in love and write love songs.
I wish I could talk to someone who'd understand.
TAPPA TAPPA TAPPA
I wish I could talk to Darcy.

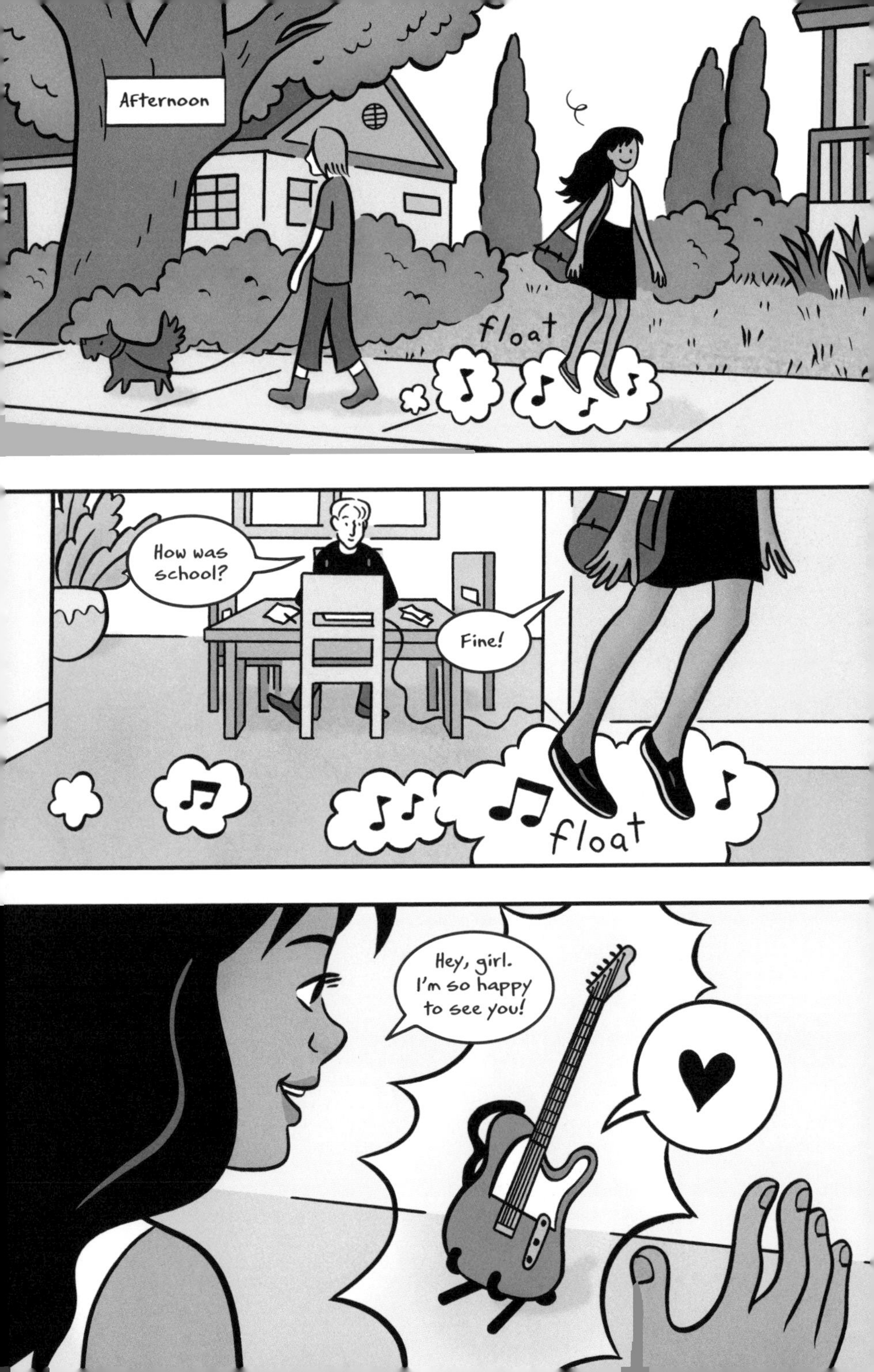
Afternoon
float
How was school?
Fine!
float
Hey, girl. I'm so happy to see you!

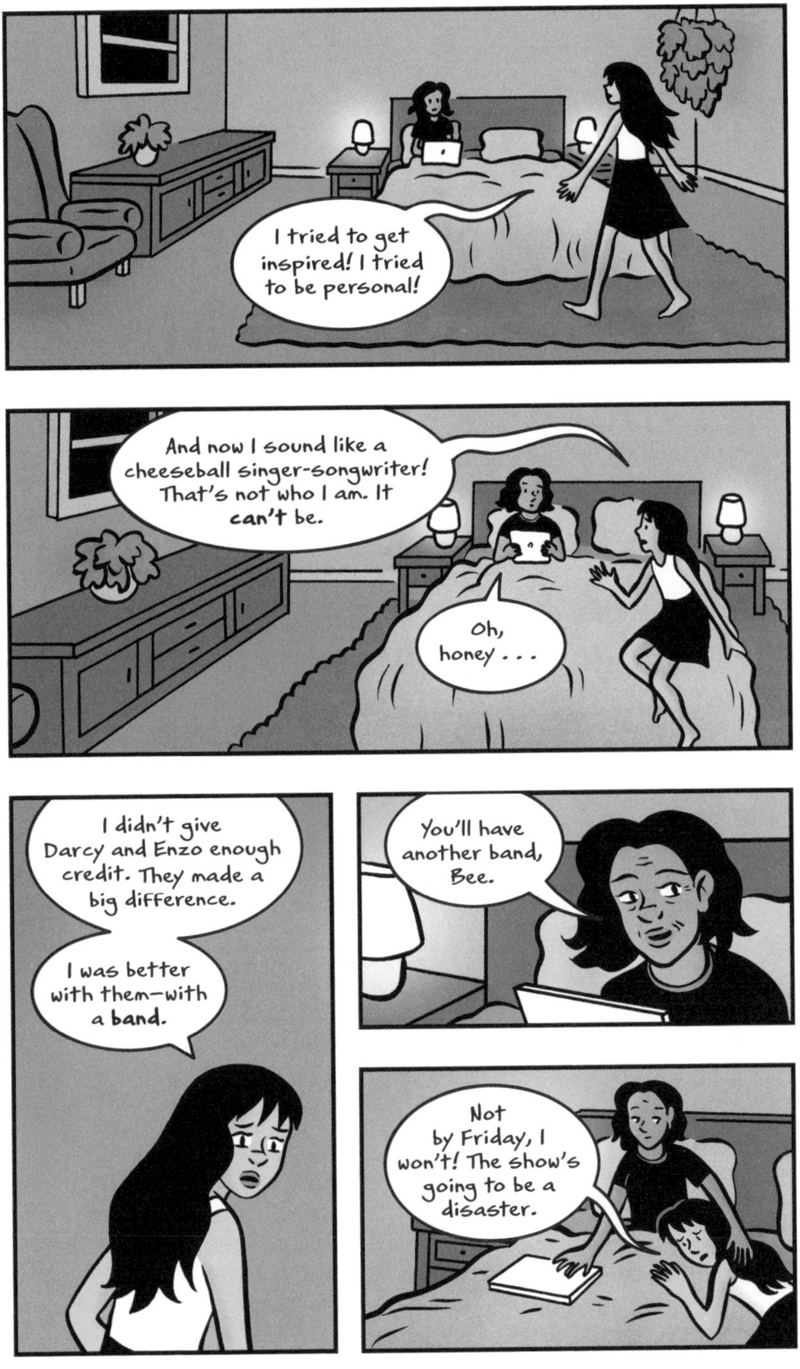
I tried to get inspired! I tried to be personal!
And now I sound like a cheeseball singer-songwriter! That's not who I am. It **can't** be.
Oh, honey . . .
I didn't give Darcy and Enzo enough credit. They made a big difference.
I was better with them—with a **band**.
You'll have another band, Bee.
Not by Friday, I won't! The show's going to be a disaster.

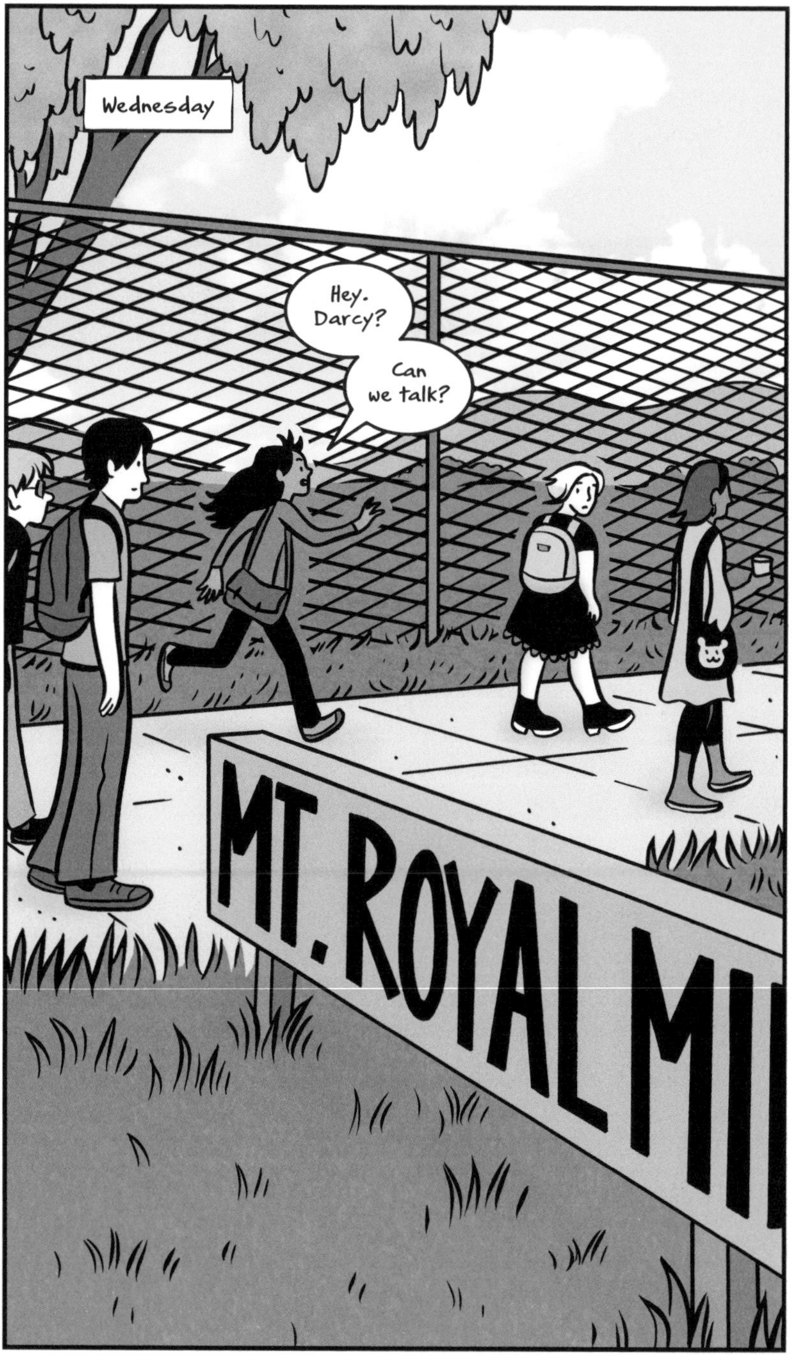
Wednesday
Hey. Darcy?
Can we talk?
MT. ROYAL MI

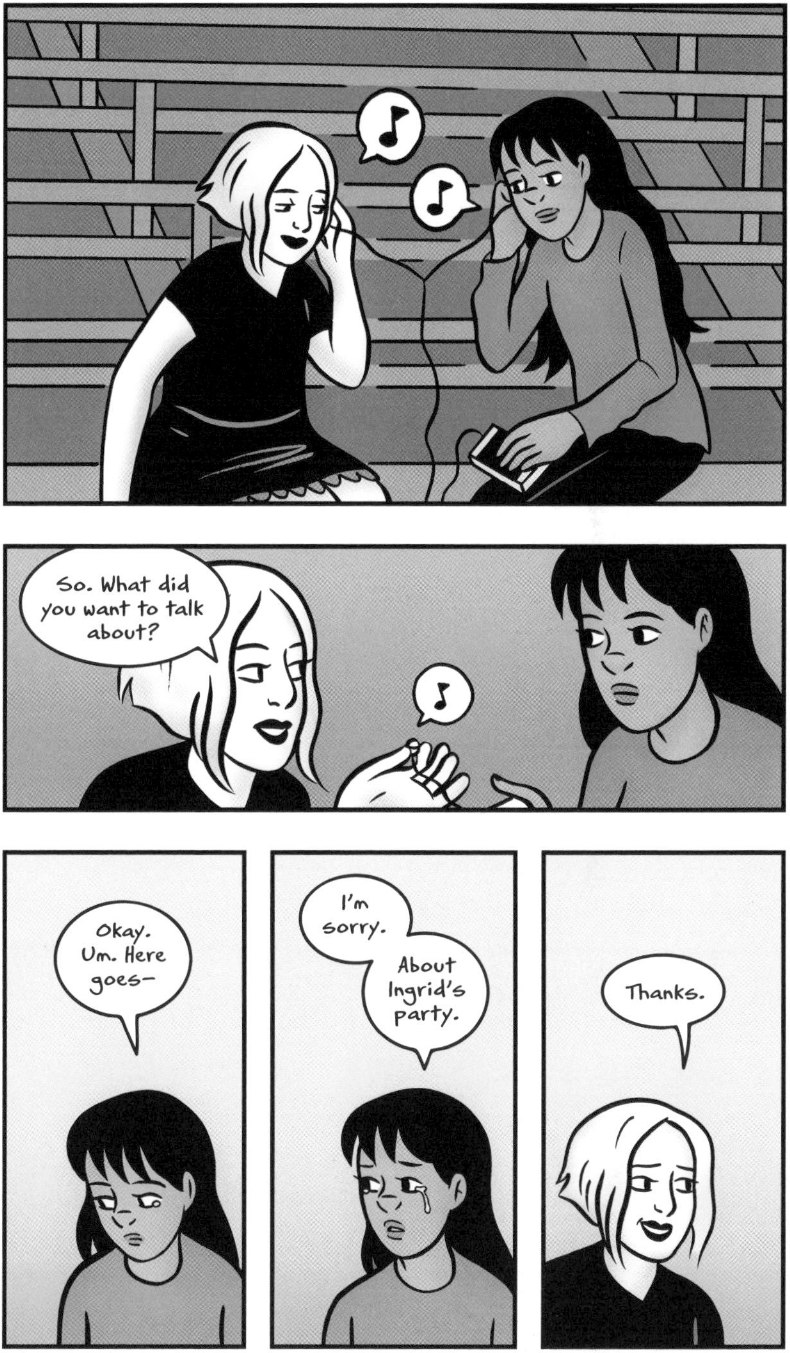
So. What did you want to talk about?
Okay. Um. Here goes-
I'm sorry.
About Ingrid's party.
Thanks.

144

Oh my God, Bina.
I'm so freaking glad I didn't lose you.
I haven't asked him yet! It might not work out!
SMACK
It's the thought that counts.
Also? We need to talk about Sporty.
Austin? Oh God. Well—
So you are dating him!
Um—
I really have to get to class. To be continued?
To be continued!

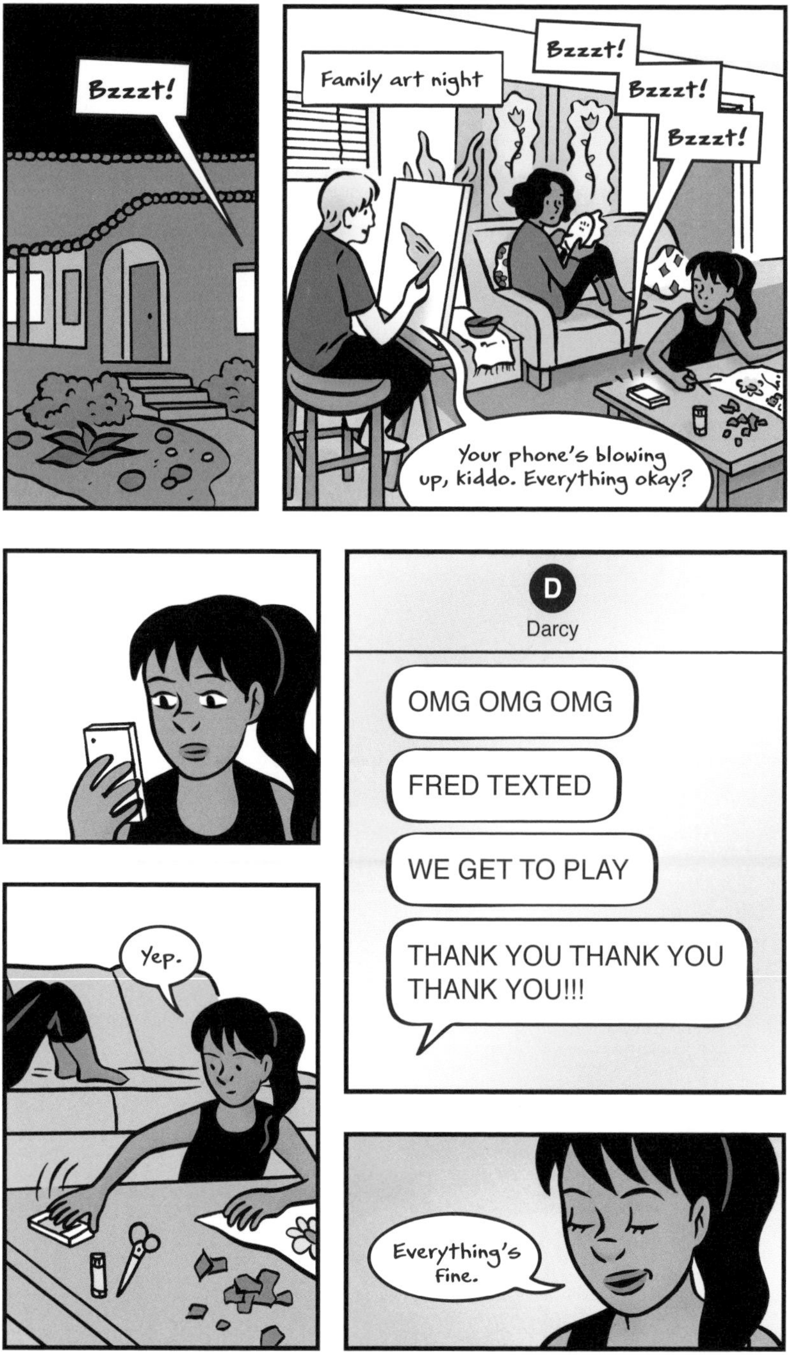
Bzzzt!
Family art night
Bzzzt!
Bzzzt!
Bzzzt!
Your phone's blowing up, kiddo. Everything okay?
D
Darcy
OMG OMG OMG
FRED TEXTED
WE GET TO PLAY
THANK YOU THANK YOU THANK YOU!!!
Yep.
Everything's fine.

December

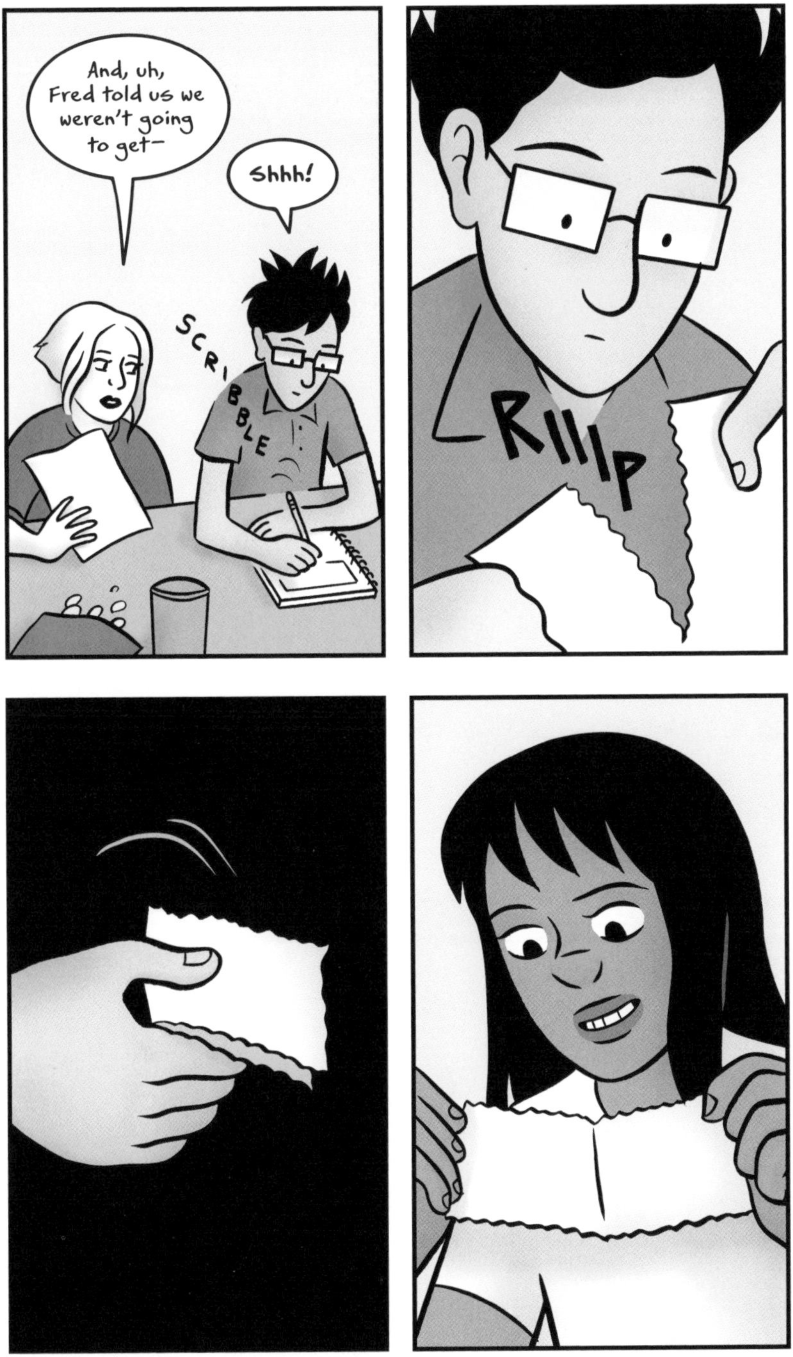
And, uh, Fred told us we weren't going to get–
Shhh!
SCRIBBLE
RIIIP

BANK OF PUNK ROCK 123
$0
Zero and 0/100 DOLLARS
for 20% of Nada
ac/Darcy

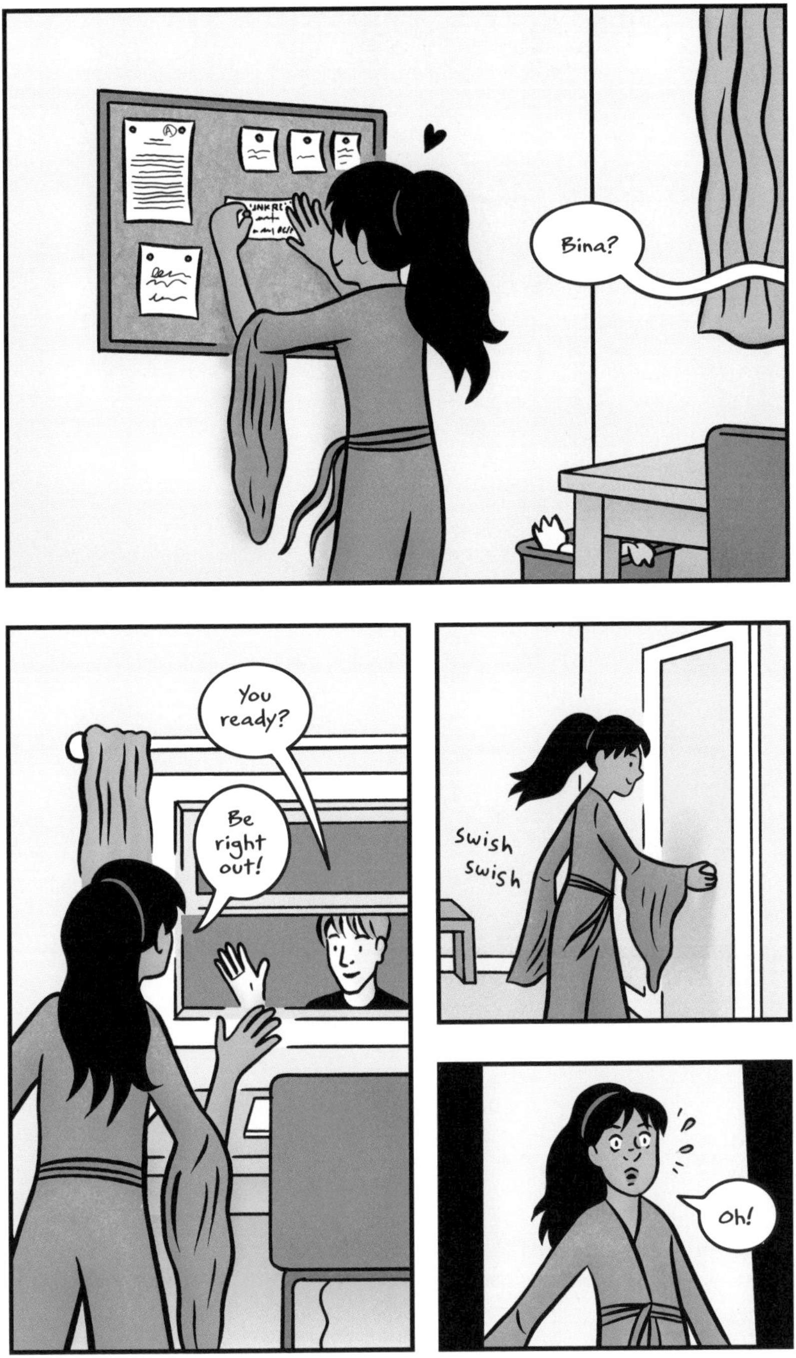
Bina?
You ready?
Be right out!
swish swish
Oh!

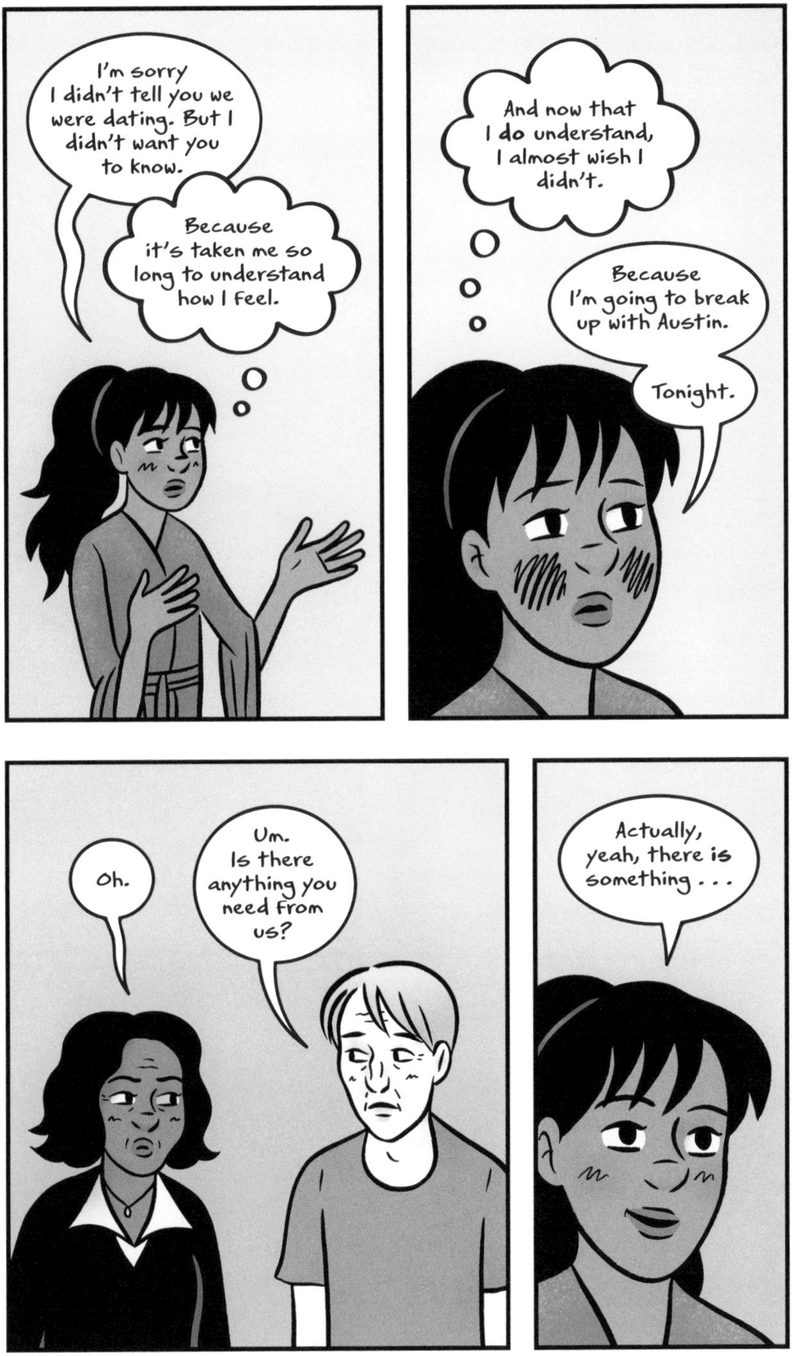
I'm sorry I didn't tell you we were dating. But I didn't want you to know.
Because it's taken me so long to understand how I feel.
And now that I do understand, I almost wish I didn't.
Because I'm going to break up with Austin.
Tonight.
Oh.
Um. Is there anything you need from us?
Actually, yeah, there is something . . .

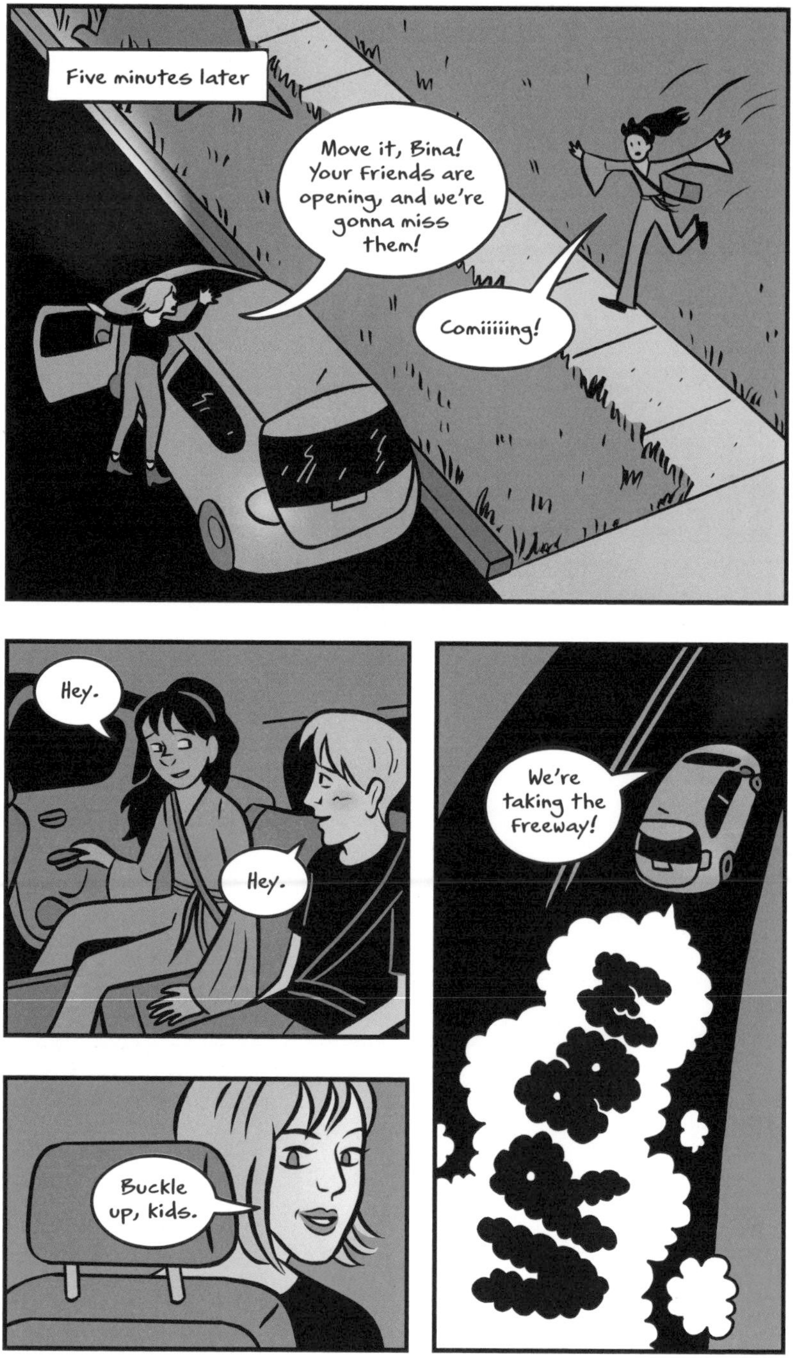
Five minutes later
Move it, Bina! Your friends are opening, and we're gonna miss them!
Comiiiiing!
Hey.
Hey.
Buckle up, kids.
We're taking the Freeway!

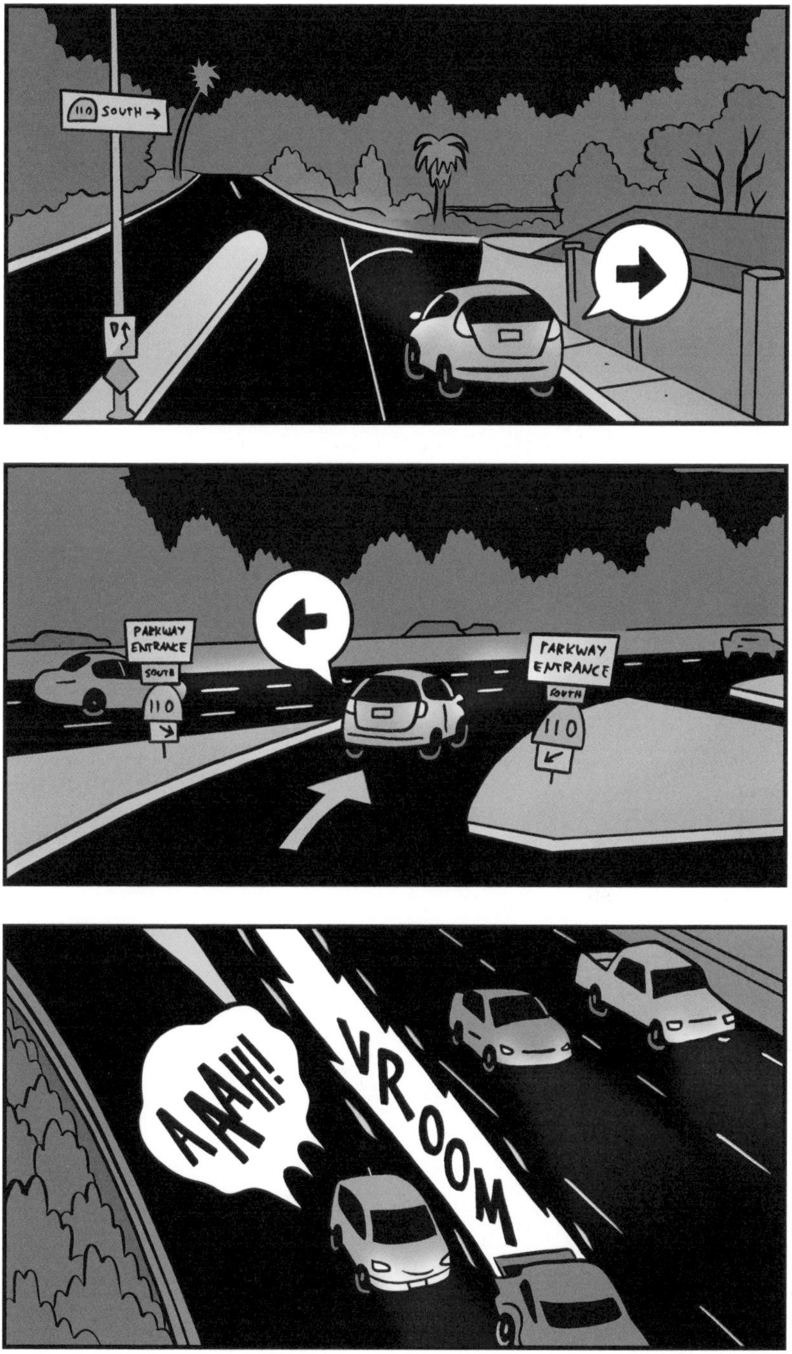
110 SOUTH →
PARKWAY ENTRANCE
SOUTH
110
PARKWAY ENTRANCE
SOUTH
110
AAAH!
VROOM

158

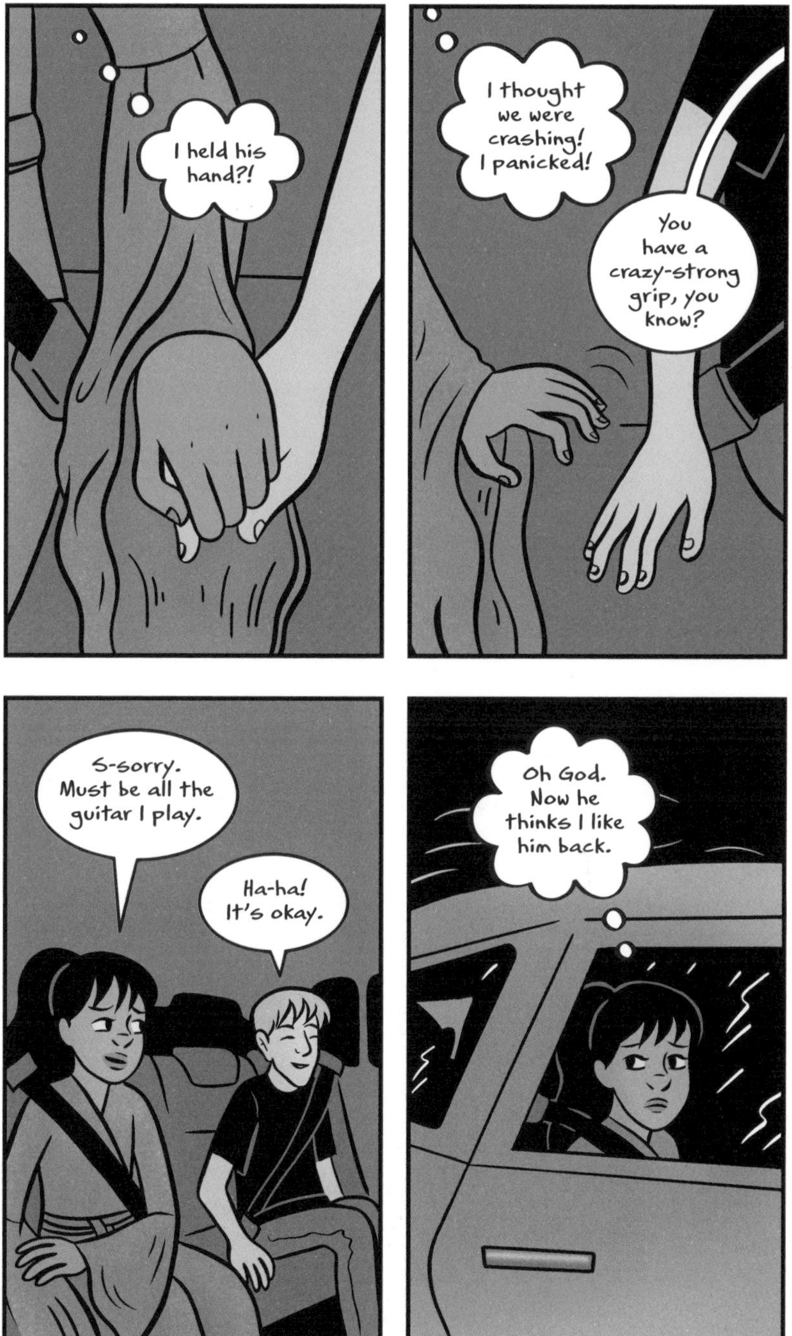
I held his hand?!
I thought we were crashing! I panicked!
You have a crazy-strong grip, you know?
S-sorry. Must be all the guitar I play.
Ha-ha! It's okay.
Oh God. Now he thinks I like him back.

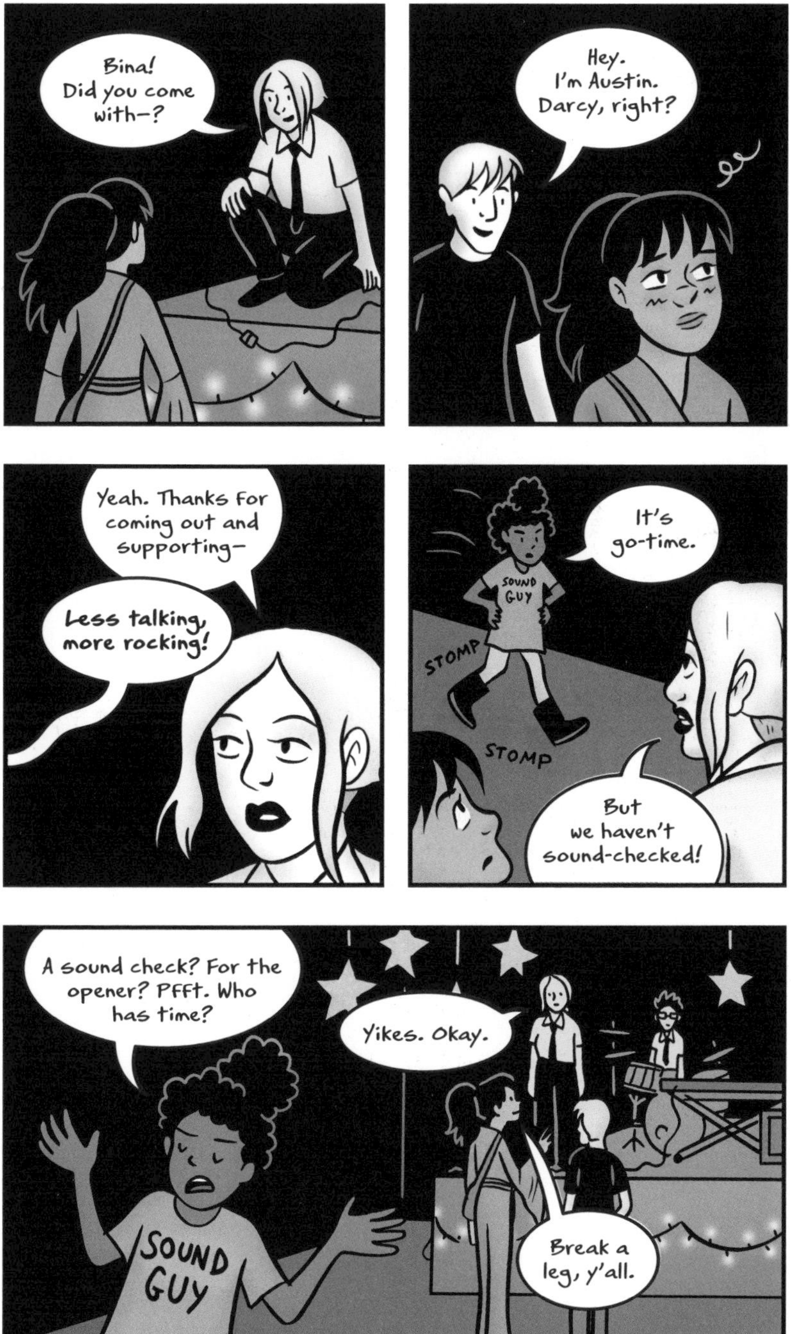
Bina!
Did you come with–?
Hey.
I'm Austin.
Darcy, right?
Yeah. Thanks for coming out and supporting–
Less talking, more rocking!
SOUND GUY
It's go-time.
STOMP
STOMP
But we haven't sound-checked!
A sound check? For the opener? Pfft. Who has time?
SOUND GUY
Yikes. Okay.
Break a leg, y'all.

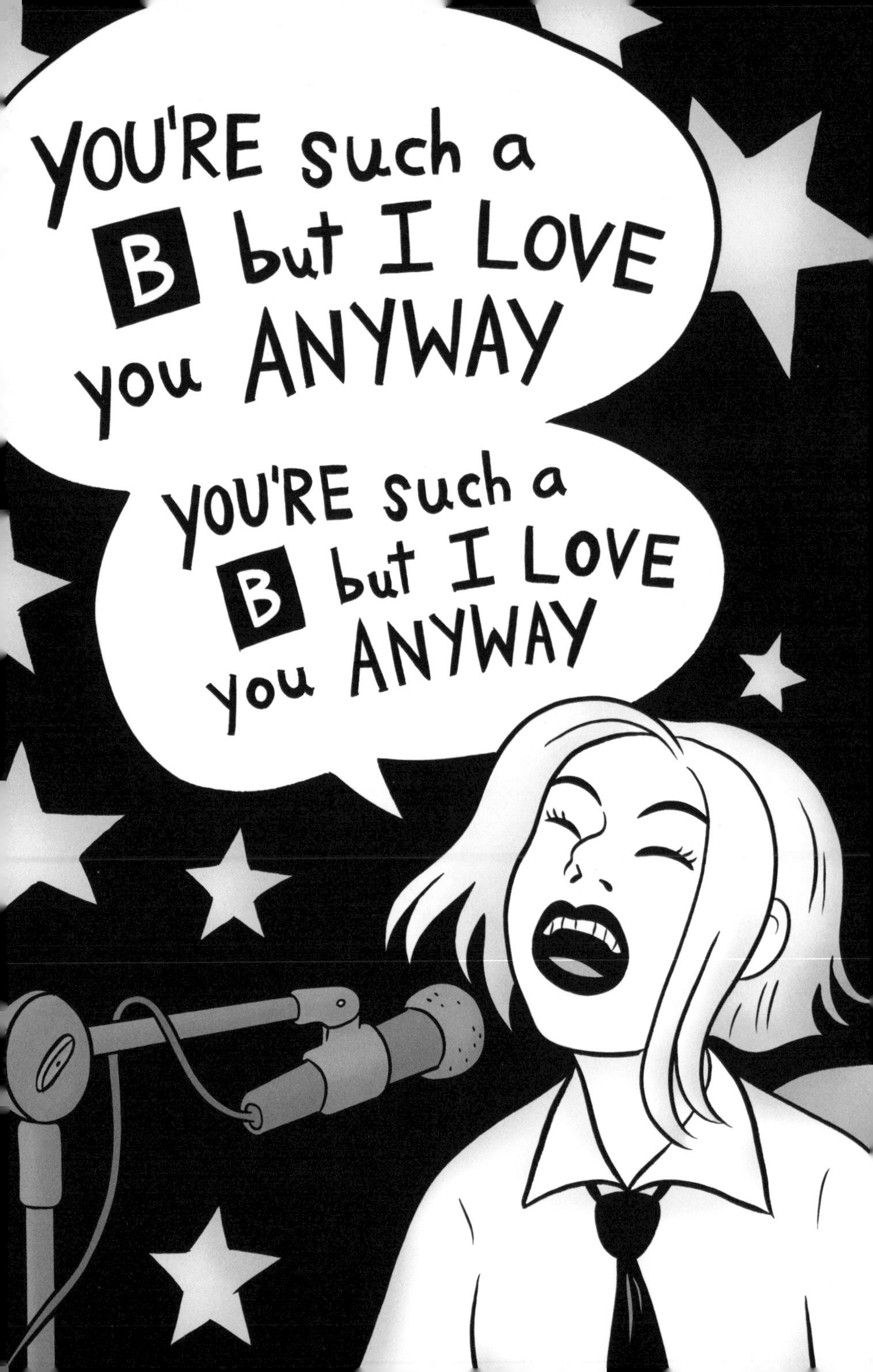
YOU'RE such a B but I LOVE you ANYWAY
YOU'RE such a B but I LOVE you ANYWAY

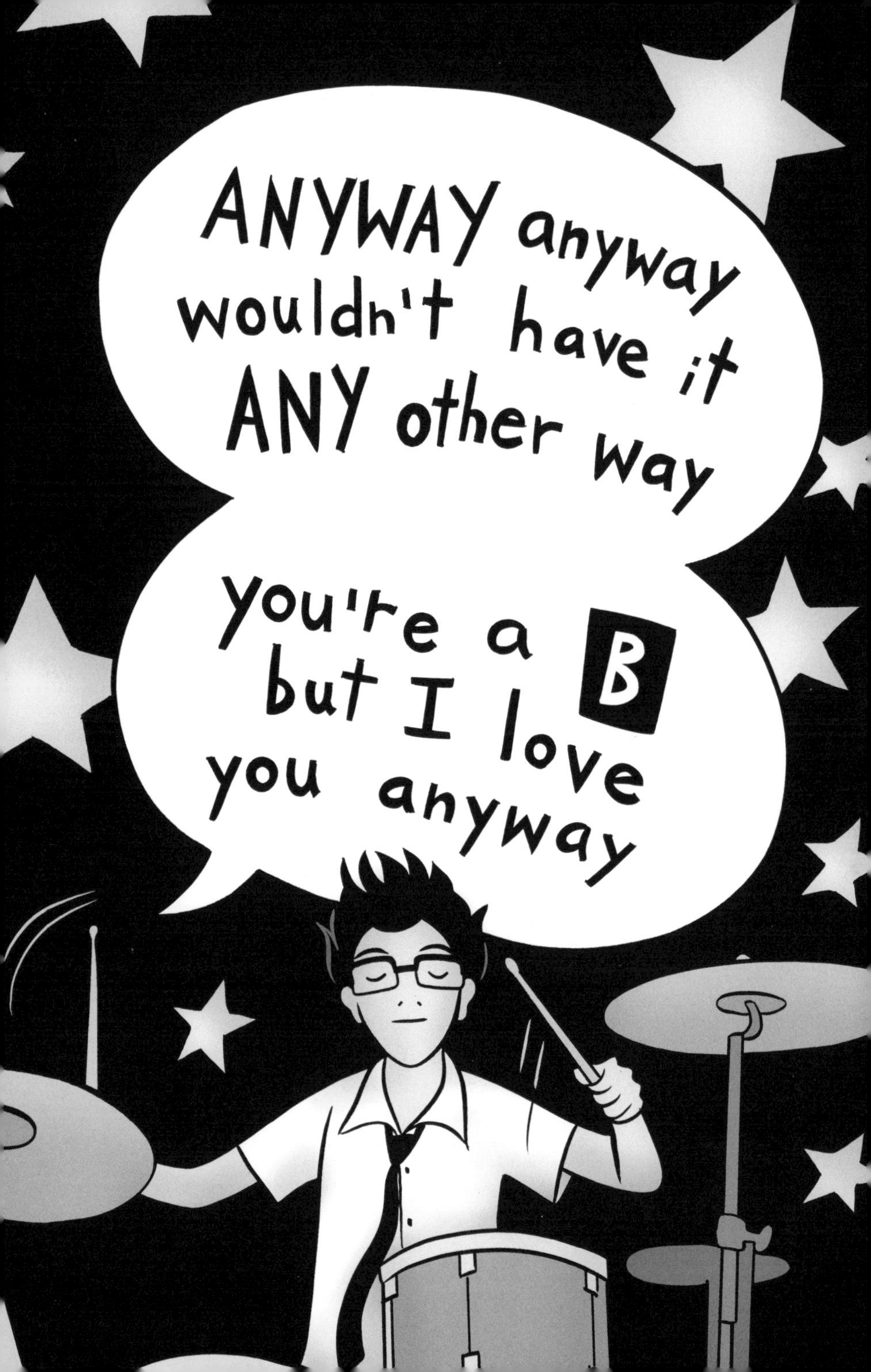
ANYWAY anyway wouldn't have it ANY other way
you're a B but I love you anyway

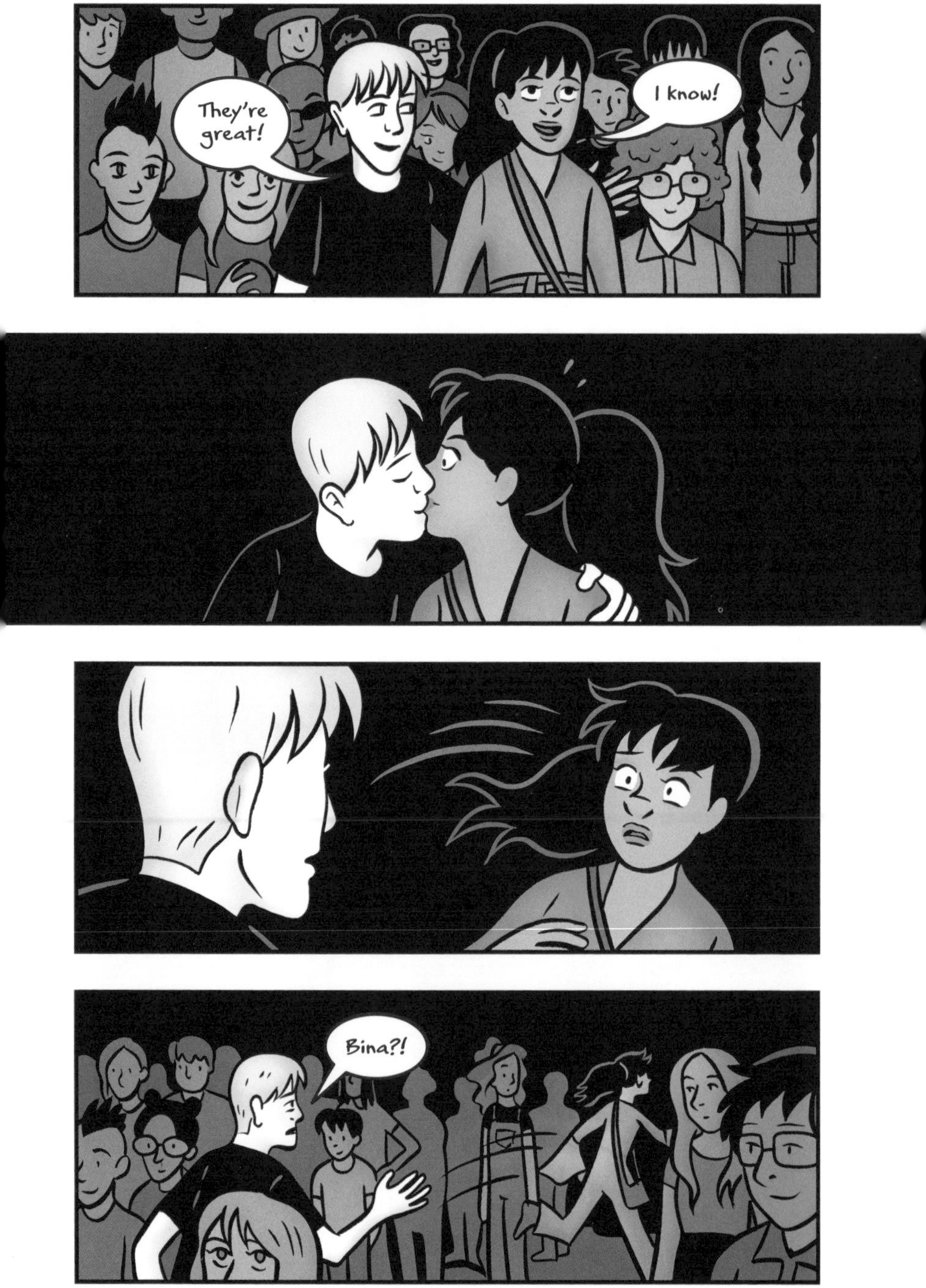
They're great!
I know!
Bina?!

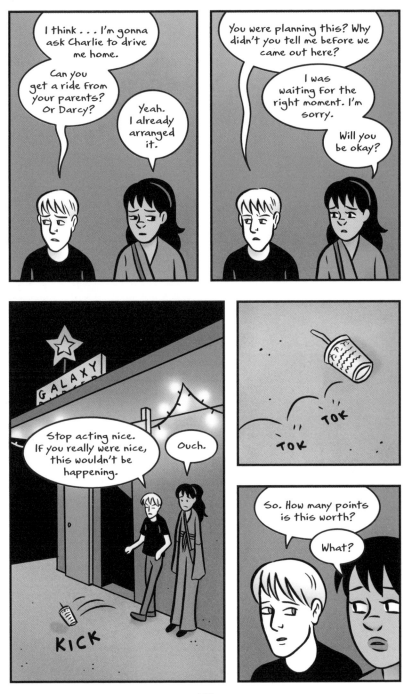

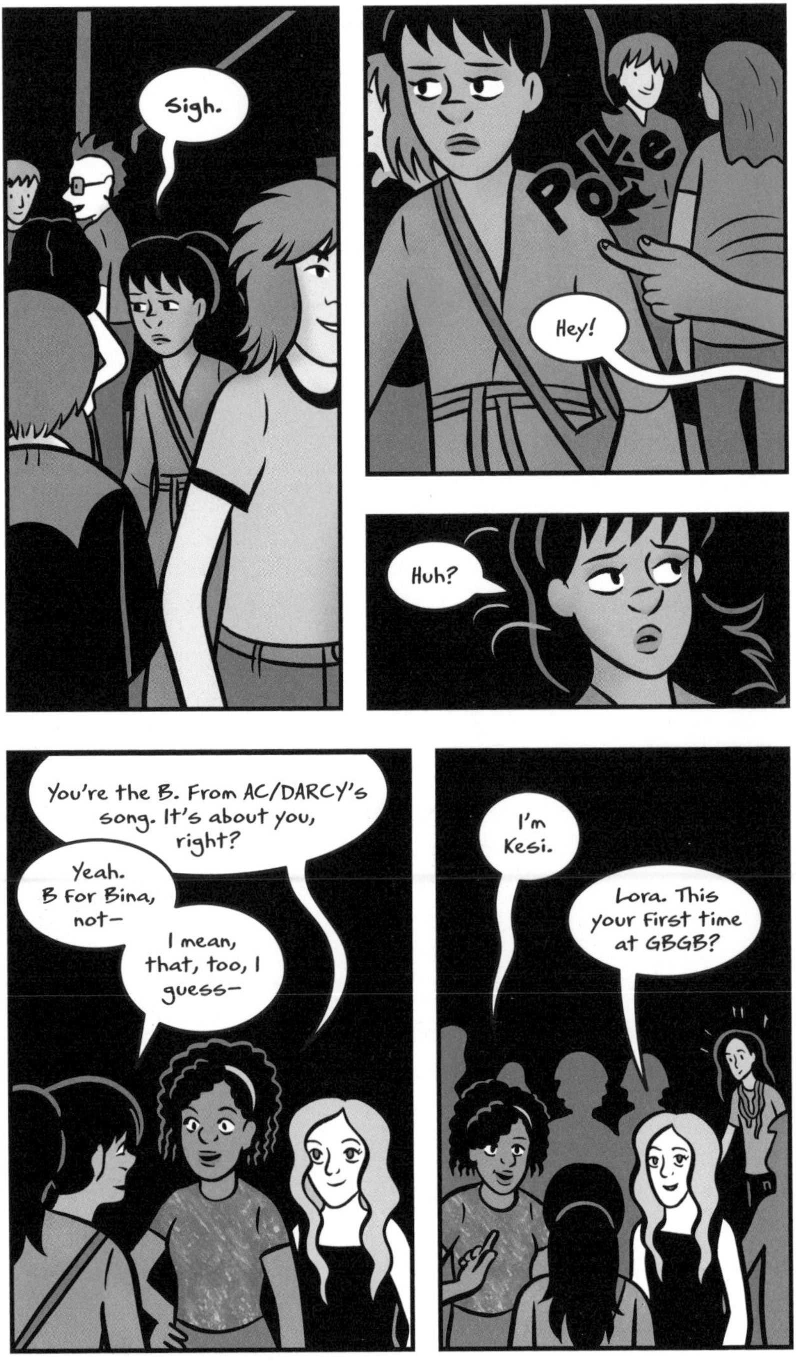
Sigh.
POKE
Hey!
Huh?
You're the B. From AC/DARCY's song. It's about you, right?
Yeah. B for Bina, not—
I mean, that, too, I guess—
I'm Kesi.
Lora. This your first time at GBGB?

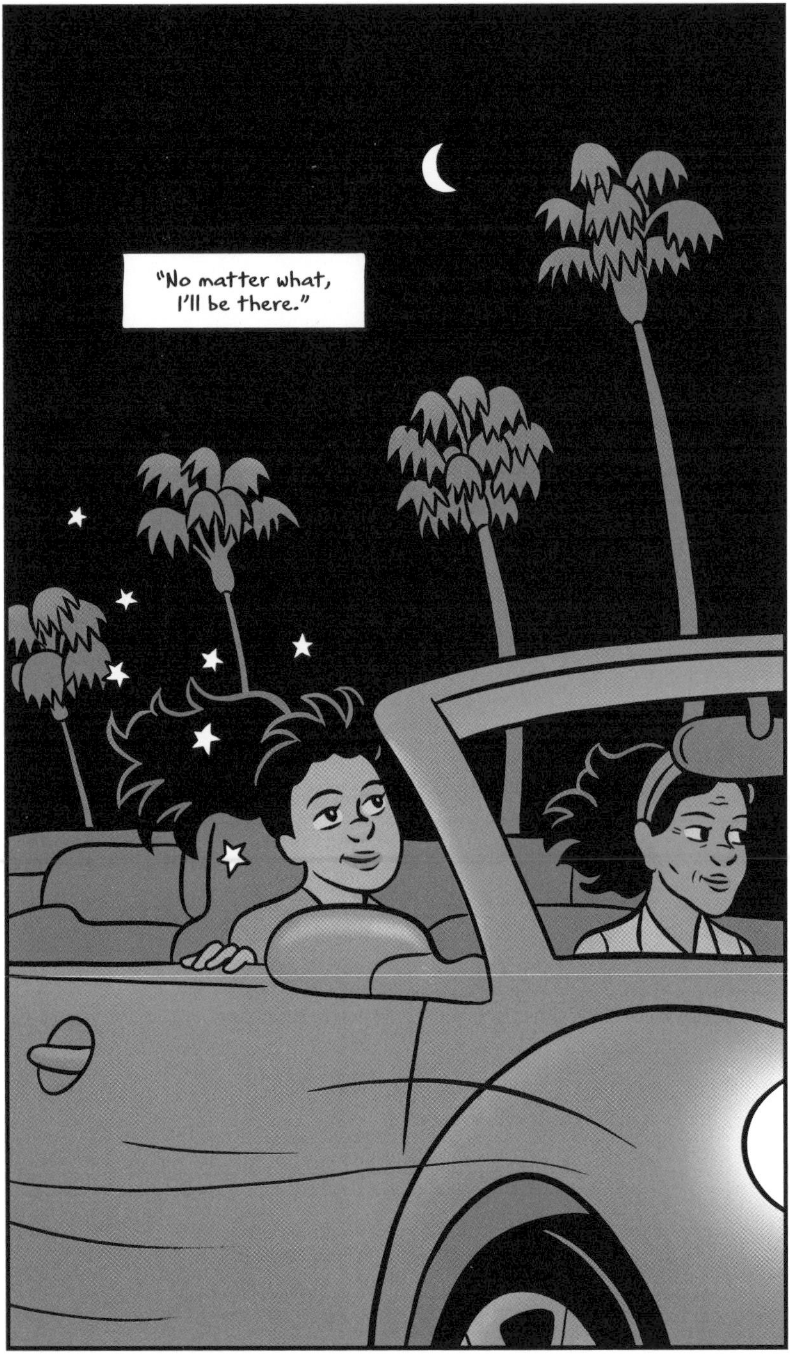
"No matter what,
I'll be there."

HOW I MAKE COMICS

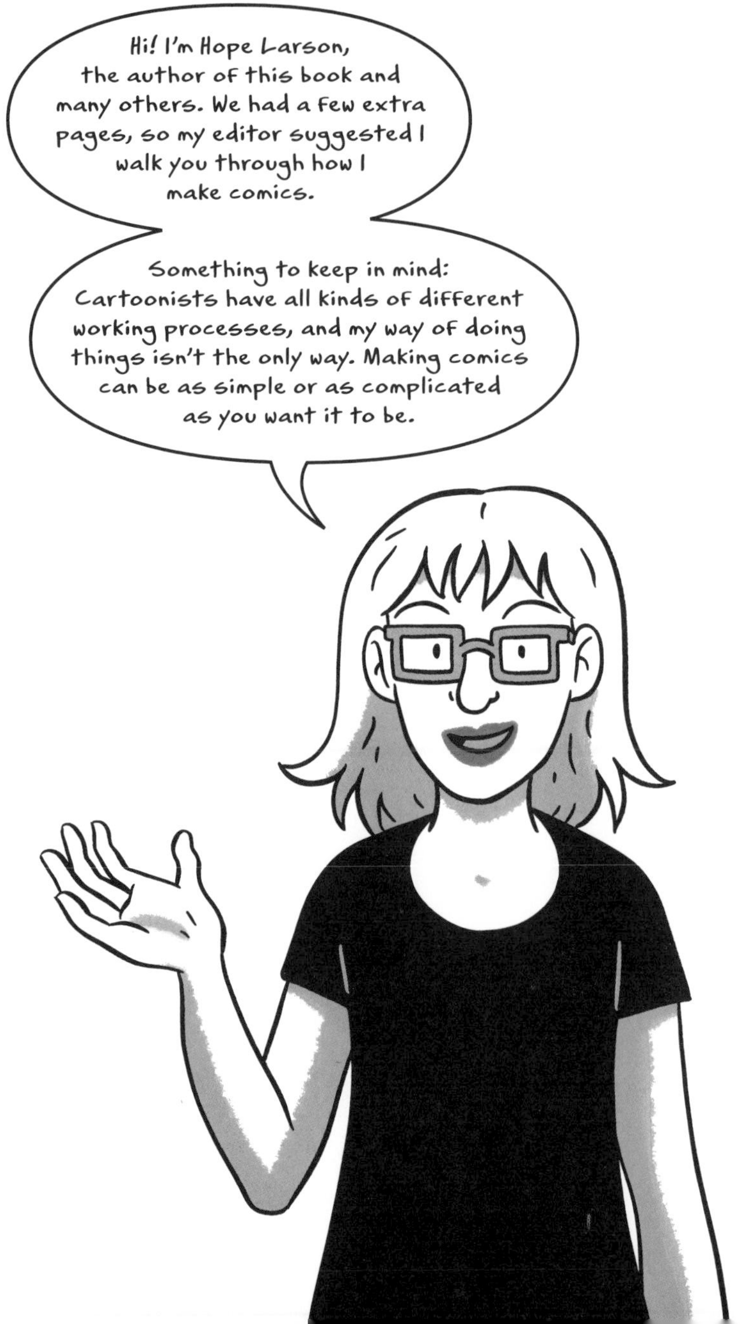
Hi! I'm Hope Larson, the author of this book and many others. We had a few extra pages, so my editor suggested I walk you through how I make comics.
Something to keep in mind: Cartoonists have all kinds of different working processes, and my way of doing things isn't the only way. Making comics can be as simple or as complicated as you want it to be.

THE SCRIPT

All my comics start with a SCRIPT. It's easier and faster for me to visualize the comic through words than to draw it all out while simultaneously figuring out the plot, characters, and dialogue. Writing a script also helps me figure out how long the book will be.

Important elements of comic scripts include:

HEADING
At the top of each page, I write the page number and the number of panels on the page. The more detailed the panels, the fewer there should be.

PANEL DESCRIPTION
I explain what's happening in each panel, including where we are and what time it is, what the characters are doing, and what emotions they're feeling.

DIALOGUE
This is anything the characters are saying or thinking.

SOUND EFFECTS
Not every page has sound effects, but I usually write these down, too.

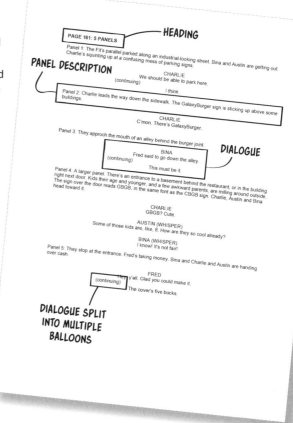

The script goes through several rounds of revisions before my editor, Joy, decides it's ready to be drawn. But even then, nothing in the script is set in stone. Things always change once I sit down to draw.

LAYOUT

I scripted five panels on this page, but when I did my LAYOUT, I decided that was too many. To make sure the environments (aka backgrounds) got a chance to shine, I reduced the panel count to three.

I do my layouts on an iPad Pro, in an app called Procreate. I like being able to move elements around, and that's easier to do while working digitally.

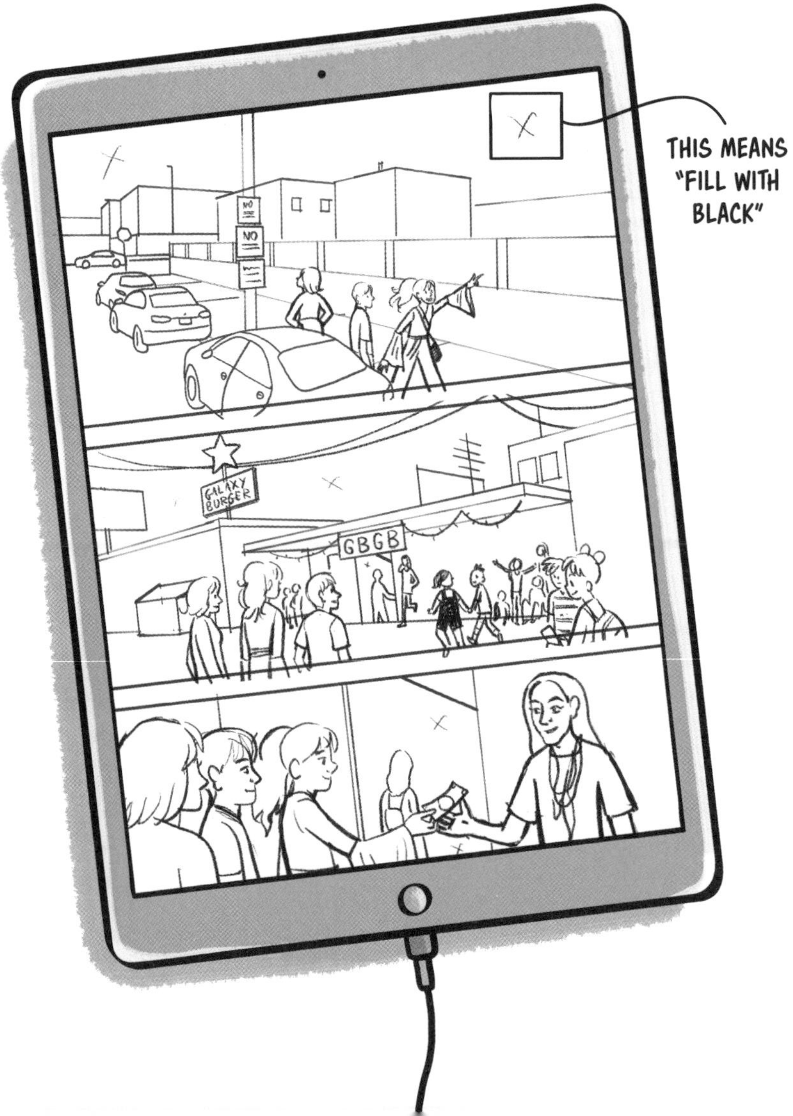
THIS MEANS "FILL WITH BLACK"
NO
NO
GALAXY BURGER
GBGB

PENCILS

Once I'm happy with the layout, I move on to PENCILS. I bring the layout into Photoshop and tint it a very light blue, then print it out on Bristol board, a kind of thick drawing paper.

I trace over the layout with an orange Col-Erase pencil—an erasable colored pencil—and tighten up parts of the drawing that weren't clear. Then I scan it back in and add the speech balloons, or "letters."

I do a whole draft of the book that looks like this, then I go over it with my editor again. She makes suggestions for improving the book even more, and I fix as many problems as I can before I move on to the next step.

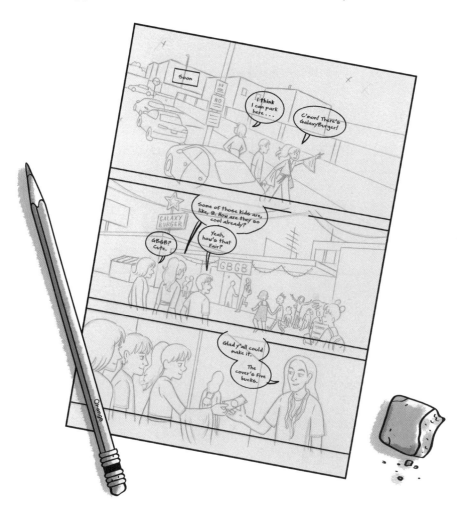

INKS (UNCORRECTED)

We've finally reached one of my favorite parts of the process: inking! This is when the book starts coming together and looking how I imagined it would. I throw on a podcast or audiobook, pull out my stack of orange-penciled pages, and start inking right over the top of them. I use a small watercolor brush and a bottle of ink for almost everything but straight lines, which require a felt-tip pen and a ruler.

Below is a scan of a page as it looks on paper, before I correct it on the computer. The blacks aren't very dark yet, and I'm still using those little *X*'s to indicate which areas will be black. I like to fill those areas on the computer, because it's faster and it uses less ink.

I leave the orange pencil lines right where they are. I can remove them on the computer without needing to erase them.

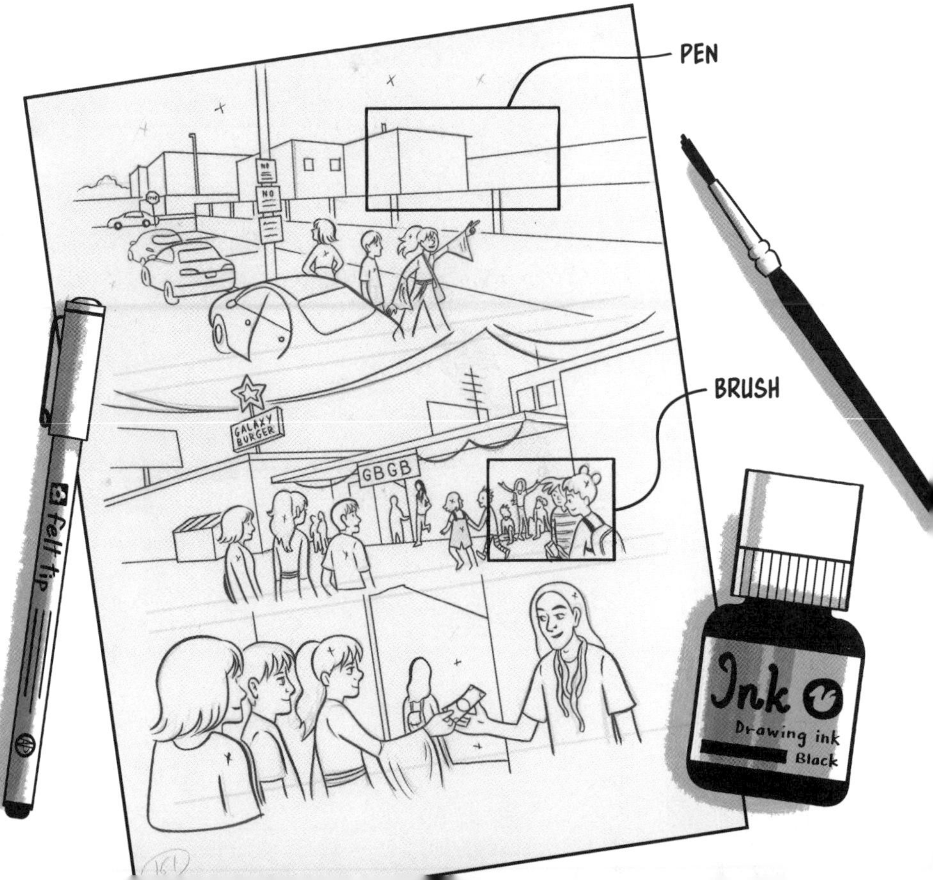
PEN
BRUSH
NO
NO
GALAXY BURGER
GBGB
felt tip
Ink
Drawing ink
Black

INKS
(CORRECTED)

I scan my inks into Photoshop and make lots of changes. I adjust the image to be black and white. I fill any solid black areas. I fix and digitally redraw any parts of the image that look wonky.

I add the letters back in. I rethink speech balloon placement, draw final balloon tails, and send the page off to the colorist!

COLORS

It takes a long time to draw a graphic novel, so having someone else to help with colors is wonderful. On *All Together Now*, I worked with colorists Hilary Sycamore and Karina Edwards. They add the tones and shading that bring the artwork fully to life.

I don't want to say I *couldn't* color a book by myself, but I would be a grumpier, more frazzled person. I'm so glad Hilary and Karina are on my team!

AND THAT'S IT!

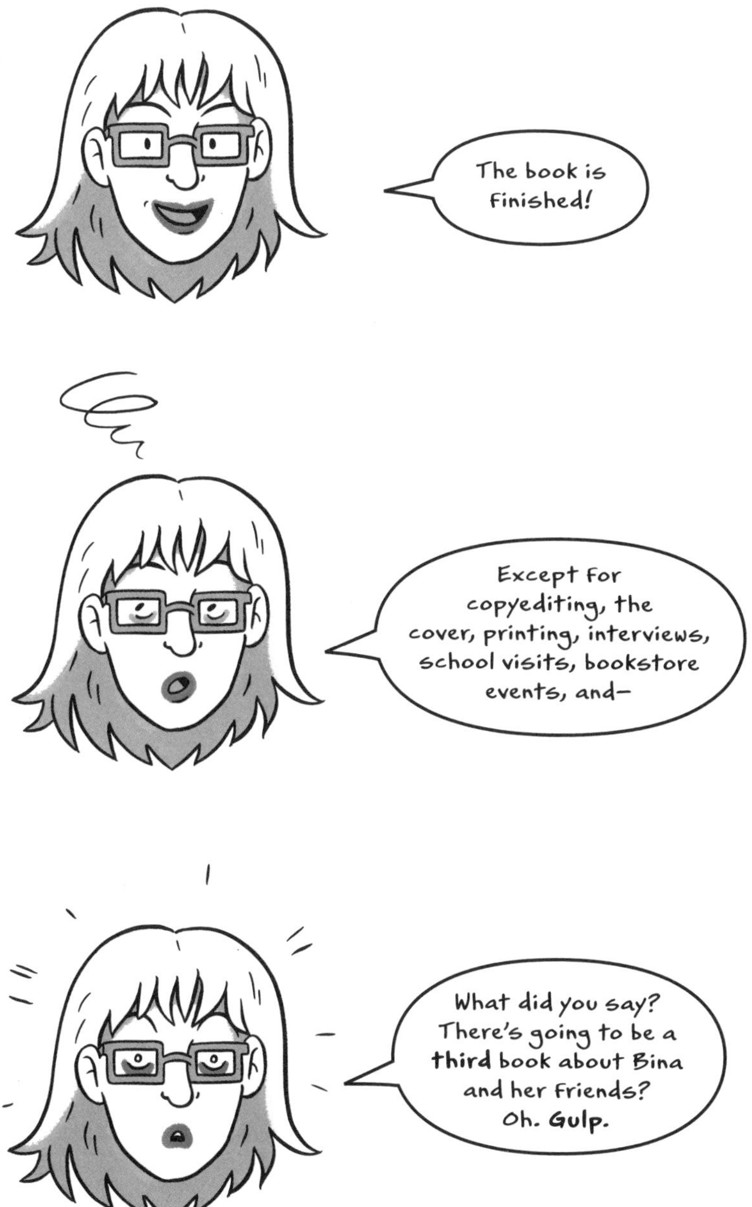
The book is finished!
Except for copyediting, the cover, printing, interviews, school visits, bookstore events, and–
What did you say? There's going to be a **third** book about Bina and her friends? Oh. **Gulp.**

OKAY, THEN. BACK TO WORK!

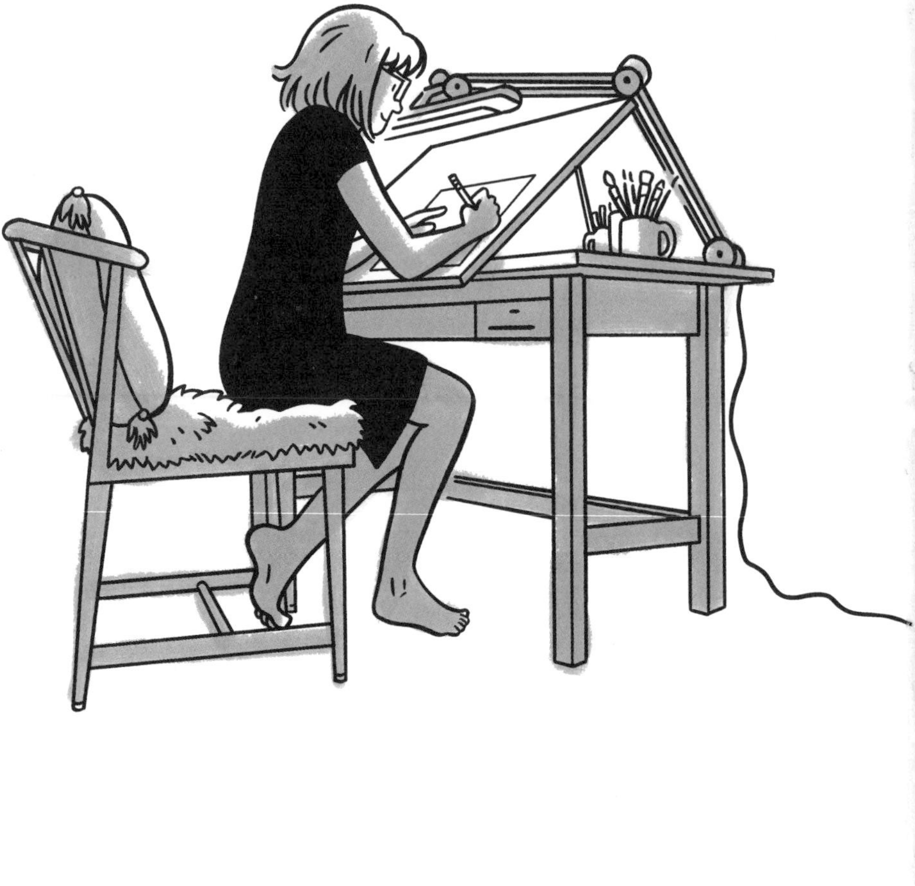